HANDYMAN

HANDYMAN

JODI LYNN COPELAND

APHRODISIA

KENSINGTON BOOKS
http://www.kensingtonbooks.com

APHRODISIA BOOKS are published by

Kensington Publishing Corp.
850 Third Avenue
New York, NY 10022

Copyright © 2008 by Jodi Lynn Copeland

All rights reserved. No part of this book may be reproduced in any form or by any means without the prior written consent of the Publisher, excepting brief quotes used in reviews.

All Kensington Titles, Imprints, and Distributed Lines are available at special quantity discounts for bulk purchases for sales promotions, premiums, fund-raising, and educational or institutional use.

Special book excerpts or customized printings can also be created to fit specific needs. For details, write or phone the office of the Kensington special sales manager: Kensington Publishing Corp., 850 Third Avenue, New York, NY 10022, Attn: Special Sales Department, Phone: 1-800-221-2647.

Aphrodisia and the A logo Reg. U.S. Pat & TM Off.

ISBN-13: 978-0-7582-2212-1
ISBN-10: 0-7582-2212-2

First Kensington Trade Paperback Printing: March 2008

10 9 8 7 6 5 4 3 2

Printed in the United States of America

CONTENTS

Coming in First   1

Not a Second Too Late   95

Third Time's a Charm   191

COMING IN FIRST

1

Now, he was the kind of guy she needed to meet.

Parallel parked across the street from the Almost Family youth services building, Lissa Malone stopped examining her reflection in the vanity mirror of her Dodge Charger to watch the guy. He stood in front of the youth building, which was constructed of the same old-fashioned red brick as every other building in downtown Crichton, laughing with a lanky, long-haired blond kid in his early teens. The kid wouldn't be a relative, but a boy from the local community who was going through a rough patch and in need of an adult role model in the form of a foster friend.

Kind, caring, and considerate enough to be that friend, by donating his free time to the betterment of the kid's life, the guy was the antithesis of every man she'd dated.

Make that every *straight* man. And then again, he wasn't the complete opposite.

The way his faded blue Levi's hugged his tight ass and his biceps bulged from beneath the short sleeves of a slate gray T-shirt as he scruffed the kid's hair, the guy had as fine of a body as her recent lovers. What he wasn't likely to have was their badass hang-ups.

He was one of the good ones. A nice guy. The kind of guy Lissa had never gone for and never had any desire to.

There was something about those bad boys that called to her. Not just their bedside manner. Though she wasn't about to knock the red-hot thrill of being welcomed home from work by having her panties torn away and a stiff cock thrust inside her before she had a chance to say hello.

She shuddered with the memory of Haden, the brainless beefcake she ended up with following her latest dip in the bad-boy pool, greeting her precisely that way three weeks ago. What Haden lacked in mentality, he more than made up for in ability. The guy could make her come with the sound of his voice alone.

Show me that sweet pussy, Liss.

Haden's deep baritone slid through her mind, spiking her pulse and settling dampness between her thighs. She caught her reflection in the vanity mirror as she shifted in the driver's seat. Her cheeks had pinkened—an unmanageable tell to her arousal—calling out her too-many freckles.

Yeah, there was definitely something about those bad boys. Something she wouldn't be experiencing ever again.

Lissa wasn't the only woman Haden could bring to climax in seconds. As it turned out, she also wasn't the only woman he'd been bringing to climax the almost two months they dated. Really, it shouldn't have surprised her. With bad boys, something always ended up coming before her. Another woman. A massive ego. Or worst of all, the bad boy himself coming before her, then not bothering to stick around to see if she got off.

She was sick to hell of coming in second.

In the name of coming in first and being the center of a man's attention if only for a little while, she was ready to give nice guys a try. Her housemate and ex-lover, Sam, claimed she wouldn't regret it, since what people were always saying about nice guys was true: they finished last, and it was because they wanted their leading ladies to come in first.

A nice guy like the well-built Good Samaritan across the street, Lissa thought eagerly. Only, a glance back across the street revealed he wasn't there any longer. Neither was the kid.

"Well, shit." *So much for opportunity knocking.*

Not that she had time to do a meet and greet. She had an appointment with the owner of the Sugar Shack candy store for a potential interior redesign job. Besides, Mr. Nice Guy was likely one among a hundred like him who donated his time to Almost Family and similar nonprofit services.

How many of those others had an ass and arms like his?

A dynamite ass and a killer set of arms, and probably a gorgeous wife or girlfriend to go with them.

Her eagerness flame fanned out, Lissa put her nice guy hunt on hold. She returned her attention to the mirror for a quick teeth and facial inspection. Finding everything acceptable and her freckles returned to barely noticeable, she grabbed her black leather briefcase satchel from the passenger's seat and climbed out of the car.

The closest she'd been able to get a parking spot to the candy store was three blocks away. She was a stickler for arriving early, so reaching the place on time wouldn't require sprinting in her skirt and open-toe heels. Hooking the satchel's strap over her arm, she took off down the sidewalk.

One block in, footfalls pounded on the sidewalk behind her. Not an uncommon thing, given the number of people milling about the downtown area on a Friday afternoon. What was uncommon was how noisily they fell, like the person was purposefully trying to be loud.

Were they in step with hers?

Sam's thing was paranoia, not Lissa's. Only, it appeared her housemate was rubbing off on her. Her skin suddenly felt crawly.

Her entire body went tense with the sensation of being watched. Followed. Stalked.

Oh jeez! Could she be any more melodramatic?

This wasn't a dark, stormy night scenario. The sun shone down from overhead and, while June in Michigan didn't often equate to blistering temperatures, a warm, gentle breeze toyed with the yellow, green, and white flowered silk overlay of her knee-length skirt. And there was the fact she was surrounded by a few dozen other people.

To prove how ridiculous she was acting, Lissa stopped walking. The footfalls came again, once, and then fell silent.

Her breath dragged in.

What if she *was* being followed? The candy store was still a block and a half away. Sprinting the remainder of the distance might be the safest route. Yeah right it would. She was liable to snag a heel in a sidewalk crack and break her neck. *Then* she would have a reason to be concerned.

Ignoring the hasty beat of her heart, she faced her overactive imagination by spinning around . . . and there he was.

Mr. Nice Guy stood less than twenty feet away. Not following her or even eyeing her up, but standing in front of a coffee shop, peering into its storefront windows.

He moved toward the shop's door, pulling it open with a tinkling of overhead bells and placing his ass in her line of vision. Once more she appreciated the stellar view. This time it was more than appreciation though. This time, just before he turned and disappeared inside, he looked her way.

Lissa's heart skipped a beat with the glimpse of pure masculine perfection.

Stubble the same shade of wheat as his thick, wavy hair dusted an angular jaw line and coasted above a full, stubborn upper lip. Eyebrows a shade darker slashed in wicked arcs over vivid cobalt blue eyes. His cheeks sank in just enough to make him look lean, hungry, and dangerous all at once. Then there was the way he filled out his jeans; his backside had nothing on his front half. Beneath the faded denim, muscles bulged and strained in all the right places. And she did mean *all* the right places.

If not for catching him joking around with the youth services kid, she would have mistaken him for a bad boy in a heartbeat. He wasn't. But clearly her body approved of him.

Heat raced into her face and her nipples stabbed to life, making her wish she hadn't relied on the built-in shelf bra of her yellow short-sleeve top to hold in her cleavage. Her breasts were way too big to be fully constrained by the flimsy little cotton bras sewn into shirts. For whatever reason, she allowed Sam to talk her into giving one a try. Probably because when she slipped out of her bedroom wearing it, he'd taken one look at her chest and offered to give her a pre-appointment mouth job.

Coming from a gay guy, that was a major compliment.

The bells over the coffee shop door sounded as a gray-haired, sixty-something couple exited. Lissa glanced at her watch. Ten minutes till her appointment. A block and a half to go.

She could spend five minutes determining if Mr. Nice Guy was single and searching and then huff it to the Sugar Shack. Or forgo the meet and greet, arrive at her appointment on time, and take Sam up on his mouth job offer when she arrived home.

As much as she loved Sam, there was no future for them beyond friendship. There probably wasn't one with the guy in the coffee shop either.

Lissa walked back to the shop anyway.

To the sound of tinkling bells, she pulled open the wood door with white and red stained-glass coffee mugs designed into its window slats. Entering the shop, she looked up at the bells . . . and nearly slammed into Mr. Nice Guy.

He stood in front of a customer bulletin board, pinning business cards up with long-fingered hands that bore neither rings nor tan lines. After tacking the last card onto the board, he turned toward her, flashed a smile sexy enough to do a fluttering number on her sex, and moved right on past and out the door.

"Well, shit." *So much for opportunity knocking.* Even worse, she was starting to sound like a broken record.

She should forget about him and get to her appointment. But between his lack of a wedding ring and that sexy smile, her eagerness flame was rekindled.

Lissa grabbed one of the newly posted business cards off the bulletin board. *Thad Davies, Handyman* was written in black, and beneath it, in bold, blue lettering, *Loose Screws Construction.* Was the company name meant to be a double entendre, and exactly how handy of a man was Thad?

Handy enough to leave her his number.

Smiling, she tucked the business card into her satchel. Later, maybe she would give him a call. Or maybe she would pick up a box of Sam's favorite sweets while she was at the Sugar Shack and use them to bribe him into making good on his mouth job offer.

"You're a bastard!"

Thad Davies sank back against the black metal rails of his headboard and sighed over the glaring brunette standing on the end of the bed's bare mattress.

Naked and flushed with the aftereffects of orgasm, she looked ready to beat the shit out of him. From what little he knew of her, she was nice enough. Her sweat-glistening tits were definitely nice, as they jostled around with her anger. That didn't mean he was ready to forget she was a client and sleep with her for free. "You play, you pay, sweetheart."

With a huff, she bounded off the end of the bed, flashing an ass that was just as nice and well rounded as her tits. "Don't call me that! And don't you *ever* come near me again."

She reached the tangle of sheets, covers, and clothing, which had found their way to the floor in the midst of their wild screwing, and started kicking them apart.

Damn, he really didn't like upsetting women. It wasn't his fault they hired him for sex and ended up falling for him along the way. Not all of them did, but more than a couple had in the five months since the woman-pleasuring division of Loose Screws started up. "You called me," he reminded her.

The brunette stopped kicking to look at him, hurt evident in her eyes. "I *thought* we had something between us."

"We do. A business deal."

The hurt left her expression as cold fury took over. Soft pink lips, which less than ten minutes ago had been wrapped around his dick and delivering him to nirvana, pushed into a hard line. Giving the chaotic pile a final kick, she uncovered a slim red purse and yanked it up by the strap. "Consider the deal off," she bit out as she shoved her hand inside the purse and yanked out a handful of bills. "Don't expect any referrals to be coming your way."

Fifties and hundreds plastered him in the chest and rained down on the bed around him. Some people might feel cheap in a situation like this. For Thad, it was all in a day's work, and he happened to love his job most of the time . . . well, what man in his right mind wouldn't?

Pushing the bills off his chest, he moved to the edge of the bed and swung his legs over the side. He rolled the condom off his deflating shaft, tucked it into a tissue, and deposited it in the wastebasket between the bed and the short black oak dresser that doubled as a nightstand. "Don't you be forgetting that silence agreement you signed."

Midway through diving down to retrieve her bra and panties, the brunette's breath dragged in on a gasp. She glared at him. "Like I would tell anyone I had the poor taste to pay to fuck you."

"You got your money's worth. All six times." Today, she'd

chosen to suck him off while he fulfilled her order of oral sex. The five times she employed his services before this, she'd been after her pleasure alone. The ecstatic cries centering each of those sessions said she'd enjoyed herself plenty.

With a final huff, she jerked the bra and panties off the floor and, not bothering to go back for her skintight white minidress, stormed out the bedroom door. Less than twenty seconds later, the front door slammed. The short lapse of time told him she'd left his rental duplex buck naked.

The neighbors would have a coronary over that exit.

But to hell with what his neighbors thought. Thad had never been a saint a day in his life and he never intended to pretend otherwise, even if the ultraconservative city of Crichton and the surrounding county preferred him to do so.

He scrubbed a hand over his face, aware that line of thinking was a lie.

He didn't want to give a damn what his neighbors thought of him and if they discovered he worked part time as a gigolo, but he didn't have any choice in the matter. Thanks to the economy being blown to shit and taking his job with the local automotive plant along with it, staying in the area meant making his money by whatever means possible.

Loose Screws, the construction company he ran with two of his former plant coworkers, was taking off slowly. And business would continue to be slow until the economy bounced back. The cold hard truth was most people didn't have the money to spend on building or remodeling.

Women did have money for sex. Or whatever else might tickle their fancy, or any other part of their mind and body.

Last week Benny pulled in a grand just for spending the afternoon alone with an eighty-year-old widow. Alone and naked, but still that was a helluva lot of dough for a few hours of small talk while being ogled by an old lady.

Speaking of his business partner, Thad should give Benny a

call and see if he and Nash needed help at the current construction site. The job was a relatively small one. It was also nearly finished, and the sooner it got done, the sooner they would get paid. Nash could avoid needing the cash by sucking up his loathing for the wealthy and asking his affluent father for a handout the man was eager to give. Benny was doing whatever it took to keep his Alzheimer's-stricken foster mother in an upscale nursing home. Thad just liked to be able to afford to eat and make rent.

After going into the half bath adjoining his second-floor bedroom and getting washed up, Thad pulled on a pair of boxers and jeans, then headed downstairs to the kitchen. He lifted the cordless phone from the counter, planning to punch in Benny's cell number while he discovered what, if any, food waited in the refrigerator.

The phone rang before he could punch the first number. Pulling open the fridge door, he hit the phone's Talk button. "Loose Screws. This is Thad."

"I need you," a low, husky feminine voice implored through the phone line.

One of the reasons he was able to charge as much as he did for his gigolo services was the shitload of testosterone the good Lord saw fit to gift him with. The carnal invitation that seemed to fill the woman's words had his blood pumping hot. His cock joined in, already hungry for more loving. Remembering this was the construction phone line didn't do a thing to calm his body. The woman-pleasuring division of Loose Screws originated because of someone calling the company, guessing it to be a hustler service by its name, and hoping one of their employees might be interested in working as a stripper for a bachelorette party.

"Then you called the right place." Letting the refrigerator door shut, Thad focused on determining if she was after business or pleasure. "How might I be of service?"

"The way the ceiling's leaking, I think my roof's about ready to fall through. I need to get it fixed before the next rainstorm."

Serious words spoken in a sultry tone. Didn't tell him a damned thing. "This need business related?"

"It's personal."

If the sigh following her words was authentic, and not just a chirp in the phone line, it would suggest she was after pleasure. Loose Screws couldn't afford for him to be wrong. "So long as your place isn't too big, I might be able to squeeze you in. Lemme check the calendar."

Thad glanced at the hot rods and hotter babes calendar hanging on the refrigerator door. His next pleasure appointment wasn't until the following Thursday, with a woman old enough to be his mother. Tammy might be as old as his mother, but with her all-over tan, shoulder-length bleached blond hair, and silicone-enhanced double Ds, she didn't look a thing like his mother. Unlike Benny's client widow, she wouldn't spend their time together staring at his naked body but would have her hands and mouth all over him.

What about the woman on the phone? Did her sexy voice go with a sexy mouth she had plans to put all over him? "Are you local?"

"According to Sam, I am."

"Come again?"

A throaty, sensual laugh most women could only accomplish with a sore throat carried through the phone line. "I thought you said loco. Sam thinks I'm crazy, but then he doesn't have much room to talk." Her voice returned to the low, husky tone. "I live about five miles out of town, in an older ranch-style."

"Sam live there too?" More specifically, was Sam her man and crazy enough to take after Thad with a gun should he catch him doing his woman?

"Yeah. Though, he's stepping out pretty soon."

A female construction client wasn't bound to let on she

would be alone when he arrived. That pretty much guaranteed it was pleasure services she sought. Until he had a better idea of her relationship with Sam, Thad wouldn't be providing those services—a quick drop-by, however, would give him a chance to confirm she was after sex... while checking out the goods he would get to work with. "I'm busy later this afternoon, but I should have time to fit in an inspection before then. What's the address?"

Her voice raised a few octaves as she rattled off the address and told him the color of the house and surrounding landmarks. "By the way, my name's Lissa, or Liss. See you in a few."

Another sigh slipped through the phone line before it went dead. His cock gave a happy little jerk in response. Thad looked down at his groin. "Hate to break it to you, buddy, but she was talking to me. Unless you want Sam putting you out of commission permanently, you'd best not get any ideas about bringing Liss bliss."

2

Lissa did a little shimmy across her bedroom in potential outfit number four, a semi-sheer peach sundress that clung to her plentiful curves and required going braless with its open back and plunging scoopneck.

Sitting on the foot of her bed, Sam shook his head. "The ho-baby look's perfect for catching a bad boy, but you're chasing after a nice guy now."

Drawing a frustrated breath, she unzipped the dress, yanked it over her head, and tossed it on the bed next to him, where the previous rejects lay. It was a damned good thing his personal taste ran to nice guys, since it was becoming increasingly clear she knew absolutely nothing about catching one herself.

Giving up on the closet, which contained a mix of moderately slutty bar clothes and casually refined work clothes and not one friggin' happy medium outfit, Lissa tugged open her middle two dresser drawers and pulled out the first item in each: well-worn, cutoff jean shorts and a V-neck, red tank top. Turning around, she jokingly lifted them for Sam's inspection.

Approval entered his brown eyes and he flashed his teeth in a smile. "Nice. Girl next door meets lady in red."

Fisting the clothes in her hands, she groaned. Of course, when she was trying to be funny, she would finally get it right.

He lifted her black bra from where she'd earlier flung it on the bed and tossed it to her. "You sure you don't want me to cancel my meeting and stick around for protection?"

She feigned a pout as she set the tank top on the dresser. After hooking the back clasps, she worked the bra around her body and her breasts into the cups. "If you followed through on your offer yesterday and went down on me, you wouldn't need to be worried about some stranger coming over while I'm home alone."

He gave her a sympathetic look. "Aw, honey, your kitty might have been happy for a few days, but in the end you would still be itching for more than I can give you."

As if that wasn't apparent by the fact she'd been parading around in nothing but skimpy panties for the last half hour and he hadn't even acted a little excited.

Because she enjoyed teasing him and knew he found it equally amusing, Lissa swiveled around to face the mirrored closet door. She bent down to slide her bare feet through the legs of the cutoffs and made a show of wiggling her black panty-clad ass in his face. His smile re-emerged as she slowly straightened, trailing her fingertips along her inner thighs. The shorts settled into place over her ample hips, and she dipped her first finger inside the right cuff and beneath the leg of her panties. Her breath caught with the flick of her fingertip between her pussy lips.

With a hearty laugh, Sam shook his head. "You're outrageous, Liss."

He might not be aroused by her behavior, but her body was turned on by the idea of him watching her finger herself. Part of her wanted to slide her shorts and panties down her legs and continue masturbating until she climaxed. A bigger part was aware of how soon Thad would be over. If she was really going to give this nice guy thing a try, she ought to practice being a good girl in return.

Lissa pulled her finger free of her panties and shorts, and grabbed the tank top from the dresser. She grinned at Sam's reflection. "I'm crazy and you love me for it." Sobering, she turned around and pulled on the tank top. "Thanks for offering to stay, but I'll be fine alone with him."

"Just promise me you will be careful. Even nice guys have their naughty days."

Really? Now there was a tidbit of info she hadn't planned on but was damned glad to hear. Maybe she wouldn't have to practice at being a good girl. Not if Thad was feeling naughty enough to put out on the first date.

As if they were even having a first date.

He was coming over to check out her ceiling and roof, while she spent the time confirming he was single and then casually convinced him they should see each other when business wasn't an issue. "He's coming over to look at the roof, not to get it on."

"So says you." Sam eyed the tank top's V-neck, and she looked down to discover her cleavage nearly busting out; either the shirt had shrunk with the last washing or she'd gained weight. "So says me if, after he sees you in that top, he's still focused on the roof, you'd best be sending him my direct—" The doorbell rang, cutting him off and, in the next instant, curving his mouth in a sly smile. "I'll get it."

Lissa's heart sped up. Thad was five minutes early. Punctuality was probably a trait common to nice guys, but it pleased her all the same. Grabbing a brush off the dresser, she moved back in front of the mirrored door and gave Sam's reflection a warning look. "Don't screw this up for me."

He placed a hand over his chest and sniffed. "I'm hurt."

"What you are is a drama queen. I mean it, Sammy. For all I know, this guy could be the one." Or he might be married with six kids. But, damn, she hoped not. "I don't want him running away because you pinch his ass as soon as he clears the door."

He dropped the offended act to flash an intrigued grin. "I only do that to the gorgeous ones, so I'll take that to mean we're talking some serious eye candy."

She nodded at the open bedroom door. "Let him in and see for yourself. Just don't get any nibbling ideas."

Typically Thad wasn't one for sizing another man up. But then, typically he wasn't greeted at a potential pleasure client's door by said client's husband. Or boyfriend. Or whatever the hell the admittedly good-looking, clean-shaven, brown-haired guy in the tailored black pants, matching tie, and mint green dress shirt was to Lissa. "You must be Sam."

With a nod, Sam slid his gaze the length of Thad, lingering a little too long for comfort in the area of his groin. Sam returned his attention to Thad's face to reveal an amused smile. "You must be Mr. Nice Guy."

"Sam was just leaving," a low, throaty feminine voice said from behind Sam.

Sam stepped back from the doorway, and the owner of that sexy voice came into view and had Thad hoping to hell she was Lissa and her interest in him was purely physical.

Pleasure clients rarely greeted him in casual clothes, preferring lingerie, tight dresses, or nothing at all. This woman's clothes were casual. The way she filled them out was anything but. From her generous breasts to her curvy hips and thighs, she was the type of woman the term *hourglass figure* was coined for.

She was also remotely familiar.

A warm smile curved her lipstick-free lips. She swept a hank of loose copper, shoulder-length hair away from her face, tucking it behind her ear before extending her hand to him. "Lissa Malone."

Despite the fact he was no saint and the hell-bent rebel years of his youth, Thad had always believed in God. Moments like this with natural beauties like her conveyed his existence that much more.

"Thad Davies." Her hand was warm in his, her skin soft. The scent of vanilla drifted to him. Not strong or perfumey, like so many of his clients wore, but the subtle scent of lotion or body wash. "So you're worried about getting wet?"

Sam gave a deep chuckle, reminding Thad of his presence. Moving next to Lissa, Sam pulled her into his arms and whispered something in her ear that had her laughing as well. He released her to give Thad a look that could mean "hands off" as easily as "treat her right," then nodded a good-bye and took off down the covered porch to the sidewalk.

Lissa looked back at Thad. "*Should* I be worried?"

Between the sensual interest in her jade green eyes now and the sultry sound of her laughter moments ago, he suddenly remembered where he'd seen her before.

In his favorite wet dream. Had to be.

Sam left them alone, but his parting look didn't guarantee it was with permission to fuck. Since Thad still wasn't 100 percent sure that was the reason he was here, he played it safe. "Possibly. I can only tell so much from what you said over the phone."

Barefooted, she turned and started walking away. He closed the door and followed, because what in the hell else was he going to do?

Lissa led him through a small, open living room that branched off in two directions. She veered to the right and headed down a short hallway to a closed door at the end of it. Glancing at him over her shoulder, she said in that ultra-hot voice, "The worst of the problems are in here."

She pushed in the door to reveal "here" was a bedroom. On the trip over, he'd assured his cock it wouldn't be getting any action, but that didn't stop it from rising to attention with the prospect. Not even the nearly overwhelming African safari theme was enough to halt the hardening effect, especially when he looked a little closer.

Mating elephants adorned the wall tapestry hanging over the bed and a trio of bronze monkeys were seeing, hearing, and doing each other on a bamboo table near the headboard. The comforter featured an entire aborigine tribe fornicating in every way imaginable. It wasn't his style, but the erotic décor suggested she was his kind of woman. Rather, his kind of client. "Nice bedroom."

"I'll tell Sam you approve of his taste."

Sam slept here? Somehow the room didn't quite gel as being entirely masculine. Neither had the way Sam's attention lingered on his crotch. Was the guy gay? Or bi? More important, did Lissa sleep somewhere else?

"As you can see, the damage is getting pretty bad."

Thad followed her gaze to the ceiling to discover there truly was water damage. Well, hell, could he be lucky enough to have this be a two-in-one call?

"Sam said he felt the ceiling last night and it's really soft."

"I don't doubt it. If you look close, you can tell it's starting to bulge." Realizing what a play on words that was, he glanced over at Lissa. She was taking a lesson out of Sam's book by ogling his groin. Only, coming from Lissa, the ogling was much appreciated. "There damage anywhere else in the house?"

Her gaze shot to his face. Freckles he hadn't previously noticed scattered across her cheeks and along the bridge of her nose with her guilty smile. That smile turned teasing, and open desire sizzled in her eyes.

She clearly wanted to make a move. The noticeably solid state of his dick confirmed he wanted the same. So why was she hesitating? Was this truly supposed to be just a construction appointment, or was her relationship with Sam the problem?

She turned away and started toward the door. "My bedroom's down the hall. We should probably get to it."

That answered that. Sam wasn't a problem. The enticing sway of her hips as she traveled the short distance to her room suggested there wasn't a problem at all.

Thad stepped into the bedroom behind her, glad to see she wasn't harboring a safari fetish. Her room was decorated in cool shades of green and blue with touches of pink mixed in throughout. The bed in the center of the room was only partially made. The sheets and comforter had been tossed back in a way that hinted she wanted him to crawl inside.

He pulled his attention to the ceiling and did a quick inspection. "I don't see any cracks or signs of water damage."

"Maybe it would help if you lay on the bed."

Something told him that was as blatant an invitation as he was going to get. It could be Lissa was a doer, not a sayer.

Going with the idea, he toed off his work boots and reclined back on the bed, with his arms folded beneath his head. The subtle scent of vanilla clung to the sheets, making his body ache with the want to say to hell with the ceiling and pull her down on the bed beneath him. "Nope. Still nothing."

"Do you want me to come over there and show you where the moisture's gathering?"

Her voice was lower than ever, and he looked over to discover she still stood near the door. Movement near her sides caught his attention. He glanced down to find her hands fisting and unfisting. Nerves? "We should talk fees first."

"You seem like a nice guy. I trust you to charge me fairly."

"Is that what you want, a nice guy?" Far from a typical request—women always wanted him at his wildest.

Thad recalled Sam's greeting words then. He'd called him

Mr. Nice Guy and flashed an amused smile. Sam must favor rough sex and agreed to this pleasure session to give Lissa a chance to experience slower loving in a manner that wouldn't mean having to go slow himself. The asshole.

"I'm really out of my element here." She let out an anxious-sounding laugh. "I've never done this sort of thing before. Sam usually handles it."

He came up on his elbows. "Why didn't he today?"

"He has a meeting now and a date later."

A date? Had Lissa made a bargain with Sam—in exchange for sleeping with another guy, he got to do the same with another girl? It was a helluva way to run a relationship, but then he wasn't here to judge.

He was here to bring Liss bliss.

The reality was he didn't have an appointment this afternoon the way he told her over the phone, just the usual Saturday night burgers and beer meet-up with the guys at McCleary's Pub. That was three hours away, plenty of time for a pleasure session.

Thad's cock throbbed with relief. His fingers itched to tear away her tight-fitting tank top and short shorts to get to the lush body beneath. Meeting her eyes, he asked as a final point of clarification, "Sam's okay with you doing this?"

She looked shocked, maybe even a little offended. Her fingers ceased their curling and uncurling to form fists. "Of course, he is."

Lissa sounded testy, but she couldn't really be put off by his question. It wouldn't make sense. More likely she'd grown tired of talking and was eager to get on with the slow screwing. Lucky for her, that made two of them.

Giving her a let's-get-busy smile, he stroked the mattress next to his hip. "Why don't you come over here and show me where the moisture's gathering?"

Her fingers uncurled. Relief slid through her eyes. She crossed the room in an instant and all but flung herself down on the bed beside him. He rolled toward her and reclined on his right elbow. She did the same, coming up on her left arm. Her tits pressed together so hard with the move, he thought for sure they would pop right out of the V-neck.

No such luck.

The mounds stayed in place, taunting him with the urge to bury his face against their ampleness and have himself a mouthful.

"Thanks for not making me feel stupid about this." Lissa's voice was ripe with lust. "I didn't know if a guy like you would think the worst of me for inviting you onto my bed when I barely know your name."

A guy like him?

Thad looked back at her face, saw how completely the desire in her voice was reflected there, and realized what she meant. That he was a nice guy, because they were officially into the game.

In true nice-guy fashion, or at least what he was guessing to be nice-guy fashion, he slowly walked his fingers across the mattress. He trailed them along her neck, up to the slightly pointy rise of her chin, and then brushed her full lower lip with the pad of his thumb.

In the background of his mind, his dick roared at him to go faster. He blocked that roar out to concentrate on the dilating of her irises and the sudden hitch in her breathing. "You know, there's a reason us nice guys finish last."

She blinked once and then flicked her tongue out, dabbing at his fingertip with moist, little licks. Pulling her tongue back in, she whispered hotly, "So their leading ladies can come first."

The freckles grew darker on her cheeks and nose. She looked shocked by her words. Probably thought she'd ruined the whole nice-guy scenario. But, hell, it was her scenario to ruin, make that alter. To show her he was prepared to give her sex as wild as she desired, he cupped her cheek and slanted his mouth over hers.

Her lips parted beneath his with the first brush. Warm air pushed into his mouth. Her tongue came next, dipping damp and forcefully inside, coasting past his teeth to rub against his own tongue in a way that wasn't even remotely nice. Rather sexy as hell and speaking directly to his cock.

Lissa's hand touched down on his back as the erotic mouth play continued. Her fingers balled in the cotton of his T-shirt before skating lower to grip his ass. She jerked her body toward him and hooked her leg over the side of his, bringing their pelvises flush, her pussy tight to his cock.

Needfully, she ground along his shaft.

Even as he thought about how damned good the contact felt, being pressed against a woman with an honest figure and real meat on her bones, a moan slid from the back of her throat, breaking near silently between their joined lips.

Normally, this would be the point where he took things over. Let the bad boy all the ladies wanted break out and do his wickedest. But he could guess that would be the same move Sam would make, and Thad wasn't about to engage her in the kind of rough sex she likely got on a regular basis without her say-so.

He pulled back from her mouth. "Do you want the lead, Lissa?"

"I want whatever you want."

"This is about your pleasure, sweetheart. If I get off in the meanwhile, it's a bonus."

"God, you're so nice." Yet not nearly as nice as Lissa thought he would be . . . unless she'd gotten lucky and caught him on one of the naughty days Sam said even nice guys had.

She wanted to be as naughty as possible, by stripping the clothes from his body and getting his swollen cock inside her aching pussy, pronto. But she didn't want to do so at the cost of jeopardizing any chance they might have at something good, maybe even something lasting.

Sure, she didn't know jack about him yet, but then that was exactly the point.

"I can be bad for you," he surprised her by saying. Surprised her even more by taking her breast in his hand through her tank top.

Her nipple heated, beaded, ached for so much more.

She wanted the clothes gone. Wanted to feel his work-roughened hands, and the calluses that would undoubtedly line them, petting every inch of her. "Don't make yourself uncomfortable," she forced herself to say.

"This is about you, remember? Your comfort. Your pleasure."

Her heart skipped a beat with the sincerity shooting from his eyes, the lean angles of his face. He really meant the words. He wanted to put her first. And Lissa wanted that so badly her entire body vibrated with white-hot need.

Increasing the pressure of the leg she'd wrapped around his, she gave his left butt cheek a hard squeeze and ground against him. Her clit tingled with the delicious press of his cock. For a second, she thought, just that easily, she might be coming. But, no, she wasn't coming yet. Not until she had him naked and panting for the same.

She tugged back the collar of his T-shirt and nipped a wet kiss at his throat. "Be bad, Thad. Be very, very bad."

Hesitation wouldn't have surprised her—he was normally a nice guy, after all. The way he took her shoulders in his hands, pushed her back on the bed, and buried his face against her cleavage shocked her to no end.

And thrilled her so completely, her pussy felt molten.

Thad lifted his head to push the tank top up her torso and over the rise of her breasts. Her bra came next, lifting and moving above the mounds and making her tits look mammoth with their tops compressed beneath the underwire.

Apparently, he was into mammoth. She caught the flicker of anticipation in his eyes before he dove down and lashed his tongue between her cleavage.

Having her breasts tongue-fucked wasn't a new experience. But with the scruff of his jaw and the stubble over his upper lip rubbing against her skin with each lash, the wicked sensation rippling through her highly aroused body felt better than ever before.

One hand plumped the mounds higher, tighter together around his tongue. Lissa took his other hand in her own and brought it to her lips, sucked his first finger between them. His breath hissed out, hot and heavy, against her flesh and she repeated the act, sucking his finger in deep, hard. Wishing to God it was his cock filling her mouth, but not about to risk pushing things so far so soon.

His tongue stopped its thrusting and his head lifted, just far enough to bring his mouth to a nipple and then take the rigid bud between his teeth and twist. Her sex fluttered with the twist, grew unbearably heavy with the next one, and started clenching for a cock that was nowhere nearby with the third rough twist.

"I want your dick in me!" She sighed over the words. Ones she'd spoken to any number of bad-boy lovers, but not ones she should have spoken with Thad.

He didn't go still as she'd expected, or give her an unimpressed look. Didn't even stop the sensual torture of his teeth and lips around her nipple. Just slid a hand down the rise of her bare belly and unsnapped her shorts with a foreboding pop that drove her senses wild.

The calluses she'd been hoping for caressed the skin beneath her panties, petted her waxed mound, and then eased into the slick folds of her sex. He wiggled his finger partway inside her. Cream seeped out to greet his entrance, and he started a slow, sweet rhythm, stealing her breath with each gentle thrust.

Though she told herself she wasn't coming until he was naked and panting to do the same, with the third push of his finger inside her juicy hole the pressure balling in her lower belly became too much to hold back. Climax rippled through her as a wave of intense pleasure that had her biting down on her lower lip and being damned glad his finger wasn't any longer in her mouth.

Lissa let out a yip of ecstasy as the tremors of sensation subsided. If orgasming with his finger inside her felt so good, how amazing was it going to feel when his cock was pumping her over the edge?

It wasn't a question she planned to let go unanswered for long. He hadn't responded negatively to her crude words, so there was no reason to pretend at being a nice girl. "I want you naked."

Thad pulled his hand from her shorts and freed her nipple of his mouth. He met her eyes with challenge glinting in his own. "Make me that way."

Her belly turned over with excitement. If that challenge was a sign, she'd found herself a closet bad boy.

Not about to waste time with wonder, she buried her hands in the back of his shirt and pulled at the thin cotton until the tanned skin of his back was free. The T-shirt came over his head and her cunt flooded with fresh cream.

Swinging a hammer clearly did incredible things to the masculine physique, because his body was easily the hottest she'd ever laid eyes on. Sculpted. Bronzed. Rock hard.

He was fucking edible.

Lissa wanted to lick him head to toe . . . and she hadn't even seen him from the waist down. Her fingers shaking with anticipation, she pushed at his chest. "Lay back on the bed. I need to see more."

A chuckle rumbled out of him. His stubborn upper lip curved in a wolfish grin, lending his slightly sunken cheekbones the hungry, dangerous edge. He sat back on his haunches to tug at her shorts. "You aren't the only one, sweetheart. I need to see the hot little pussy that soaked my fingers."

"Not if I see your big, hard dick first."

His grin kicked higher, reflecting his like of her hard talk.

Heart pounding against her ribs, she scrambled to escape his weight and get him naked first. They tugged at each other's clothes. Pulling at zippers and yanking at hems, rolling together on the bed, their mouths finding each other in the chaos and fusing, tongues licking, rubbing together, teeth clicking with their wild tumbling and impatience. Then their mouths falling apart as they rolled once more, and the bed disappeared from beneath Lissa's back.

She thudded onto the carpet with an "oomph." The breath hitched out of her in time with the sound of Thad hitting the floor. Somewhere below her, or off to her side. She couldn't tell. Couldn't see a damned thing. In the midst of all that rolling and tumbling, the sheets had gotten wrapped around the top of her head.

She swiped them away from her face to discover they were wrapped around her middle as well. The left side was still tucked beneath the mattress, creating a short wall.

"You okay?" Thad's voice came from the other side of the wall.

"Yeah. You?" she tossed back, clawing at the sheets, wanting back to her quest of stripping his made-for-licking body. Or maybe she'd already gotten him naked. She'd lost focus there for a while.

Lissa tore at the sheets again, grunting when they refused to give way. "I can't get out of these things!"

Callused fingers touched down on her inner thighs, stilling her pointless fight. Denim and silk teased against her legs, coasted over and free of her toes. His voice came out raspy. "Too bad for you. The view down here's incredible."

Her belly tightened. She felt suddenly vulnerable. Naked. So awesomely hot and wet with the knowledge he was eyeing her bare cunt.

She let her thighs fall farther apart. The telling catch in his breathing was ecstasy all its own. But, damn it, not the ecstasy she wanted to be experiencing. She couldn't even reach down to spread her lips for him. "I can't get to you."

"Good thing you don't need to. Like I said, this is all about you. Your pleasure."

A whir started up on the other side of the sheet wall. A whir she recognized as one of several vibrators she kept stashed under her bed . . . and he'd found and was about to use on her.

3

She trusted him, Thad assured himself, so he would have to trust her in return. He'd obviously been sidetracked by trying to figure out what Lissa called him to her house for—construction inspection or pleasure. Getting her to sign a silence agreement before he laid a hand on her had completely slipped his mind.

He wasn't about to demand she sign one now.

What he was going to do was take the pink vibrator, with its rabbit-shaped clit stimulator, he discovered under her bed and use it to drive her wild.

Lissa opened her legs wider and her pussy lips parted, exposing her blood-red clit. He'd seen a lot of women this way, stripped as bare as possible. Still, the sight of her cunt slick with cream and clenching in anticipation of his invasion had his balls drawing tight. She was wet enough for him to slide inside her right this minute. Much as he wanted to bury himself between her fleshy thighs, he wanted to make the moment last more. Because she was a good paying client and they deserved the best.

Angling the ears of the clit stimulator toward her right thigh, he buzzed it gently against her skin. Her leg jerked and a whimper came from the other side of the short wall of pale green sheets. He touched the ears down on her other thigh with the same light buzz. Her sex clenched. Juices trickled from her hole, lifting her sexy scent on the air and making his mouth water with the want to taste her.

Bringing the vibrator partway up her thigh, he brought the ears down on her sensitized flesh as he bent forward and licked the length of her slit.

Lissa ground against his tongue. He lapped at her folds, and she writhed and moaned, "I want your dick in me. Now!"

He wanted to put it there, before the damned thing split open his best jeans. First, she was getting a second orgasm.

Drawing back on his knees, Thad gave her plump pink cunt a slap. She squeaked out another plea for his cock. He laughed, relieving a small part of his tension. Hard to believe he thought her a doer not a sayer just a short while ago. "Be a good girl and maybe I'll give it to you."

"I never would have guessed you for a tease."

"All part of the job." He grimaced with the slipup. Some women got off on the idea he was a stud they paid to fuck. Others lost all trace of desire the moment they remembered he was only theirs for the duration of the session.

Before she could give his words thought, he brought the plastic ears of the vibrator to her clit and buzzed it full on.

Her pussy flooded with scarlet. Her ass lifted off the floor and she attempted to pull her legs together.

He used his shoulders to push them back apart. "Don't be getting any ideas about fighting the pleasure. Wouldn't want to have to spank you to keep you in line."

Actually, he would love to swat her round ass, watch the supple skin turn pink, but that wouldn't be happening this time around.

He lifted the ears from her clit. She sighed, obviously thinking he was going to follow her order and slip his dick inside her. Grinning, he used his fingers to spread her labia farther apart and eased the shaft of the vibrator inside her instead.

Lissa gasped with the penetration. Then moaned, loud and long, when he rocked the dildo deep inside her, bringing the buzzing bunny ears right back tight to her clit. He gave her a handful of seconds to adjust to the overload of sensation, and then added his tongue to the mix, licking the wet flesh surrounding the vibrator. Dipping between the bunny ears to nibble at her clit.

She bucked hard against his mouth. The dildo slipped farther inside her. Her breath caught loudly. "I'm going to come," she wailed. "I don't want to come."

Thad's licking stopped short. He lifted his head to eye her over the wall of sheets. Fuck, if that wasn't a mistake.

She had those huge tits in her hands, her fingers wrapped around the nipples. Pinching, pulling, tugging them into furiously hard, red points. She'd managed to get his zipper undone and his cock partway out of his boxers when they'd been messing around on the bed. Now it twitched hard, escaping his clothes entirely. One look at her freckled cheeks and blood-swollen lips and he knew he wouldn't be delaying her order a second longer. He needed to get his dick inside her before he came on the carpet.

Only, by the sounds of things, she'd changed her mind about that order.

Holding tight to his need, he asked, "You don't?"

Lissa sank her teeth into her lower lip and gave her head a shake. Copper tendrils of hair swept against the sticky skin of her neck. "Not without you inside me," she said thickly. "Fuck me, Thad."

His heart stampeded with the desperation in her words and the pleading in her hazy green eyes. If it was a wet dream he remembered her from, then those had to be the words she was shouting to him in it.

Yanking a condom from the pocket of his jeans, Thad sheathed himself with a speed born of years of doing precisely that. To the sound of her anxious panting, he pulled the vibrator out of her body and took hold of her soft butt cheeks. He tipped her hips up to allow for the deepest penetration possible and then held his breath and pushed his cock inside.

Her pussy sucked him in greedily. Her ass bucked in his hands. "Yes! Oh God, thank you. Yes!"

Those were words he'd never been able to resist. The feel of her cunt milking him with her building orgasm was equally irresistible.

Gripping her ass cheeks hard, wishing he could see her fondling her luscious tits, he shoved into her creamy hole again and again. Alternating the speed when her sex clamped down tightly around him to ensure her clit was getting hit at the right angle for ultimate pleasure.

Lissa purred with her release. An honest to God purr that reminded him of all the cloth and metal animals getting it on in Sam's room. "You are *such* a nice guy," she panted as her juices flooded around his cock. "Sooo nice."

The words were about as far off as they could be, but Thad wasn't in the mind-set to quibble. Shit, he wasn't in a mind-set at all. Every ounce of his brainpower thundered through his body, building pressure at his lower spine and snugging his balls painfully tight before they finally gave way.

His cock exploded, cum pelting latex at breakneck speed. He pinched his nails into her bottom with the force of the climax, aware it probably hurt but not really giving a care just now.

The way her pussy hit him with another wave of cream said she didn't give a care just now either. That or she got off on the pain. Kink was fine by him. Using the sheets to tie her to the bed and take her helpless body in every way imaginable sounded pretty damned fine too.

Only, he'd done his job and, unless Lissa paid for another screw, he wasn't going to be touching her again, let alone tying her up spread-eagle so he could eat her out.

Thad let go of her butt and pulled out of her. Generally, he used the minutes following sex to make small talk and stroke the client's ego—whatever it took to see she called for his services again. That he'd considered having Lissa again, when work wasn't an issue, told him small talk and ego stroking were bad ideas.

He came to his feet to find her lying with her eyes closed, hands filled with her breasts, breathing coming short and fierce. Giving her time to come down, he left the bedroom to search out a bathroom. He found one immediately next to her room, and washed up and righted his clothes before returning to the bedroom. She laid on the floor yet, eyes open now and breathing more regular, but still with her tits in her hands.

Hell, that was distracting.

Her eyes met his and her lips curved in a satiated smile. He'd never noticed before how much smaller and thinner the top one was. The imperfection should have helped to turn his testosterone off. Instead it made him want to drop down on the floor and see if her upper lip felt or tasted any different than the bottom one.

Thad returned her smile but otherwise stood still. "I hate to ruin the moment for you, sweetheart, but we need to talk fees and paperwork."

Her eyes fell back closed on a sigh. "I feel like a limp noodle. I don't know that I can move, let alone walk to the kitchen."

"What's in the kitchen?"

"I didn't figure you could quote me accurately without seeing all of the damage. There's some moisture gathering in here and then that bad patch I showed you in Sam's room, but the roof's also leaking over the kitchen."

Thad's gut did a slow tightening with her serious tone. Lissa thought he meant fees and paperwork in regards to working on her house. For fixing her roof. Which meant she really had called him here for construction services. Was that it? "What kind of moisture are we talking about?"

Opening her eyes, she attempted to push to a sitting position, only to fall back on the carpet when the sheets around her middle refused to budge. "I don't know. I specialize in interior design and decorating. Most anything building related beyond that is out of my realm."

Though the last thing he wanted to do right now was touch her, he couldn't very well let her continue to flounder around on the floor. Bending down, he lifted her up and planted her on her feet. He fumbled around with the sheets for a while before deciding they were never going to ease up from this end and yanked the other end out from under the mattress. Finally, he was able to get her free. Get all those curves out in the open. Those gorgeous tits inches from his face and her hairless pussy nearly as close and still smelling of her climax.

He'd never allowed a construction client to become a pleasure client in the past for good reason. Unfortunately, he had the sinking feeling he hadn't done that this time either.

If his gut was right, Lissa didn't have a clue he was a gigolo. "When you were talking about moisture gathering before, did you mean on your ceiling?"

She fell into a lazy stretch that did wickedly carnal things to her body. "Of course, I meant on my—" Both the stretch and her words stopped short. Color rose into her cheeks, bringing out her freckles in masses once again. "You thought I was propositioning you," she said quietly, clearly embarrassed about it.

"I didn't mean to sound that way. I'm attracted to you, obviously, but I never meant to get you right into my bed."

She looked around the room, as if she was searching for a way to set things right, and then forewent the search to fling herself back on the bed. "There's the moisture spot. I can never find it except when I'm laying in bed. A trick of the lighting, I guess."

The trick of the moment wasn't the lighting, but the way she got his cock raging all over again with her flounce and how it resulted in a whole body jiggle.

Thad forced his gaze to follow her finger to the ceiling. He still couldn't see any water damage and he wasn't about to lie down beside her to find it. "I'd like to take this job on, but I'm not sure that'd be such a good idea after what just happened."

Lissa shot up in the bed. The pleading was back in her eyes, though for entirely different reasons. "It was a mistake. It won't happen again, I swear. Unless you want it to. Not that I expect you to want it to. You're too nice of a guy to sleep around."

Where the hell did she get this nice-guy impression of him? Was she a friend or relative of a previous construction client? Is that why he thought she looked vaguely familiar? "Where did you hear about Loose Screws?"

Sliding off the end of the bed, she went to the dresser across from the foot of it. She grabbed a T-shirt and tugged it over her head. "I pulled a business card off a bulletin board in one of the downtown shops."

She'd covered herself up for his sake, Thad knew. But the T-shirt skimming just south of her sex and her nipples pressing against the thin fabric were in some ways more erotic than having her stand naked before him. He focused on her face. "You don't know any of the company's past clients?"

"No." She frowned. "Should that concern me?"

So much for her trust. Not that he could blame Lissa for rescinding it after what went down. He wasn't a nice guy, but her behavior now suggested she was usually a nice girl. "They've all been happy with the end results. I can give you a list of references if you'd like."

Her smile came back. "Not necessary. Like I said, I trust you."

Damn big mistake there, giving that trust right back again. Of course, it wouldn't matter in his decision making, since Loose Screws couldn't afford to turn down this job. "My partners and I will fix your roof, on the condition you don't say anything to them about what happened."

"Oh. Okay."

She looked chagrined, like she thought he was disgusted with himself for sleeping with her. Knowing the strange way most women's minds worked, she probably thought he was put off by her fuller figure.

Hell, if she knew the truth. . . .

She couldn't know the truth, but he also wouldn't leave her thinking the worst. "For the record, I want it to happen again, but it's not going to. I need to keep my energy saved up for activities that pay the bills."

"He was such a nice guy." Legs dangling over the edge of the kitchen counter, Lissa lay back against the white and blue Formica and pouted at the water-stained ceiling. Thad had been gone more than an hour and she still couldn't stop moping over his parting words. "All he cared about was my pleasure, Sammy. Just *me*. That has never happened before."

"I always put your pleasure first when we were an item, so I'll assume present company doesn't count. As for lover boy, don't you worry, honey, he'll be here Monday morning wearing nothing but a tool belt and that suck-u-licious smile."

She laughed. "You wish." Sobering, she admitted, "So do I." But the odds were next to zilch.

Thad had put her needs first for a short while, but his primary focus was on work. It proved what a nice guy he was, to tell her the truth of his priorities instead of dragging her into a relationship the way so many past jerks had done, Sam non inclusive. True to his word, Sam had always put her first, but that was years ago, back before he realized men were more his style.

As if to contradict the thought, Sam moved between her thighs. He bunched her ankle-length skirt in his hands, lifting the gauzy green material up and away from her legs and planting a wet kiss on her inner thigh. Lissa shot to a sitting position with the unexpected move and the flutter of arousal that accompanied it.

He grinned. "Sean's not expecting me for another half hour. Would a friendly kitty lick cheer you up?"

"Probably. But *I* don't have the time for it. I have another appointment with the Sugar Shack." *Liar.* She had plenty of time before the meeting and, since she rarely worked more than a few hours on Saturday, had no plans to spend it in her basement office.

So why was she turning Sam down? He was a god with his tongue. Thad had been just as gifted, but then Thad wasn't here, offering up his oral services.

Sam slapped her thigh. "You're a terrible liar, Liss."

She used to get wet from his love slaps. Even when he'd done it teasingly the last few years, she'd enjoyed a little buzz of sensation. Today, his playful swat made her wish it was Thad's powerful body sandwiched between her thighs.

Easing Sam aside, she pushed off from the countertop and let the skirt fall down around her legs. "I *do* have an appointment."

"Not for another hour, when the candy store shuts down for the night. I heard the message on the answering machine this morning."

"Oh." She should have known better than to attempt to lie

to him. She just didn't want his paranoia striking and making him say something ridiculous, like suggesting she'd gone and set her heart on Thad being the one to finally put her front and center. Not that the suggestion would have been so ridiculous, considering that was exactly what Lissa had done.

Really, who could blame her for getting her hopes up? He'd seemed so perfect: hard, bad-boy outer shell with a soft, creamy, nice-guy filling.

"You know the real reason so many nice guys finish last?"

She was sick of the question, but answering it was preferable to thinking about Thad's creamy filling and bemoaning the fact she'd never gotten to taste it. "So their leading ladies can come in first."

"The other reason," Sam said seriously.

She frowned. "I didn't know there was another one."

"It's because they're afraid to put themselves out there. Sounds to me like you caught Thad on a naughty nice-guy day, which was just fine until his head cleared enough to consider his behavior. He probably felt guilty as hell over hopping into bed with you so quick and came up with the first excuse he could to avoid falling to temptation a second time."

Lissa's heart beat faster. Was he suggesting there was still a chance of her being Thad's number one, assuming his personality measured up to his dynamite body? "You think work isn't his first priority?"

"Could be it is. Or it could be he's intimidated by his lust for you. He's going to be here next week, working on the roof. If you really want a chance with him, use the time to get to know him with your clothes on."

"I can do that." How hard could it be to forget the rigorously sculpted torso hiding beneath his shirt? Her sex tingled as the vision of her hands running over his muscled, suntanned chest flashed through her mind. Maybe it would be a little difficult. "Just in case things don't work out, the kitty lick offer will still be good, right?"

Sam gave the laugh that said she was being her shameless self again. "Give me a few hours advance notice and I'll have my tongue primed and ready."

Dark brown eyes glistening with amusement, Nash took a drag from his cigarette while he considered Thad from the opposite side of the wood pub table. He let out a puff of smoke, followed by a bark of laughter. "She thinks you're a nice guy. Damn, man, now I've heard everything."

Thad hadn't told the guys the whole story of what went down with Lissa, just that in order to get contracted for her roof job, he had to convince her he was a nice guy. "Go ahead. Yuck it up." He sent a pointed look Benny's way. "But remember when you can make bills next month who you owe for landing us another *legal* job."

Nash stubbed his cigarette out in an ashtray. "Gertie's requests might not exactly be legal, but she already took care of next month's bill. Had such a fine time ogling Benny Boy up, she invited him back for seconds last night."

"This time she touched." Benny winced. "We've got to have an age cutoff. I can't handle being stroked by an eighty-year-old. I just kept seeing the wrinkled faces of the residents in Mom's nursing home." With a second wince, he grabbed his mug of beer from the table and took a long drink. He wiped the residue from his blond mustache with the back of his hand. "Christ, I can't go that route again."

Thad and Nash gave nods of understanding. The burgers and chips arrived seconds later and the guys fell into companionable silence as they ate. Thad was halfway through his olive burger when Benny asked, "What's she look like?"

"Who?" Thad questioned, though he knew exactly who Benny

meant. The woman Thad had spent the afternoon telling himself he wouldn't be touching again.

"Lissa." Benny confirmed his guess.

Thad studied the olive cheese sauce oozing out the side of his burger. "Average."

"Liar." Nash popped a chip in his mouth. "She's hot. I can tell that much by the way you say her name like it's enough to give you a semi."

Was the hardening effect hearing her name had on his dick that obvious? Thad sent Nash a quelling look. "Sorry to disappoint you, but Lissa's"—damned hot. A sex kitten, once she got past the whole good-girl persona. Potentially attached—"a nice girl."

"Nice girls like to be naughty too," Benny observed.

"I'm telling you, she's not worth wasting talk on. She might even be married. She lives with a guy." Some asshole that would leave her alone with a stranger who was clearly hot for her body. Only, hell, Thad had no right calling Sam an asshole. He had no idea what his relationship with Lissa was, but if she was truly a nice girl, then he wasn't her husband or lover. "Just lay off the flirting around Liss. You guys know how damned bad we need this job."

"All right," Nash agreed soberly. A heartbeat later, his mouth curved in a shit-eating grin. "We promise not to flirt with your girlfriend."

"For fuck's sakes, she's not my . . ." Thad caught the defensive note in his voice and stopped himself. "Nothing. She's nothing."

Only, if Lissa was nothing, just another woman he slept with and then went on his way, why was he shifting in his seat like he'd never even done over a girl as a teenager and feeling guilty as hell about lying to his buddies in the meanwhile?

4

They should be able to be adult about things and disregard what happened yesterday. But just in case they couldn't, Thad wanted to find out before he started working on Lissa's roof. Quitting the job midway through would both leave her in a bind come the next rainstorm and scar Loose Screw's image in a way the construction division of the company couldn't afford.

Thad parked his truck next to a red Dodge Charger he recognized as Lissa's. He made his way up the gravel drive and along the sidewalk, which was separated from the front of the white ranch-style house by a row of tiger lilies. He was no flower guru, but the summer he spent helping to beautify downtown Crichton through the city's youth services correction's department made certain he knew the names and markings of most local flora.

At fourteen, his punishment for illicit behavior had been a court-mandated curfew coupled with community service, or time in a juvenile detention center, his choice. Now, at thirty-two, if his illicit behavior as a gigolo was uncovered, there would be no options. His ass would be headed straight to the clink.

The thought of doing time roiled his gut and strengthened his reason for being here, knocking on Lissa's front door. Two minutes passed without a response, and Thad tried knocking again. Since her car was in the drive, it followed she would be home.

Unless she was out somewhere with Sam.

Early afternoon on a Sunday that place could easily be church. Knowing that wasn't enough to stop his dislike of the guy from surfacing. Sam would be a client of Loose Screws as much as Lissa would—it was time Thad started remembering that.

Another series of knocks without a response and he gave the doorknob a twist. Finding the door unlocked, he pushed it in. "Hello? Anyone home?"

More silence.

Damn. He should have called ahead. He hadn't because he didn't want Lissa to be prepared for his visit. Encountering her when her guard was down and genuine Liss shining through would be the true test of his ability to keep his hands off her.

Walking into the house, he considered the way the living room branched off in two directions. Yesterday, he'd gone right and arrived at the bedrooms and bathroom. Today, he wasn't up to finding Lissa alone in her bedroom. Or, worse, finding her and Sam paying homage to the elephants screwing on his wall hanging by doing the same.

Going with the safer route, he veered off to the left. A good-sized kitchen with white and pale blue linoleum flooring and an attached dining room opened up. Hushed music drifted from somewhere nearby. He followed the muted strains to a closed door on the far side of the kitchen. Amped-up music would explain why Lissa hadn't heard him calling. If she was behind the door, she also wasn't liable to hear him if he tried calling out again now.

Feeling too much like the rebel teen who'd been caught breaking and entering almost twenty years ago, he pulled open the door to reveal a semidark stairwell. Rock music blasted his ears as he started down the stairs. The lyrics from "Lick It" registered and his gut tightened with the idea he was about to walk in on Lissa giving Sam head. He should turn back, get the hell out of the house, and call ahead next time he wanted to drop by. The idea he could get to the bottom of her relationship with Sam and, in doing so, potentially eradicate his want for her had him continuing on.

Thad reached the bottom of the stairwell . . . and froze.

Twenty feet to his left, Lissa sat rocked back in a maroon, wheeled office chair. Her bare feet were propped up on a desk in front of a lit computer monitor and her head reclined back, copper tresses flowing over the chair's top edge. Her eyes were closed. Her lips glistening with shiny red he attributed to the sucker making its way along the curve of her cheek and down the front of her throat.

"You gotta lick it, before you stick it. . . ." She sang a notch or two above the music, pumping the balls of her feet on top of the desk as her left hand continued the sucker's descent along the column of her throat, past her collarbone.

Her white sports bra should have looked puritan, virtuous even. But the way she was reclined back gave him a perfect view of the line of her generous cleavage and destroyed every ounce of innocence.

In time with the next verse to "stick it," she pushed the sucker between her breasts and started a thrusting game to mimic the way he'd tongued her tits less than twenty-four hours ago. Thad's cock pulsed with the memory of sucking her erect nipples into his mouth as her pussy tightened around his finger with her climax. His shaft pulsed that much harder when Lissa's lips parted on a rapturous cry, suggesting she was doing far more than sucker-fucking her breasts.

He looked to the right side of the basement, half expecting Sam to be sitting there, watching the show while he pumped his meat in his hand. A shuffleboard table and dartboard pitted up against the wall and a short wet bar with two backless stools extended out from the corner. Both stools were empty.

Sam wasn't around and neither should Thad be. But he was here, was watching, and was anxious as hell to discover exactly what she was doing in that chair.

Where the right side of the basement had concrete flooring, the left side was carpeted. Between the pounding beat of the music and Lissa's now-and-again cries, he was able to move soundlessly across the gray tweed flooring. Five feet away from her, the angle he approached her at uncovered the fact she wore men's black boxers. She wasn't having any problem filling out the area designed to accommodate the male anatomy either. Her right hand snaked beneath the waistband, her knuckles pushing at the cotton material from the inside out.

He didn't need to see her pussy to know her fingers were pumping away inside it. But he wanted to. Wanted to strip the boxers down her legs and watch her masturbate until her juices were running along her thighs. If she wasn't a potential construction client, he would probably do just that. She *was* a potential client, and Loose Screws damned well needed her business.

Pushing out deep breaths meant to calm his raging dick and the thundering of his pulse, Thad let her continue to sing and sigh along with the music. Right up until the moment the sucker left her sports bra and started down the soft rise of her belly to the boxers. Her hand lifted up in the boxers, creating an opening for the sucker to slide into while flashing a glimpse of her damp, hairless mound.

No way in hell could he stand idly by while she slid that sucker into her cunt and proceeded to fuck herself with it.

"Sorry. Didn't realize you were busy." He shouted the lame words.

The sucker stilled beneath the edge of the boxers. Lissa's eyes flew open, slanting toward him dark jade and heavily lidded. Blinking at him, she pulled the sucker from the boxers. Then she did something he never saw coming. She closed her eyes again and pulled her right hand free of the boxers to move it to the slit at their front and part the material, making a perfect frame for her sex.

Her feminine lips plumped up, blood red and slick with arousal. She brought the sucker to her mouth and gave it a thorough tonguing. Juicy wet, she trailed it back down her belly, over top of the boxers, and along the slit of her labia.

On a sharp inhale, Thad brought his hand over his throbbing cock through his jean shorts. He had to stop her. He would never be able to work for her after watching her get off with the sucker. But then, he would probably never be able to work for her after seeing what he already had, so he might as well let her finish what she started.

A naughty smile curved Lissa's lips as she parted her sex. Using her index finger to stroke her clit, she twisted the head of the sucker against her hole. A moan trembled above the blatant music and her feet went flat and still on the computer desk. She gave her clit another stroke, followed by a flick of her fingernail that shot her hips forward, propelling the sucker partway inside her sheath.

Vivid freckles broke out on her cheeks and nose. Juices pushed out around the ball of the sucker. Grinding the sucker all the way inside her pussy, she pumped the hard candy against the walls of her sex. Her pelvis shot forward with each pump, and she angled the sucker stick to rub across her clit in time with the thrusts.

Her breathing turned to ragged pants that stole his mind from the music and the knowledge he'd given up on holding back and was stroking his cock through his shorts. All his attention centered on Lissa's sensual moves.

Her hips bucked off the chair once again, hovering in the air for a long moment before falling back on the seat with her low, husky moan. Her pussy spasmed around the sucker. First clenching the candy tight and then pushing it partway out of her sex along with a flood of cream. "Yes, Thad! Just like that. Fuck me just. Like. That."

His hand stilled on his dick. What the hell was she doing shouting his name?

The answer was irrelevant. Hearing Lissa call his name out with her orgasm was enough to have him moving behind her chair and pressing his mouth over her upturned one. Her lips parted and her tongue slid eagerly against his. She tasted of cherry sucker and sex, and Thad wanted to lick her everywhere.

Her left hand came up to curl around the back of his head and drag him down for a longer, wetter kiss. He sucked, nibbled, licked, and ate at her mouth, until her light vanilla scent and the potent aroma of her juices became too much to disregard.

Releasing her lips, he turned his head in search of her hand, pulling the first two fingers between his lips and lapping at the juices coating them. His balls went snug as the hot taste of her zeroed straight to his overaroused cock. "Shit. This just makes me want to lick your pussy all the more."

Lissa's breath rushed out on a sharp exhale. She jerked her fingers from his mouth and shot up in the chair. Her feet dropped to the floor and the cream-drenched sucker pulled from her sex to go sailing across the room.

Shock passed through her eyes. Her lips moved. She had to be speaking quietly because he couldn't hear what she was saying over the music.

Noting a small silver CD player on the shelf above her computer monitor, he hit the Pause button. "What did you say?"

"You scared the crap out of me!" She swiveled in her chair

to face him, looking guilty as sin and twice as tempting. "I thought I imagined you standing there."

Thad's gaze fell to her crotch. Her legs were a couple inches apart and the opening she'd made in the boxers hadn't quite closed up. "I tried knocking, then calling out to you, but the song was obviously working its magic."

"*I* was working. The song was my mood music." Her voice dared him to deny her.

He'd never been known for turning down dares. Or a hot woman with her pussy hanging out. "Decorating a sex lounge?"

"Seriously doubtful in this county."

The truth in her words hit home. Crichton was a bedroom community and not in the respect that people publicly talked about what went on between their sheets. He had to stop talking to Lissa about sex. "I thought you might have clients outside the area."

"I do. But none of them own sex lounges." She jerked her chin at the computer monitor and the digital rendering of a store layout on the screen. "I'm pulling together design ideas for the Sugar Shack."

"Since when do they sell X-rated candy?" The words never should have left his mouth, but her lips were still glistening cherry red from the sucker, distracting him.

She shifted in her seat before crossing her legs and hiding his prize. "They don't. I got stuck on ideas and thought an orgasm might help to clear my head. I didn't know I had an audience for real."

Even if she thought she was only fantasizing, it didn't sound like something a nice girl would do. Neither did tossing out the word *orgasm* like they were discussing the weather. So maybe she wasn't a nice girl. Or maybe she was. Either way, it didn't matter. Thad was taking himself off this job and away from Lissa.

Nodding toward the dartboard and shuffleboard table on the opposite side of the basement, he asked offhandedly, "How do those figure in with your work?"

"When I finish a job and a client tells me how much they like what I've done with their place, Sam and I come down here to celebrate."

"Where's Sam now?"

Lissa winced at the edge in his voice. Sam had been right about Thad feeling like a victim to his lust around her. The way he was acting now, uptight and barely sparing her a glance, made it clear she'd pushed him too·far with her masturbation show.

At first, she really had believed he was a figment of her imagination, but then she'd known better. The sizzling want in his cobalt eyes had been too arousing to let pass. Being a good girl was turning out to be a big job. After tasting the carefully restrained hunger in his kiss it was also a job she wasn't about to give up on.

Standing from the office chair, she crossed her arms over her breasts, hiding her barely dressed state as much as possible given her limited resources. "Sam's at his own work. He's the curator at the field museum. They just got a new lion exhibit in and he wanted to be there to see the display plans he put together were followed."

Thad finally met her eyes. A calm smile curved his scrumptious lips, suggesting he'd filtered the last several minutes from his mind. "I never got a chance to finish my inspection and was hoping to wrap it up today. Since I won't be working the job, I want to be able to give the guys as good of a supply and man-hour estimate as possible."

"You *what?*" Jeez, oh man, Lissa better really be imagining things now.

His apologetic look was all too real. "Working on a roof is dangerous enough without being distracted, and that you definitely do to me. Nash and Benny are good guys. You'll be impressed with their work."

"But I don't trust them. I trust you."

His gaze narrowed on her. "Why?"

"You're a nice guy." He didn't look convinced it was enough, so she added, "You've never given me a reason not to trust you. A lot of men would have taken advantage of catching me masturbating."

A self-deprecating smirk tugged at his lips. "I tried."

"You got sucked into the moment. The second I realized I wasn't imagining your presence and told you so, you stopped trying."

Thad's smirk turned into a smile so wide she thought for sure he would start laughing. What was it with her that her attempts to be serious ended up amusing people, and vice versa?

He smiled at her a few more seconds and then looked toward the stairwell. "I have to be somewhere at three, so I should get started on the inspection."

Lissa pouted behind his back. Apparently the words were her cue to get started on accepting she had no chance with him. So much for her dip into the nice-guy pool. She should be glad she'd failed so miserably. Bad boys never cared enough to put her first, but they also didn't make her sulk. "Do you want my help? I'd rather not get up on the roof, if that's okay by you."

"Scared of heights?" he asked without looking back.

"No. Of falling and breaking something important. I like my body just the way it came assembled."

His gaze moved back to her, zipping from her bare feet to her hair, which she'd only gotten around to finger combing so far today. The heat in Thad's eyes when he met hers said he liked her body plenty himself. Just not enough to give in to the naughty urges she surfaced. "I shouldn't need any help. I just didn't want you to hear someone on the roof and decide to break out your gun."

"I prefer a Louisville Slugger as my weapon of choice."

"You play ball?"

She sighed. Another attempt at humor down the drain. She did have a baseball bat, but she didn't use it to take out unexpected guests. "I was in a softball league the last few years, but I've got too much going on now to keep up with practice and games."

He nodded at her computer monitor. "Business is good for you?"

"Yes," she answered succinctly. Lissa realized he was making small talk then, instead of attempting to hightail it up the stairs. Idle as the conversation was, it could be her one chance to put him at ease around her. She smiled warmly. "I signed a new contract last night."

"You're obviously great at what you do to be pulling in clients right now."

"Actually, hiring an interior designer is more cost-efficient than most people think. As much as anything else, my job is to help save money while making more space available in an established environment." She recalled what Thad said yesterday, about needing to concentrate all his efforts on activities that paid the bills. Maybe that wasn't just an excuse not to sleep with her. "Business isn't so good for you?"

He shrugged. "Things are pretty slow on the construction side. The way the economy is, I'm surprised we're seeing as much work as we are."

"What else do you do?"

What looked like discomfort, probably over the idea she wanted to know more about him after he effectively turned her down a second time, registered in his eyes. "Just, uh, general handyman stuff."

"I have quite a few connections. If you were to work on my roof and impress me with your many talents, I might be encouraged to put in a good word for you." Lissa hadn't meant the sexual talents she'd gotten a sampling of yesterday, but Thad's hesitant expression said that was how he took it.

She sighed. So much for setting him at ease. After that comment, the chance of her being the center of his attention, even for the handful of days he worked on her roof, was as good as gone.

"You're kidding me?" Thad barked into his phone. He glared out the kitchen window at the neighborhood lights cutting through the black night and wished to hell he could somehow redo this day. Starting with not going over to Lissa's house and ending by magically making Benny's foster mother's health get better instead of taking a grim turn for the worse.

"I wish I was," Nash returned morosely from the other end of the phone line.

"So do I," Thad agreed, careful to put the right amount of sympathy into his voice this time.

He knew how close Benny was with his foster mother, how the woman had turned him from a kid who took comfort in hurting himself to a good-hearted man, and he hated the thought of him sitting at her hospital bed, praying for the improbable. But Thad also couldn't get past the reality that, with Benny out of commission, Nash was going to need help with Lissa's roof. Loose Screws couldn't afford to hire someone, even short term, which meant that help would have to come in the form of Thad himself.

Shit. He was screwed.

He would never be able to play the nice guy for however many days it took to re-lay her roof. As he'd cautioned, he would be physically up on the roof, while his mind traveled to her basement office and thoughts of her loving herself up with a sucker.

Then again, maybe he wouldn't be screwed. Maybe he would be so distracted he would fall off the roof and break his pecker. It would bring an abrupt end to his gigolo services and every chance he had with women in the future, but right about now that didn't sound like such a bad thing.

Inhaling the fresh scent of springtime in the country, Lissa started around to the backside of her house. A huge, ugly green dump bin had been dropped in the yard this morning and was now in the process of killing the grass with its hulky weight. Typically, she loved the three acres of grass and another two of woods that made up the backyard. Today, she could've cared less. Thad was on her roof, stripping up thirty-year-old shingles and tar paper.

That he was only here because his partner's mother was gravely ill faded her good mood some, but not enough to stop her anticipation for the possibilities that lay in the week ahead.

Five days of roofing work. Five days to get him to change his mind about them by proving she was okay with coming in second to his job. All right, so in the long run she wasn't okay with it. But for now, knowing he was the kind of guy who would put her first as soon as feasibly possible, she could handle it.

Lissa reached the metal ladder leaning against the side of the house and extending up to the roof. She tipped back her head and shielded her eyes from the late morning sun. The scraps of roofing material flying over the side of the house to land in and around the dump bin told her Thad was on the roof, but she couldn't see him.

It was for the best he was out of sight. No use getting her hormones riled up before heading out to meet with a supplier, even one who happened to be her friend. "I have to run into town," she called out. "Do you need anything before I leave?"

"Will Sam be around?"

"A lot of times he comes home for a quickie lunch. Why?"

"In case any questions come up." Thad's head came into

view followed by his body encased in worn jeans and a white sleeveless T-shirt that clung to his heat-dampened torso. He did a toe-to-head assessment of her practical low-heeled sandals, casual charcoal gray slacks, and burgundy knit top. A warm smile claimed his mouth. "You look nice, Lissa."

She wet her suddenly dry lips. "You look hot."

Seriously, who knew sweat could be so appetizing? If she thought there was a chance of him allowing it, she would risk scaling the ladder to get on the roof and lick the perspiration from his hard body.

He wiped an arm across the sweat beaded on his forehead. "It's muggy out today. Not the best condition for working on a black roof."

"If you want to take a shower to cool off, I don't have to go right now." Lissa winced at the raising of his wickedly arched eyebrows. God, what a mouth she had. She might as well have offered to skip her meeting to stay home and wash his balls with her tongue. "I don't think that came out right. I meant the shower can be tricky to run and I would be happy to stick around to get it working for you."

"Thanks for the offer, but I'm good for now." He peeled off his T-shirt and tossed it aside. Glistening golden tan skin dusted with wheat-colored hair and inch after inch of rippling sinew came into view to do a swelling number on her sex.

"You look hot." Nice. She sounded like the broken record he'd made her that first day she spotted him, outside of the Almost Family building. "Hotter. You look hotter now." Yeah, like that was so much better.

Thad's eyebrows raised again, staying that way long enough to suggest she was treading in unsafe territory. But really what fun was there in playing it safe?

It wasn't fun she was after today, Lissa scolded herself. Today, and probably tomorrow and the next day too, her goal was to relax him enough around her to allow them to have a friendly conversation. Once he saw sex wasn't the only thing on her mind, she would convince him she was fine with his putting work first for the time being . . . and then she would get him naked.

But no naked time today.

Ruefully, she dragged her gaze away from his honed torso, down the rungs of the ladder, to the safety of the grass. "I'm leaving now."

"Sure you aren't feeling too distracted to drive?"

She darted a look back up at him. He was smiling, in amusement, or relief she was going? Uncertain, she attempted an innocent smile. "What would I have to be distracted about?"

He looked at her a few seconds, just looked with his deep blue eyes so intense she wanted to wriggle out of her work clothes and into his arms. Without responding, Thad turned and bent down to pull at a strip of shingles near the roof's edge. Only, he had responded, Lissa realized, by placing his lusciously tight ass in her face and giving her a whole new distraction.

Since his back was turned, she allowed a few seconds of ogling and then hurried around to the front of the house. She was almost to her car when Nash called from behind her, "Wait up, Liss."

Ignoring him sounded like an incredibly good idea. But since he probably wanted to ask her a question about the house, she couldn't do it. She turned back to find herself inches away from another naked, sweaty, beautifully sculpted chest.

Nash had been on the other side of the roof the last while, taking down a supply list. Obviously, no matter what a guy was doing, being surrounded by dark shingles on a sunny, humid day required going topless.

He hit her with a smile that deepened the cleft in his chin and oozed bad-boy charisma. "If there's something going on with you and Sam, you have no chance of getting lucky elsewhere."

Hard bodied. Cocky. Undoubtedly naughty. A week ago she would have assured him Sam was a friend and then demanded he pin her up against her car and do all kinds of wicked things. Now, all she could think was that he wasn't Thad. "If that's your attempt at a come-on, it sucks."

Good humor flashed in Nash's eyes with his laughter. "I don't hit on the object of my friend's lust, but if I did, I guarantee it wouldn't suck." He sobered to reveal, "Thad thinks there's something going on between you and Sam and until he learns otherwise he's not going to be putting his hands back on your merchandise, if you catch my drift."

Thad had told his partners about their sleeping together? It didn't seem likely given he made her swear not to mention it as a condition of Loose Screws taking on her roof job. But then, how else would Nash know about them? And was he suggesting Thad was only keeping his hands off her because of Sam?

Lissa's body hummed with hope. "What do you know?"

"Nothing. And if you let on to Thad I suggested to the contrary, I'll deny it. All that should matter to you is he's a nice guy who could use a good woman in his life. A good, *single* woman."

"I'm single, but I can't make any promises about being good." She bit her tongue over the words, cursing Shameless Liss for slipping out with her excitement. But woohoo! There was a chance for naked time with Thad today yet.

Nash's amused smile returned. "I can see why he likes you. He *is* a nice guy, but he's also got a wild streak. He would never say it to your face, but he likes his women with spunk. The kind who aren't afraid to take charge and stake their claim."

"I need to go." Not around to the other side of the house to yank Thad off her roof and onto her lap either. Later, hopefully, she would get him to relent to his lust so they could get naked and be the center of each other's attention for the rest of the day—better yet, year. First, she had to be a good girl and somehow manage to turn off her overeager hormones long enough to meet with her supplier.

"Thanks for the insight." Nash nodded in reply, and she walked the last few feet to her car. Opening the driver's door, she turned back. "Watch yourself around Sammy. He's not my lover, but he is gay and has a thing for pinching hot guys on the ass."

Tammy Anderson, Lissa's custom furnishings supplier, opened her office door to greet her with a friendly smile. For a woman in her mid-fifties, she didn't look a day over forty. Tammy confessed to having bodywork done, to go along with her dyed blond hair, though there wasn't a single mark on the visible portions of her body. In a silk chartreuse scoopneck top and silver crop pants, plenty of skin and the majority of her ample breasts showed.

Tammy settled into her chair behind an L-shaped desk. Catalogs, swatches, and paperwork were organized on the long side of the desk, off to her left, and a slim silver laptop sat in front of her. "I was wondering if you were going to make it in today."

Lissa glanced at her watch as she took a seat across the desk. "It's one after eleven. Wasn't our meeting at eleven?"

"Yeah. But in the six years we've worked together, you've never arrived less than ten minutes early."

Wow. She was right. Arrival time hadn't even crossed Lissa's mind during the short trip into Crichton. All she could think about was Thad and how she was going to seduce him once she got back home. "My house is being re-roofed. I took the time to make sure the guys didn't need anything before I left."

Tammy narrowed her light blue eyes, giving Lissa a skeptical once-over. "Something's not right here, Liss. You have construction men slaving away on your roof and we're meeting in my office? Tell me these guys are ugly."

"They're ugly."

Tammy gave a dry laugh. "I *bet* they are."

"They are." Lissa smiled impishly. "Unless you're into sweaty muscles, tight asses, and cocky grins." Nash's grin was cocky anyway. Thad's grin only turned that way when she managed to make him forget he was a nice guy.

If not for this meeting, she could have him grinning that way right now. Have her hands running all over his nude, sweaty body. Her mouth wrapped around his cock. Her tongue licking from base to tip and back again.

Her eyelids fluttered shut as she imagined the hot, silky, masculine taste of his seed and then him tasting her in return. Sliding his tongue in and out of her pussy while he taunted her clit with his fingers.

"Paging Lissa. Is Lissa Malone still in this office?" Tammy's voice piped into her steamy thoughts, opening Lissa's eyes.

Tammy smiled amusedly. "We need to reach a decision by noon if you want this order to go in today."

Lissa looked down to discover cabinetry and room accessory catalogs on the desk in front of her. When had they gotten there? "Sorry. I'm distracted."

"You've got hot roofers at home. Who could blame you?"

Really, who *could* blame her for not being able to concentrate after what Nash revealed about Thad? The news was simply too incredible for Shameless Liss to cast aside. And Shameless Liss was exactly what Thad was going to get.

In approximately ten minutes.

Tingling with excited energy, Lissa pushed back her chair and picked up an armful of catalogs. "One day isn't going to make any difference on this project. Can I take these home to go over tonight and e-mail you the order in the morning?"

"Only if you promise to attach pictures of your roof under

construction. You know, when the half-naked studs are on it, with their tight asses bent over and their beefy arms pounding away."

"You got it." Though it wasn't visions of Thad's arms but another part of his anatomy pounding away inside of her that filled Lissa's mind and heated her through as she sped back home.

5

Heart slamming in her chest with anticipation and the reality Thad could still reject her, Lissa stepped out of her car. She hurried up the driveway and along the flower-lined sidewalk to the front porch. Nash sat on the edge of the covered porch, chewing on the end of a pen cap as he jotted notes on a clipboard. She moved in front of him, casting a shadow over the clipboard.

The pen stilled in his hand. He looked up at her and lifted the cap from between his teeth. "What's up?"

She glanced at the roof and then back at Nash. Given what he told her about Thad's taste in women, he was all for them hooking up. That being the case, she let her intentions come through in a dirty-girl smile. "I'm going to need Thad for a one-on-one job for at least the next five hours. Take the rest of the day off with pay."

Approval shined in Nash's eyes. He capped the pen and stuck it under the metal lip of the clipboard. "Yes, ma'am." He stood. "Remember, he won't say it to your face, but he's into spunky women who aren't afraid to take charge and make their claim."

Every stimulated cell in Lissa's body was counting on that fact. She turned and watched Nash walk to a tan S-10, her gaze wandering to the seat of his jeans out of habit. He climbed into the cab and started the truck, giving her a thumbs-up through the open driver's side window as he backed out of the drive.

She waited until the truck pulled out of the driveway and disappeared down the tree-lined stretch of gravel road before heading inside the house. Sam was at work, which left choosing an outfit to entice Thad with up to her. Then again, selecting an outfit would be moot now that she was operating under the idea he secretly wanted a bad girl.

All she needed to put her plan into action was protection.

A well-padded bodysuit would ease her anxiety over voyaging onto the roof. Since the outfit sounded about as unappealing as a girl could get, she settled on sexual protection, lifting a condom from her top dresser drawer and returning outside. Her stomach flip-flopped as she started up the ladder to the roof. The thought that Thad was up there, sweaty, shirtless, and waiting for her, kept her climbing.

Her belly tightened with her first step onto the roof. Then she caught sight of him, thirty feet away. His biceps glistened in the sun, muscles bunching in a way that shot heat directly to her core as he yanked at one of the few remaining shingles on this section of roof. Desire fought back nerves, and she moved as fast as possible toward him.

Seeming to sense he was no longer alone, he called over his shoulder, "Hey, man, can you toss me the shingle shovel? I can't get this bitch off."

His crude language told her he guessed her to be Nash. It also suggested Nash was accurate and a not-quite-so-nice guy lingered just beneath Thad's surface. Her pussy dampened with expectation. "Sorry. My hands are full."

Thad's head whipped around, eyes narrowing as they met Lissa's face. "I thought you were afraid of—" His gaze fell on the condom in her hand and he stopped short to frown. "What are you doing, Liss?"

"Giving you what you want." The words came out breathy.

Standing, he crossed to where the shingle shovel lay. He grabbed the shovel and returned to scrape at the shingle. "You know I want you. You also know I won't sleep with you again and why."

"You need to put making money front and center in your life. I get that and I'm okay with coming in second."

He stopped scraping to give her a doubtful look. "I don't buy it."

Smart man. If she was talking about the long term. "Right now, all I want is to feel your mouth on mine and your cock sliding inside me. If you decide you want the same, I'll be on the back porch." She started walking. Turning back after three steps, she flashed a naughty smile. "Naked."

"Nice girls don't act this way."

"I never said I was nice." Just led him to believe such in the hopes it would aid her cause. According to Nash, all she needed on her side was her everyday unabashed personality. "If it helps to sway your decision, remember I'm paying for your time."

"So basically I'd be your gigolo?"

He didn't sound put off by the idea, which led her to believe her sensual invitation was beginning to bring out his wild streak. Her smile widened. "Yep. My paid stud."

"What if I really was a gigolo?"

"You'd be the envy of thousands."

Thad gave up on loosening the son-of-a-bitch shingle to watch Lissa continue across the roof. She gingerly crossed to the other side of the peak and then disappeared from sight.

Did he dare buy her words? Was she only after sex without promises and did she really not care if he was a gigolo?

He was willing to bet both answers were no, but he was also rock hard and raring to cross over to the other side of the roof to discover if she really was naked on the back porch. Considering she already risked climbing up here and the pitch was almost flat over the porch, the odds were favorable she was lying nude on the yet-to-be-stripped shingles, with her bare thighs spread and her succulent tits filling up her hands.

His dick twitched as the erotic image planted itself in his head. Nearly certain he would live to regret it, he started over the roof peak.

Lissa came into view immediately, speeding his pulse. Every one of her generous curves was exposed, the sun beating down to shimmer against her skin, lightly tanned in the areas clothing didn't normally hide and creamy white in the others.

His attention strayed to those other areas as he moved closer. Her hands weren't massaging her breasts, but crossed leisurely over her stomach. Her legs not spread in invitation, but straight out and bent slightly at the knees. He kept going until he was next to her, inhaling her sultry scent—vanilla touched with the musk of arousal—and discovered her eyes were closed.

Well, hell. Here he was feeling ready to bust out of his jeans and there she was looking ready to doze off while she caught a few rays. "For someone who was afraid of falling off the roof and breaking something yesterday, you're looking mighty relaxed."

"It's a façade."

Her voice was even lower and huskier than normal, and it coursed a shiver of want along Thad's spine. "Give me your hand. I'll help you get down."

She opened her eyes to reveal dark green hunger. Her lips curved in an eager smile. "I meant it's a façade if I look relaxed. I'm anxious as hell. You've had your eyes on every inch of me a couple times now. I've yet to see you naked below the waist."

Lissa came up on her knees in front of him, revealing she'd used her clothes as a protective layer between her body and the shingles' rough finish. She tugged on his tool belt. "Get down here and let me fix that."

His shaft pulsed with the command in her words. "I still don't think this is a good idea." Loving on the roof, or loving at all. Even so, he went down on his knees.

His skin was already so hot he shouldn't have detected the warmth of her hands. But he felt that delicious heat in every part of him as she placed her palms on his bare chest and ran them slowly down his torso to the tool belt.

Eyes on his, smile growing a little naughtier with each passing second, she eased the buckle open and set the tool belt aside. "Don't think. Turn off your mind and listen to your inner bad boy."

Yeah, he could do that. Had done it a hundred plus times before—not listened to his inner bad boy, but let his naturally naughty self shine through. Only one thought niggled at him. "Sam is—"

Her fingers went to the front of his jeans, popping the button and easing down the zipper. "Not an issue."

Bending her head, she flicked her tongue across his nipple. Thad sighed over the contact and the heady sensation shooting from the instantly erect disc to his groin. With the next damp flick, her fingers pushed through the split in his boxers, finding his cock, wrapping around the solid length and pumping.

The breath hissed out of him. He took her sides in his hands, stroking her warm skin as she started working her tongue's way down, laving along the muscles of his abdomen, dipping into his navel. She moved lower still, until her ass was plumped up lushly with her position and her tongue almost stroked over his cock in time with the pump of her fingers.

Lissa lifted her tongue and pulled her head back. Her fingers came next, freeing his aching shaft to the humid air. The pitch of the roof was nearly nonexistent as he'd guessed, so fear of falling off wasn't an issue. Being reported by the neighbors for indecent exposure could be. Belatedly, he looked around, only to find she didn't have any nearby neighbors.

Even if she had neighbors, he probably wouldn't have cared a second later, when she flicked her tongue back out and lashed the wet tip across the head of his penis.

His heart rate spiked. Pre-cum pearled in her wake. Thad reached forward and cupped her plump ass cheeks in his hands, caressing the soft flesh.

Stroking his inner thighs, she went back for a second tongue lashing. Then blew on the moist, pink head of his cock. "You hearing that bad boy yet?"

Louder than he ever recalled hearing him. "Starting to."

Her fingers went to his balls, fondling their weight as she pressed her face nearly flush with his groin. Her lips came down on the side of his shaft. She kiss-nibbled his straining flesh, trailing her tongue along the sensitive vein at the underside, before asking, "What's he saying?"

He shuddered with the loss of contact. Tightening his hold on her ass, he pulled her closer. "He wishes you'd hurry up and start sucking his cock."

Lissa let go a deep throaty laugh. "Sounds like my kind of guy. There's nothing quite like a good cock appetizer before lunch. Nothing other than having one as the main course, that is."

Her mouth moved to the head of his dick. No teasing games, just parting her lips and taking him inside. An inch and then two. More until the moist heat of her mouth enveloped all she could take.

Feathering his balls with one hand, she cupped the base of his shaft in the other while her tongue and lips possessed his cock. She sucked him hard and deep, again and again, pushing him to the edge too damned quick. Months had passed since he'd experienced pleasure for the sake of pleasure alone. Since he hadn't fucked a woman without being paid for his services. He wasn't going to feel guilty for coming early and before her. Not when he knew he could and would be hard again in minutes.

Tension pulled at his spine, bringing him back on his bent legs. Lissa's beautiful tits rubbed against his thighs with each pump of her mouth, and a primal growl registered in his throat.

Thad lifted his hands from her butt to grip her hair in his hands. His fingers tightened reflexively with her next suck. His balls went taut. "A couple more sucks, sweetheart, and you're going to be getting more than a mouthful."

Lissa's mouth lifted from his cock before he could make good on the vow. He groaned with the abrupt departure. "That wasn't a warning. You could have finished your appetizer and I'd have been good for the main course ten minutes from now."

Looking pleasantly surprised, she rocked back on her bent legs. The flush of her cheeks had her freckles at an all-time redness and the color of her aroused nipples was just as vivid. She grabbed the condom from beside her laid-out clothes. "Remind me of that come dinnertime."

So she planned to do this again? How many times and was it still with the idea she didn't mind coming in second?

He hadn't felt bad about wanting to come in her mouth before she found her release, but the thought of putting her second, after his pleasure clients, had his gut knotting.

Her fingers touched down on his hypersensitized dick, working the condom on and bringing his thoughts up short. Her legs parted to expose the juices leaking along her inner thighs as she attempted to crawl onto his lap.

Thad took her arms in his hands and turned her away from him. "On your hands and knees."

She purred out a murmur of approval. "Do I detect a bad boy coming out?"

Actually, he'd been thinking the position would cause the least damage to their bodies should the clothes slip away. But he would happily be a bad boy. Would he ever.

"I'm bad, Liss." He urged her down on all fours and took in the view from behind. Round ass. Fleshy thighs trailed with cream. And those stunning tits backdropped by the woods that rose up an acre away. "More so than you could ever imagine."

From behind, he skimmed a hand up the inside of her right leg, teasing his fingertips along her upper thigh and then dipping them shallowly into her pussy. "Your cunt's dripping wet for me." He worked a finger in deeper and she sucked in a breath. He let out his own breath, whispering hot air across her backside. "Your asshole's pretty pink and puckered for attention. Where should I have you?"

He pulled his finger from her sex to tap it at the rosette of her ass. "This hole." He brought two fingers back to her pussy, petting her swollen lips. "Or this hole. I can't decide."

Lissa shifted her weight back and down, taking his fingers partway inside her slick sheath. "Stop teasing and fuck me already."

As much fun as teasing her was, Thad had no choice but to give in. His balls were full to bursting. Taking his cock in hand, he guided it to the mouth of her pussy from behind. "This hole." He eased the head of his shaft inside her. "We'll save the other one for dessert."

Releasing his erection, he took her hips in hand. He pushed into her, gasping with the forceful clench of her sex. She rocked back hard, panting with the action and nearly spilling his seed in the process. But that wouldn't be happening. Now that they were joined, he wasn't coming until she did.

He moved his hand to the front of her mound, intending to stroke her clit and bring her to a faster climax. She beat him to it, lifting one hand from the roof to rub a finger against her clit.

Her finger caressed the side of his shaft with each of their mutual thrusts, bringing his need that much higher.

Before he lost control, he gathered up a handful of breast and twisted at her nipple. Lissa's pants became moans and then squeaks. She gave in to orgasm with an elated cry. But she didn't call his name out this time. Thad made up for that, by doing something he never did, and called out her name as he came seconds later.

Lissa leaned an elbow on the wet bar counter and dipped her potato chip into the dip container. Thad sat on the basement bar stool next to her, eating in something she never thought he would attain around her—comfortable silence.

She cast the lean angles of his profile a sidelong look as she chewed. The man definitely had a wild streak. He'd whipped out more than a few bad-boy tricks on her the last two days and once again this morning, when he arrived to work early. Part of her had been expecting him to revert to his nice-guy ways after their sexcapade on the roof. He hadn't. And he also hadn't shown any more concern about her saying she was okay with coming in second.

Maybe he was operating under the idea that when her roof was done so would the sex.

The thought made the dip taste sour.

If she wanted him to be around after her roof was finished, she needed to start spending more time around him when sex wasn't involved. She needed him to know she was after more than the physical. "Nash could have shared lunch with us. I don't feel the need to have sex with you every time you take a break."

Half-eaten sandwich in his hand, Thad looked over. "Really?"

His expression was unreadable, but his tone suggested he thought she was full of shit. Lissa frowned. "Of course, really. Do you think I'm just attracted to you for your body?"

"And my staying power."

Oh jeez. That sounded like something one of her cocky bad boys of days past would say. Had she unleashed his wild streak a little too thoroughly? "So you've forgotten I was drawn to your nice-guy qualities? Even if you were a total submissive when it comes to sex, I would still respect you."

His mouth curved temptingly beneath an upper lip that always seemed in need of a shave. "Just respect?"

She yanked her attention back to his eyes. It would be easier not to think about sex around him twenty-four/seven if she didn't love the feel of his stubble against her skin so much. If his almost-bad-boy smile didn't get her wet on sight. "I don't think I could do a submissive guy. Nice guys, sure. But subs are pushing it."

Interest climbing into his eyes, Thad set the sandwich down on a paper plate and swiveled on his bar stool to face her. "What about a Dom?"

"I already know you aren't one. That much came clear the moment I found out you volunteer with Almost Family. Maybe a Dom would do that, but I . . ." Lissa trailed off with the abrupt narrowing of his eyes. Damn, his mouth.

The almost-bad-boy smile evaporated. "Nash talked to you," he accused.

She shouldn't pin this on Nash. But she couldn't very well tell Thad the truth. And really he hadn't said Nash talked to you about my volunteering, just that Nash talked to her and he had. "Not much. What he did say was for our benefit."

"What was that?"

"That you're a nice guy who likes to let his bad-boy streak out to play and you prefer your women on the spunky side."

He smiled in the self-deprecating way she'd seen him do a time or two before, always when she mentioned his being nice. "I'm not that nice, Lissa."

Whatever the smile was about, telling him he was nice obviously wasn't cutting it. Examples were needed. "You're here."

"What does that have to do with anything?"

"You didn't want to work on my roof. The only reason you are, and for that matter that we're sleeping together, is because your partner's mom is sick. If you weren't nice, you would have called me and told me the job was off as soon as you found out Benny couldn't do it."

Thad didn't even consider the words, just tossed them aside with the shrug of a well-built and, for once, shirt-covered shoulder. "Like I said before, business has been slow. Loose Screws needed this job."

"What about your involvement with the youth services facility? Don't tell me you're being some kid's foster friend because you think word will spread and somehow help to promote the construction company."

Heat registered in his eyes, and not the sexual kind she'd become accustomed to seeing. "My involvement is personal. I know what those kids are going through. They think they're all tough and cool and nothing can touch them, but they're wrong. I do what I can to make them see that before they end up in a jail cell or gunned down in the street."

Lissa drew back on her stool with the force of his words. *Who was he?* She didn't know him well, but she wanted to. She wanted to understand why he felt so negatively about himself to not be able to see his own worth.

She sat forward again, tempted to reach out a hand, but his expression was closed off and she had a feeling he would reject her touch. "I don't know what your life was like before for you to be able to relate, but I do know you're a nice guy now. That boy you're spending time with is lucky to have you. I'd like to meet him sometime."

"No." The word snapped out. "Outsiders can't be brought

into a foster friend situation that easily. You'd have to go through a bunch of channels and fill out more paperwork than would be worth your while." Thad stood, gentling his voice just a little to say, "Thanks for lunch. I need to get back up on the roof and make up for the time we lost messing around the last couple days."

Thad stepped off the ladder and onto the roof. Nash was already back from lunch and working on laying an edge section of new shingle. The thought of charging his ass off the roof was tempting. Thad settled on growling, "Why the hell did you talk to Lissa about me?"

He lifted a bare shoulder in a shrug, but otherwise kept working. "I didn't say anything special. Just that you're a nice guy like you said to say."

"A nice guy with a wild streak and a taste for spunky women."

"You are."

"I'm *not* a nice guy." Why would anyone even suggest that? Lissa might not know any better, but his partner damned well did. Nash had laughed over the idea of Lissa believing him nice less than a week ago.

Nash glanced over. "Sorry to break it to you, but we've been friends for damned near a decade and I can personally attest to the fact you are definitely a nice guy. The only reason I give you shit to the contrary is because you think you're a badass."

Thad didn't think he was a badass. He'd quit thinking that way when he'd been involved with Almost Family on the youth end nearly twenty years ago. That didn't change the facts. "How many nice guys do you know who screw for money?"

"You make women happy. Give them something good to think about on long, lonely nights." Nash glanced at the cell phone tucked into the edge of his tool belt. "Speaking of happy women, Tammy couldn't get a hold of you so she called the construction line to say she'd be a few minutes late tonight."

Thad's gut roiled even worse than it had in Lissa's basement, when she'd hinted to the fact she would like to become more involved in his life by meeting Seth, his youth services kid. "I forgot about her pleasure session."

"I'd take her off your hands, but I already have my own appointment lined up. I'm sure Tammy would understand if you canceled."

Would she?

Thad registered his line of thought and grunted. It didn't matter if Tammy would understand. It didn't matter if sex with Lissa felt like more than a bodily experience. And it didn't matter if her time-and-again comments about what a nice guy he was actually made him feel a little good inside. He was a gigolo, end of story. "She's one of our best customers. I'm not about to risk that by canceling."

Nash eyed him seriously. "You know if you wanted to quit the woman-pleasuring side of things, I'd be happy to give you a loan to get you by for a while."

"Bullshit you would. Giving me a loan would mean asking your old man for a handout. You'd rather slice off your own finger."

"I prefer to get by on my own. That doesn't mean I wouldn't ask him for money for a good cause."

And what? Ending Thad's need to make money via sex so he could get more serious with Lissa was a good cause? Not even close. "I suggest you talk to Benny about helping out on his mother's medical and nursing home bills if you want a good cause."

With a snort, Nash returned to laying down the shingles. "I already did and he turned me down. He's just as damned stubborn as you."

There was a difference between stubborn and stupid, Thad vented as he headed to work on the roof above Sam's bedroom. Being in debt to his partner for the sake of a relationship that probably didn't mean a thing to him and probably wouldn't last beyond Friday would be stupid.

The wood over Sam's room had rotted with the too-long unattended water damage and required replacing before new roofing could be laid. Thad took his frustration out by hauling up sheets of OSB and driving nails for a good half hour before voices carried up to him from the house beneath. Not from Sam's room, but the bedroom a few feet away. Lissa's.

"Home for a quickie?"

Her question stopped the hammer in Thad's hand midswing.

"Why?" Sam's voice was a mixture of humor and sensuality. "Is your kitty ready to collect her raincheck licking?"

Thad tensed with the implication behind the words. Lissa told him Sam wasn't an issue when it came to her and Thad sleeping together, but she never said she and her housemate weren't lovers. Maybe the man was as Thad first thought, and into sharing his woman with other men rather than taking the time to pleasure her right himself.

"Maybe tomorrow," Lissa replied. "She already got her daily licking this morning."

A few seconds passed and Sam asked, "You still think he's a nice guy?"

"I know he is." She spoke with a conviction that made Thad feel guilty as hell for his basement behavior at the same time it warmed him through. "Why?"

"The more I see him and hear about how he acts around you, the less he rubs me that way."

Lissa laughed. "Sammy, honey, he doesn't rub you at all. Seriously, quit with the paranoia. Thad is a nice guy. He just happens to fuck like a bad boy."

"I hope so. But if it turns out he's another Haden—"

"Then get your tongue ready. I'll be collecting my raincheck licking with interest."

Who was Haden? The last guy who couldn't put Lissa first, so he just strung her along because she had an uncanny way of making him feel good about himself?

Thad wasn't going to compare the behavior of some prick he didn't know to what he was doing with her. Mainly because he no longer knew *what* he was doing with her. He just knew the thought of Sam going down on her and Lissa sounding eager to let him made him dislike the guy more than ever . . . and hate himself in the meanwhile for allowing her to get to him this way.

6

Tammy kneeled on the floor of her sex room. A twelve-by-twelve square of contrasting black and white walls and furnishings solely dedicated to her pleasure, or her pain should the mood serve. Her hands were roped behind her back and a wooden biting rod with black rubber tassels captured between her teeth. Black rubber bedboots raised to mid-thigh and hooked to a matching garter belt. She wore no panties to heed Thad's sensual torture. The scanty rubber clinging to her upper half was merely a frame for her large, exposed breasts.

Her pleasure sessions were something to anticipate. She made him play out the role of Dom as thoroughly as a man who wasn't one could accomplish. And his body responded to the trust she instilled in him and when she purposefully stepped out of line, so he would have no choice but to slap her breasts or toy with her pussy to the point of explosion, only to withhold release, sometimes for hours.

Standing above her, he ordered, "Down. Ass in the air, legs together."

She went willingly, touching her forehead to the cold, carpetless floor. Raising her ass in his face, she widened her thighs, exposing the rear of her slick cunt. The crack of his palm against her bottom was automatic, a rote response to her offering herself up against his order not to do so. His cock responded to the smack of flesh against flesh. The tensing of her asshole. Her murmurs of barely contained rapture.

From the moment he'd stepped into Tammy's sedate town house and then this room that was anything but sedate, his body had been riding the same rock-solid rails as every other visit before this one. But his mind wasn't on this woman.

His mind kept bringing up Lissa.

Son of a bitch. Thad didn't want her in his head. He didn't want to like that she truly believed him a nice guy. He sure as hell didn't want her going down to Almost Family and meeting Seth.

Only, he couldn't lie to himself. He did want all of that.

More, he wanted to know that Sam was nothing more than a guy she turned to when no one else cared enough to hold her. He wanted to know that if he had the time and ability to put her first, she would never want Sam's touch again.

"What's the matter?"

The concern in Tammy's question and how completely it fell out of character with the sub she was playing forced his mind to focus on the present. He didn't have the time or ability to put Lissa first, and he wasn't accepting a loan from Nash when he knew damned well what getting the money would cost his friend.

This was his job and he could do it. "Nothing. I've been fighting a virus all week that just crept up and made me a little light-headed. I'm okay now."

She turned her head to the side, kissing her cheek against the floor and spilling her bleached blond hair over the lower half of her face. Through light blue eyes rimmed in shallow age lines and smudged mascara, she studied him. "You look damned fine to me. But if you aren't feeling it, I can take a rain check."

Like the kind Lissa got from Sam for her kitty lick?

Thad's bodily arousal died with the unwelcome thought. He shook his head. *Time to forget about her. Time to get to work.*

"I'm sure it's nothing contagious." Going to the row of black metal drawers built into the wall, he pulled out a blindfold and a vibrator. He returned to Tammy. Turning the vibrator on, he buzzed the head against her clit from behind.

She quivered, releasing a sigh of ecstasy, and he pulled the vibrator away from her sex. "Back, *now*. Or I'll be forced to fuck you with this vibrator all night, never letting you relent to release."

A tinge of a smile crossed her lips before she faced forward and sat back on her haunches. "Yes, sir."

With her meekly spoken words, he tossed the vibrator aside and slid the blindfold over her eyes. Next would come the collar with the front ring for inserting her rope leash. All he had to do was cross back to the drawers and pull the collar and rope out, put them on her, and begin her punishment.

But he couldn't do it.

Fuck, Lissa was still in his head. Telling him she knew he wasn't a Dom because of his involvement with Almost Family. She was right. He could never be a full-fledged Dom, but he enjoyed being a slave to a woman's command, which was what truly took place in these sessions with Tammy. What he wanted to take place with Lissa. "Shit."

"I don't think you're okay," Tammy observed.

No, he wasn't. Because Lissa, and her too damned many nice-guy comments, had destroyed his love for his gigolo work.

Acceptance washing over him, Thad bent to remove the blindfold and untie Tammy's wrists. "I can't do this."

She gave him a reassuring smile as she stood, massaging the

tender skin along her wrists. "Don't stress yourself. I'll schedule a doubleheader for next week to make up for it."

He should explain he wasn't really sick, that when he said he couldn't do it, he meant beyond today. But Tammy was a good woman from what he knew of her, and he wasn't quite ready to sever all ties. Just in case whatever it was emerging between him and Lissa ended up being nothing more than bad judgment and one day in the future he could regain his love for this job.

With a pointless promise to call to let her know when he was feeling up to a pleasure session, Thad let himself out of the town house. He climbed into his truck and grabbed his cell phone. He punched in Lissa's number as he backed out of the short driveway. Warmth speared through him when the phone picked up on her end and she murmured a husky hello.

After the way he'd left her house this afternoon, without even saying good-bye, he wasn't sure how she would act toward him. But then, she *had* stood up for him against Sam. He smiled cockily, feeling good all over with the realization she'd put him first. "Hey, Liss. What are you up to?"

There was a brief hesitation that had his smile dipping. Then she said, "Nothing you want to be witness to. Sammy's helping me wax."

Thad's fingers curled around the steering wheel while his mouth pushed into a hard line. It was possible she waxed her legs, but it was a certainty she waxed her mound. The thought of Sam's hands touching her so intimately boiled his blood.

Sam would be out of the sexual picture soon, he assured himself, if he was ever in the picture to begin with. "I was able to pull some strings with Almost Family," he lied; his approval was all it took for her to share in his afternoon with Seth. "Looks like you're going to be able to join Seth and me tomorrow."

"That's awesome!" Lissa's excitement burst through the phone line. "I was wrong, you aren't a nice guy. You're amazing."

He pulled the phone away from his ear and groaned. How the hell was a guy supposed to think the worst about himself around her? Maybe it was a blessing she'd entered his life, or maybe it was a curse he would live to regret when he couldn't afford to pay bills and his lenders came after his sorry ass.

"Seth says you're flossy."

Lissa stopped licking her chocolate marshmallow ice-cream cone to look over at Thad. He sat beside her on a millpond park bench, licking his Blue Moon cone with teasing flashes of an ice-cream-dyed blue tongue. They'd taken Seth down to the city's batting cages this afternoon, where Lissa had shown off her hitting skills, and then grabbed dinner at the boy's favorite pizza place before dropping him back at Almost Family.

He was a good kid, even if he did have a sizeable chip on his shoulder. Seth reminded her of Thad in that way, and it was probably why she knew from the instant Thad introduced them she was going to like Seth.

She definitely liked Thad.

The way he nurtured the kid without making him feel silly or childish tugged at her heartstrings. The way he'd wrapped his arm around her shoulders several times over the course of the afternoon gave her hope, that despite his basement behavior yesterday, he planned to continue their relationship—or whatever you wanted to call it—after her roof job was finished.

Thad's arm was over the back of the bench now, his fingers beneath her loose hair idly stroking her nape. Lissa's smile had as much to do with the intimacy as his words from Seth. "Tell him thanks for me." Or was flossy not a compliment? "I think."

He laughed. "It means you're hot, sexy"—wicked heat entered his eyes—"that he'd do you given the opportunity."

She fell into the kindling invitation and the resulting dampening effect it had on her panties. How she managed to be a good girl and keep her hands off him for the last thirty-some hours was a mystery. "Seth's not so shabby himself. I might just have to give him a call in four years, when he becomes legal."

"You plan on being single in four years?"

Where had that question come from? And did it suggest he'd changed his mind about being able to put her first? "I'm not in any rush to the altar, if that's what you mean." She took a lick of her ice-cream cone, allowing herself a moment of wistful thinking before asking, "Have you ever been married?"

Thad's eyebrows drew together. "Why 'have I ever been married'? Why not 'do I ever plan to get married'?"

"It's hard to believe such a nice guy with such a flossy bod would have remained unattached for so long."

"That's it!" His fingers left her nape, his arm lifting from the back of the bench.

Glaring, he came to his feet in front of her.

Lissa tensed, not exactly sure what she said to set him off. Not exactly sure what to expect of him since she'd never seen him look quite so upset. And not exactly afraid of his anger either. He was acting just like a bad boy, and every cell in her body buzzed with expectation. "*What* is it?"

"I told you I'm not a nice guy, but obviously telling isn't enough." Ice-cream cone in his right hand, he dropped to his knees on the grass in front of her. His left hand moved to the hem of her jean skirt, shoving beneath to yank the crotch of her panties to one side. "You need proof."

Her heart raced. Her pussy fluttered. Then she remembered where they were, and her head whipped around as she took stock of their public surroundings. Twenty feet away, ducks bathed in the millpond, which was fenced off and surrounded by a wooden walkway. A playground underlain with cedar chips sat off to their right. Sumac trees and the red-brick backs of downtown businesses lined the area behind their bench. No other people were in sight, but that didn't mean they couldn't appear from around a building corner or business's rear exit at any second.

Icy sensation shot through her sex in the next instant, sensuously stinging her tender flesh and stabbing her nipples to life in response. She snapped her attention back on Thad to find his right hand buried beneath her skirt, where his left had previously been. "What are you doing?" she gasped.

"Cooling you off." He grinned lecherously. Something cold and creamy she quickly recognized as his ice-cream cone ground against her labia.

"Oh God!" Her pussy was going to be stained blue, the same as his tongue. Perversely, the idea turned her on all the more.

She wriggled, writhed, wanted to cry out for him to push the ice cream deeper inside her. But, for once, she was too afraid and not nearly shameless enough to voice the words. "We're in the middle of the park. People could see us." Her clients.

Why wasn't he concerned about his own?

"I haven't seen anyone since we got here. They decide to show up now, that's their problem."

"Couldn't this hu—" The edge of the cone brushed her hyperaware clit, spreading delicious pleasure through her cunt and making her whimper. "Hurt your image?" she managed to finish.

Thad's eyes lifted to hers just long enough to reveal his sincerity. "Right now, sweetheart, all that's on my mind is you."

Lissa's heart skipped a beat. The risk of being caught faded away. He was putting her first. Again. Verbally.

She smiled so wide it hurt and then barely stifled her shout as his head moved between her thighs and his tongue pushed into her pussy. The hot, wet invasion of her icy cold folds was pure ecstasy, pleasure at its finest. Gripping her ice cream cone in one hand, she grabbed his head with the other and brought his face flush to her pelvis.

All but the back of his wheat-colored hair disappeared beneath her skirt. His cone fell to the ground, streaking her bare inner leg with blue on its way down. His tongue sank deeper. Stubble chafed along her clit as he suckled her from the inside out. Heat coursed through her body, up to her breasts and face, down to her toes.

Between her heightened awareness from his initial chilly penetration, his putting her first, and the incredibly skilled action of his tongue, release came swiftly and forcefully. She sank her mouth around her ice-cream cone, moaning around its dark brown peak as climax ripped through her.

Too quickly, he pulled his head from beneath her skirt and sat back down beside her. Her legs felt like rubber, along with most of the rest of her. Wanting to make him see he was the center of her own attention, Lissa forgot about her weary state to slide off the bench. She landed on her knees in the grass, barely missing his forgotten cone.

Thad chuckled hoarsely. "Did you in that much, huh?"

She tipped her head back and moved into the vee of his powerful thighs. With one hand, she jerked down the zipper of his jeans. With the other, she opened the slit in his boxers and coated his stiff cock in chocolate marshmallow ice cream.

His breath sucked in. His fingers dove into her hair. She smiled naughtily and dipped her head to lick at her sweet meat treat. "Think again, bad boy. It's your turn."

"Nice to know one of us is getting some."

At the sound of Tammy's voice, Lissa stopped whistling and looked up from washing the Formica surface of her kitchen countertop. "Just because I'm in a great mood doesn't mean I'm getting some."

Tammy flashed a "get real" smile that creased a bare minimum of age lines around the corners of her mouth. "Yeah, it does."

"Okay. Fine. I'm getting some." To make up for their hiatus between Wednesday morning and Thursday evening, Thad had given her some twice last night and once again this morning. Lissa felt achy and wonderful. "I wanted this guy I've been sort of seeing to be right for me, but I didn't know if it would work out. Honestly, I'm still not sure. You know how I adore my bad boys, and he leans more toward the nice-guy side. At least, I think he does. He seems to think he's Satan's long-lost brother."

Tammy set her briefcase against a floor cabinet. She propped her elbows against the countertop, apparently not in any hurry to get their meeting started. "What's he like in bed?"

"I have no idea." Tammy gave her a confused look, and Lissa clarified with an impish smile. "We've yet to actually have sex in a bed. The floor. The roof. The couch. The basement. The park." Though she just finished washing the area of usage, she refrained from tacking on the countertop Tammy currently leaned against.

Tammy raised a hand, the palm of which bore the signs of time the rest of her body lacked. "Stop! You're making me horny."

Lissa gave her a dubious look. "Since when do you go so long without getting laid that talking about someone else's sex life makes you horny?"

"Since my stud got sick."

"If you promise not to proposition them, I'll let you drool over my stud and his partner for a while." Lissa glanced up at the ceiling, aware she wanted to ogle Thad's hot body for her own selfish reasons. "They had to make a final supply run but should be back and up on the roof any minute now."

"A construction stud. Way to go, Liss." Tammy grinned approvingly. "I knew you could never hold yourself back with half-dressed babes pounding away on your roof. Literally, from the sounds of things."

"I just hope I don't live to regret giving in."

"Falling for him?"

"Like a rock." Since her roof was on the verge of completion, Lissa hoped to heck the signals he sent her yesterday were legitimate and that Thad was falling for her too.

Hammering from overhead minutes later indicated the guys were back. Lissa tossed the dishrag she'd used to wipe the counter down into the sink and then followed Tammy out her front door. The last section of roof to be finished was over Sam's bedroom. Thad had finished laying the new plywood yesterday, and now he and Nash just had to get down the weather shield and new shingles.

Lissa and Tammy rounded the corner of the house in time to see Thad climbing the top rungs of the ladder, with a bundle of plastic-wrapped shingles over his shoulder.

Tammy gave a low whistle. "Nice ass. Back. Whole package."

Lissa smiled smugly, her fingers already itching to get back on the whole package. "He's mine and he looks even better in the buff."

Thad appeared to become aware of their presence. After he stepped on the roof and unloaded the shingles, he turned back to flash a delectably sexy smile. His gaze drifted from Lissa to Tammy, and his smile vanished.

Tammy's breath pulled in audibly, stealing Lissa's wonder away from the roof and Thad's change of expression. Tammy's expression had changed as well, from admiring to wry. "Uh, Lissa, I have some bad news. Your stud . . . is my gigolo."

7

"Fuck," Thad breathed between his teeth as he stared down at Lissa and Tammy on the grass ten feet below. He'd never seen either one of them angry. Tammy looked more disappointed than actually upset. Lissa looked plain pissed.

"You say something?" Nash asked from where he kneeled on the roof, nail gunning new shingles in place.

"Yeah. My last rites." Thad nodded toward the ground. "The shit just hit the fan."

Nash came up beside him and looked over the edge of the roof. "Whoa. There's been a time or two I wouldn't have minded to be in your shoes, but now isn't one of them. Good luck, man."

Feeling like his balls had shriveled up, Thad climbed back down the ladder.

Tammy gave him a dry smile. "Feeling better?"

He sent her an apologetic look and then focused on Lissa. Her freckles were out in full force. This time it was safe to say they had nothing to do with arousal. "Not even close."

Lissa's mouth opened. Instead of the yelling he expected, she calmly said, "I should have listened to Sam. He said you rubbed him the wrong way, and he almost always knows what he's talking about."

Who the fuck is Sam to you?

He wanted to shout the question and get the answer out there once and for all. But this was hardly the time. She might be acting calm, but a storm raged in her jade green eyes, and it was only a matter of seconds before it opened up on him.

Before she could let loose, he pointed out what he'd been trying to get across for days. "I told you I wasn't a nice guy."

Her mouth fell open for a split second. Then her eyes narrowed and she let the fury out. "There's a hell of a lot of difference between being a bad boy and being a paid fuck. I guess this explains the reason why you could sleep over only one night this week—the rest of the nights you had another woman to stick your dick in."

Thad hated making women he didn't care about feel bad. He cared about Lissa, and knowing how much this was hurting her tore at his heart. At the same time, he hadn't promised her anything. He'd thought to discuss making their relationship monogamous tonight, with the notation not to expect any fancy dates since he wasn't liable to have a penny to his name for the foreseeable future.

Apparently, that wouldn't be happening now. "You said you could handle coming in second to my work."

"Short term in relation to your construction and handyman work. Long term . . ." She trailed off with a shake of her head. When she spoke next, both her expression and voice were back to calm. "Nothing. We never would work out long term, but obviously not because you're a nice guy." She turned to Tammy. "We should get started on our meeting." Without waiting for Tammy's response, Lissa started toward the front of the house.

"You said if I really was a gigolo I would be the envy of thousands." The words were lame. But still he thought they might be enough to stop her.

She kept walking. "I thought we were talking hypothetical."

"I haven't slept with anyone else since the day I met you."

That did stop her, to toss over her shoulder, "It doesn't matter." She started walking again. "Honestly, Thad, it doesn't matter to me what you do. We had fun. Now I'm ready to move on."

"So am I." Tammy lifted a slim shoulder in a shrug. "Lissa and I have been business associates and friends way too long for me to continue using your services."

"Blow." Sam held a tissue up to Lissa's nose, making her feel like a big baby.

She probably deserved to be treated this way, given how much blubbering she'd done since learning Thad's true nature, so she sat up on the couch and gave in to Sam's order.

Clucking his tongue, he wadded the tissue up and tossed it into the kitchen wastebasket. Normally, it was kept in the cabinet under the sink, but he'd observed her sniffling wasn't slowing and brought the basket out to the living room. "I can't believe you, Liss, getting all emotional over some oversexed jerkoff. This isn't your style."

"I thought he was a nice guy with a bad-boy appearance. I thought he was *the one*." To finally put her first. To possibly even spend the rest of her life with.

Oh jeez! Could she have made a worse judgment call?

Sam sank down on the couch next to her, throwing an arm over her shoulders and hauling her up against his side. "Aw, sweetie. You could never be happy with a truly nice guy. It was worth a try, but bad boys are your thing."

She nuzzled into his big body, wishing he would revert back to liking women. Only, it wouldn't matter if Sam was into girls again. Because the idea of him and her together in a manner that exceeded friendship no longer appealed. "Did he really have to be *so* bad?"

"Not that I'm saying he deserves it, but let me play devil's advocate for a second and point out that Thad said he hasn't had sex with anyone else since you came along. Tammy confirmed he hasn't slept with her. If he relies on sex to pay his bills, then he's risking the wrath of his financers for you."

Lissa had thought of that, wanted to cling to the knowledge, but how could she? Thad had to make a living and, given what he told her about the construction business being so slow and his grim outlook on the economy, he felt his body was the only way to do it. "Maybe temporarily, but he would never give up being a gigolo."

"You don't know that. Sure, he needs money, but for the right woman he could turn to flipping burgers."

Was there even a chance he could care about her that much? He had to care some, or he would never have bothered to make excuses for his behavior.

She forced out a laugh. "I almost would rather have him selling his body than hiding it in a too-tight sweater and dorky bowtie at some fast-food joint."

"Remember when I warned you to be careful? I didn't just mean physically."

"He gave me an ice-cream mouth job. That's not playing fair!" Truthfully, Thad's allowing her to spend the afternoon with him and Seth had meant so much more, but it was less painful to dwell on the great sex they'd shared.

Sam unwrapped his arm from her shoulders to sit forward on the couch. He wiggled his eyebrows. "It just so happens we have ice cream and I have a tongue known for making men and women scream in ecstasy for miles around."

Lissa smiled faintly. "Thanks, Sammy. As much as I love you, I'm not going to be asking for any more kitty licks. You're way too kind for me to take advantage of you like that."

He stood. "I'll accept the compliment and you'll take advantage of me one more time."

Maybe she should. Just because she no longer felt sparks between them didn't mean oral sex wouldn't help to cheer her up and ease her onto the road to getting over Thad.

She came to her feet and reached for the sides of her cotton shorts. "All right. It can't hurt anything, right?"

Sam's hands closed around hers, stilling them before she could pull her shorts and panties down. "Sorry, sweetie"—mischief gleamed in his eyes—"but I have something a little different in mind."

"You must be Thad."

Over the phone, Ginger sounded on the quiet end of things. In person, she was nearly as big as he was—the ruffled blue dress covering her from throat to ankle only made her seem bigger yet.

She was also mauling him.

She had her tongue in his mouth two seconds after she stepped through the front door of his duplex. His natural reaction was to kiss her back. But he didn't feel even a little turned on as she wrapped her arms around his body and pulled him flush against her.

Her chest was an inch, maybe two lower than his, and her big, soft breasts crushed between them. He thought to give them a little hand loving in the hopes of getting his arousal started up. Ginger pinched his ass through his jeans, then released him before he could touch her breasts.

Brown eyes slid along his body. Her painted pink lips opened on a murmur of approval. "Mmm. Mmm. Mmm. If you screw as good as you kiss, I'm in for a fun night!" She kicked the door shut, then reached to the back of her dress. "No time to get naked like the present."

"Wait!" Thad held up a hand.

Worse than feeling uneager for the pleasure to come was the guilt that gnawed at him.

He fucked up with Lissa. Not by withholding information on his gigolo job, but by getting involved with her in the first place. His damned dick just hadn't been able to say no to her curvy body and light vanilla scent. And now his head and heart were wrapped up in things.

She'd moved on. Had probably spent the entire last week naked in Sam's arms, living out the sexual acts portrayed in the man's bedroom furnishings.

His chest tightened, and he flushed thoughts of Lissa and Sam far away. Faking an excited smile, he gestured to the couch. "Go ahead and have a seat. There's some paperwork to take care of before we get naked."

Ginger swayed her hips seductively as she crossed the carpet to the couch and took a seat. She flashed an expectantly toothy smile.

"I'll be back in just a minute," Thad said, and hurried to the staircase and up to his bedroom.

He had the thought to lock himself inside and wait for her to go away. Then he realized how chickenshit he was acting and crossed to the short black filing cabinet that held Loose Screws paperwork.

The top drawer was barely open when he felt something rubbing against his ass. Make that someone.

He straightened and swiveled around. Ginger caught him in her arms and buried her tongue back between his lips. Her hand darted between them to find his cock through his jeans. Her tongue still wasn't doing anything for him, but the stroke of her fingers along his shaft was enough to start it hardening.

He should stick to policy and make her sign the paperwork and get payment up front this first time. But now that his body was beginning to get into things, he didn't dare stop.

Taking over the kiss, Thad pushed her back on his bed and kneeled a leg on either side of her hips. He cupped the side of a breast, brushing his thumb over where he guessed her nipple to be, though it was hard to tell, given how padded her bra seemed.

Ginger let out a squeal of delight. "Ooh, you are a bad boy!"

You're a nice guy.

Lissa's time-and-again words rallied through his mind and froze his thumb. She didn't believe them any longer. Could he convince her to again? More important, was he a nice guy?

Nash claimed he was. Benny hadn't been around enough to ask the last couple weeks. Thad barely saw his folks, since they lived states away, and their opinion was liable to be skewed anyway. Seth . . . Seth might be proof of his hidden nice guy.

Sure, he'd started volunteering with Almost Family because he knew what the kids who came through the center were going through. But that wasn't the reason he stayed with the program for nearly five years and three different boys. He kept going back because after they got to know him, those kids looked up to him. They made him feel good about himself. Just like Lissa had.

Shit. He hadn't messed up by sleeping with her.

Thad jerked his tongue out of Ginger's mouth and pushed off the bed. "I'm sorry. I'm not going to be able to service you." He wasn't going to be able to service any woman again. Not until Lissa was reconvinced of his nice-guy ways, and then he would only be servicing her.

Ginger sat up on the bed, eyeing him worriedly. "Are you feeling sick?"

"No." The truth was he couldn't recall feeling better in his life. "I stopped doing the gigolo service a couple weeks ago. I shouldn't have taken your call."

Disappointment curved her lips down. She stood from the bed and brought her hands to her breasts, massaging them with her fingertips. "You sure you can't keep your doors open one more night? I'll make it worth your time. Name your price."

"I can't help you."

"Three thousand."

Thad nearly choked over the amount. The benefit wouldn't be worth the cost, but that was a helluva lot of money. "For one hour?"

She rubbed her hands together and preened. "Is that a yes?"

"No. I'm sorry. I'm not for sale." He added under his breath, "I don't know how the fuck I'm going to afford to live, but I'm through with this business."

She tskked as she started toward the bedroom door. "That's too bad. I was ready to go as high as five thousand to get a taste of your suck-u-licious man pole." Reaching the door, Ginger called out, "Looks like he's all yours, sweetie."

What the hell? Who was she talking to and what made her think some other woman would gain access where she'd been denied?

The other woman in question stepped through the doorway, and Thad's heart raced. "What are you doing here, Lissa?"

She nodded at Ginger, who was suddenly grinning. "Chaperoning Sam. I was a little concerned he might get carried away and end up taking you in the ass."

"Sam? I don't know what . . ." Ginger's brown eyes and familiar smile registered then. He resisted the urge to scrape his nails across his tongue in an effort to get the man saliva out of his mouth.

Jesus, he'd kissed a man!

The knowledge of who Ginger really was had him taking a closer look. Because he knew what Sam looked like out of drag, he could see masculine features now. But if he hadn't known what Sam looked liked out of drag, Thad would never have known he wasn't a female. Being a skilled cross-dresser didn't label him a homosexual, but what about the open pleasure Sam took in kissing him? Might he just be gay as Thad had once considered? In which case, he wouldn't have spent the last days loving up Lissa.

Thank you, God.

Lissa's narrow upper lip curled into a sneer. "What? You're good enough to sleep with half the county but not kiss my best friend?"

"He was some sort of test?"

Her sneer relented with her nod. "I know where I rank compared to your work."

Thad caught the meaning behind her words. This was his chance to convince her that she was right—she came first and foremost. He hadn't planned on doing it with an audience, but he was taking whatever opportunity he got. "Do you?"

"A few nights ago, when it hit me the only reason you slept with me to begin with is because you thought I called you to set up a pleasure session, I wasn't sure. But, yeah, now I think I know."

Then why wasn't she smiling?

Movement at her sides had him looking down to discover her fingers fisting and unfisting. Nerves. She thought she knew how she ranked in his life but was still afraid of learning she was wrong. "Before I'll even kiss a client, I require they sign a silence agreement. I never made you sign anything."

A hint of a smile played at her lips. Her fingers came uncurled and stayed that way. "Maybe there's a bit of nice guy in you after all."

Thad smiled back at her in full force, wanting to reassure her once and for all. "I'd like to think so."

"Just so long as there isn't a lot of nice guy." Lissa's mouth curved in a playful grin. "Sammy assures me I could never handle being with a nice guy in the long run. I have a huge weakness for bad boys. The only problem I've found with them is they never know how to get their priorities straight."

With the mention of Sam's name, Thad looked to where the man had been standing only to find him gone. He should have apologized for his senseless loathing of the guy before he took off. But then, Sam never knew he'd been silently hating him. And, right now, Thad was too happy to have Lissa all to himself to care.

He ignored his urge to go to her. He didn't want any false impressions between them this time and that meant sharing the bleak reality of his financial situation. "Until the economy swings back enough to get more business going with the construction side of Loose Screws, I'm going to need to find another job. I can't promise I won't put that other job first for a while. I have to be able to afford to survive."

Lissa's smile didn't wane. If anything it grew, as she crossed to where he stood in front of the bed and wrapped her arms around his neck. Humor flashed in her eyes. "Lucky for you, I'm counting on that other job coming in first. Lucky for me, that other job is providing endless pleasure sessions to yours truly. I have a nice little nest egg put away with your name on it."

"You're going to pay me to sleep with you?" He laughed over the irony.

"For a few weeks. By then, I should be able to use my connections to find you some more construction jobs. I can't promise they'll be enough to support your business partners, too, but frankly I don't care who they're dipping their wick in."

Thad mellowed out with the honest affection in her eyes. Warmth slid through him. He felt really good about himself, pauper and all. "You care about my wick?"

She brushed her mouth against his, just a gentle touch. Pulling back revealed mischief gleaming in her eyes. "Only because you're kick-ass flossy."

"Keep that up and in four years Seth will be giving me serious competition." Thad let out another laugh that stopped short with the press of her mouth against his. Harder this time. He parted his lips and her tongue came inside, hot, silky, so much better and ten hundred times more arousing than Sam's had been.

Rising up on her toes, Lissa rocked her body into his, pushing her pelvis against his, sinuously grinding her pussy along his cock until his entire body ached for release.

She sucked at his lower lip as she pulled away. "I guess you'll just have to be sure I'm not still single by then."

It took a few seconds to remember what they'd been talking about. Then he realized she was implying she wanted a lasting future with him. That news was too good to allow him to keep his hands off her a moment longer.

"Guess so." Thad scooped her up in his arms and settled her back on his bed.

He leaned over her to reclaim her mouth, but she turned her head to the side. "We're actually going to do it on a bed?"

He slid his lips along her bared throat, kissing the vanilla-tinged skin at her pulse point. "Yep. But don't worry your bad boy's still inside me. He thinks as soon as we finish up here, we should climb up on the roof for round number two."

Lissa shuddered out a sigh with the wet flick of his tongue. Then she gasped, "B-but your roof is at a huge slant. I could fall off and break something important."

"It's called pitch, sweetheart," he responded in between nibbles as his fingers went to work on the buttons of her shirt. "I promise not to take you up there and let you break something." The sides of her shirt gave away, and he buried his face against the generous swell of her cleavage above the lacy black cups of her bra. "I love your body way too much the way it came assembled."

In case there was any doubt in her mind, he proceeded to show her how sincere that love was well into the night.

NOT A SECOND TOO LATE

1

She couldn't handle this.

She. Could. Not. Handle. This.

She had to get out of here, both her hiding spot inside the coatroom and the country club as a whole, before it was too late.

Genevieve Louton's fear wasn't of male strippers arriving at her bachelorette party and corrupting her virginal eyes, which weren't nearly so virginal as most believed. The fear was of her party taking the final step toward feeling like a late-afternoon tea gathering, by her mother breaking out the crumpets and jam.

For God's sake, why had Tia invited her mother?

Risking being spotted, she poked her head around the corner of the coatroom entrance to lock sights on her mother. Debra Louton flitted around the closed-off event room. An untouched flute of champagne rested in a slim hand freshly manicured with French tips to match her pristine winter white pantsuit. Devoting a few minutes to chat up each woman in the place, Debra was the perfect mother of the bride, and the pastel streamers, table drapes, and romantic music provided the perfect ambience.

If this was a bridal shower.

When, in a moment of anticipation, her best friend Tia let slip she was planning a surprise bachelorette party, Genevieve had been thrilled. Finally, a chance to break out of the overgroomed web spun at the hands of private schooling, etiquette lessons, and her parents' ability to make her feel she owed them no less than perfection for all the time and money they'd invested in her.

Genevieve had envisioned drunken stupidity, crude humor, and dancing men with rock-hard, sweaty, naked bodies they were only too happy to let her and her friends ogle till the wee hours of the morning. Even when she learned the party was being held at the pretentious Deevy Isle Country Club, she'd held out hope for the kind of feel-good girls' night that resulted in lifetime memories.

Instead she got love songs, finger sandwiches, and her twin seven-year-old cousins giggling together while they ran their fingers through the pastel-pink frosting of her heart-shaped cake.

And the guest of honor hiding in a coatroom for fear her mother would see her.

She was being pathetic. Or a good daughter. The lines had a way of blurring far too often lately.

Genevieve looked away from the girls' destruction of her cake to catch a flash of Tia's cropped, reddish-orange hair. After ensuring her mother's attention was fully engaged, she made a beeline through a few dozen party guests, most of whom she didn't even recognize, toward her friend. She grabbed Tia by the shoulder, halting her in her tracks.

Tia spun around on black pumps. The sedate shoes were no more Tia than her friend's sensible gray slacks and lavender cashmere turtleneck sweater.

Genevieve's attire was closer to Tia's style, and the reason she'd been hiding. One step into the event room, she'd realized saying she had on the littlest and loudest outfit of the group would be the understatement of the century.

Now that she'd come out of the closet, everyone could see what she was wearing. Women, young and old, were staring, measuring. Disapproving.

Her mother was never going to forgive her.

Genevieve glanced toward the section of room where she last saw Debra. Oh hell, she was missing in action.

Anxiety gripping her, she looked back at Tia. "What is this?" She smoothed her hands along the hem of her shirt in an attempt to make the midriff-baring bright pink top magically stretch to cover her navel and the faux piercing that bejeweled it.

Why had she ditched her coat in the car?

Oh right, because she thought she might be too smashed to remember it later. Fat chance of that! "Where's the loud music? The cheap booze? The naked hunks?"

Sympathy shooting from her hazel eyes, Tia patted her bare arm. "Sorry, Gen. I had them on order. Then Allison got wind of things." Her gaze slid to Genevieve's cropped top, tiny skirt, killer heels, and body glitter, and she frowned. "She assured me she would tell you about the change in plans."

Genevieve closed her eyes on a sigh. Tia didn't need to say another word. Her younger sister Allison was nearly a carbon copy of their mother, with the added bonus of ruing Genevieve for having the gall to be born first, thereby earning the right to run the family-owned estate collection company upon their father's retirement. Allison hadn't told her about the change in plans on purpose. She wanted to make Genevieve look like a fool when she showed up in tawdry, totally off-season clothes and party makeup. Their mother would throw a conniption and demand their father take her to hand, never mind Genevieve was a fully grown woman. Then the whole mess would be turned over to her fiancé Tom's hands.

Tom would laugh in her parents' face.

Letting out another sigh, Genevieve opened her eyes. Tom would *never* laugh in her parents' faces, and not just because her father was both his boss and godfather, but because he shared their mindset. Tom would agree she looked like a strumpet and then assure them she would never leave the house dressed so trashy again.

As if he had the right to dictate what she wore!

Only, he did have the right, or at least he would in a month, when he became her husband. Because that was the way things worked for the deep-rooted, moneyed families of Deevy Isle.

Covering her face with her hands, she groaned. "I'm too young for this. Or old. Or tired."

"Seeing as how Allison invited your little cousins and your grandma, and they seem to be having a good time, option one and two are out." Tia pulled Genevieve's hands away from her face. "You *do* look tired."

"Exhausted." Not in the physical sense, but in a way that had to do with living up to too damned many expectations, very few of which were her own.

"I don't know how you've lasted this long without cracking. I've only lived in the area a few months and put on just enough of a my-shit-doesn't-stink pretense to keep my family's name respected, and I still feel like telling the majority of the island to fuck off."

Typically, Tia's forthright attitude, at least around those who knew the real her, was the one thing sure to keep Genevieve sane and seeing the humor in life. But tonight, not even that was working. Tonight, she wanted to run away. To have the bachelorette party she deserved. One that didn't include minors and mothers and a sea of pastel clothes, cakes, and table trimmings.

"Would it be so wrong to disappear?"

"If Allison didn't assign me the job of letting the chefs know every time a food tray gets low and then check in every ten minutes to make sure I'm actually doing it, I'd have been gone long ago."

Genevieve looked around the room in search of her sister. She skimmed the far side of the room and her belly cramped when she found herself staring into her mother's horror-filled eyes. Lips pushed into a tight line, Debra started over.

"Crap. I've been spotted." Genevieve grabbed Tia's hand, giving it a quick squeeze as she darted a look toward the event-room door and then back at her fast-approaching mother. "Cover me, Tia. Please."

Worry entered Tia's eyes. "Where are you going?"

"I don't know. Just away." She glanced back in Debra's direction. T minus fifteen seconds, and only that long because her mother had to weave through tables and chairs, along with party guests.

Genevieve let go of Tia's hand and stepped one foot toward the door. "Tell her I had to use the bathroom. Or, better yet, that I realized how wrong I dressed for the party and ran home to change. That should miff Allison and buy me a half hour."

"Will you be back before the party's over?"

Another glance at her way-too-close mother revealed the woman's nostrils flaring like an enraged bull's. "Not if I get lucky."

The way the black-haired babe in the hot-pink belly-baring top, silver miniskirt, and matching stilettos kept eyeing him up from her stool at the bar, Nash was going to get lucky tonight.

Not that he didn't get lucky a lot of nights.

But those other nights he was getting paid. Tonight, he was in his stomping ground of McCleary's Pub, tossing back longnecks while he shot the shit with Thad Davies, his longtime friend and coworker. Eight months ago, he and Thad had been working skilled trades with the local Michigan automotive plant. Then the economy went to hell and the plant was idled permanently, taking their jobs with it.

Nash could have gone to his old man for a loan. Or hell, moved back in with his folks and mooched off them from here to eternity. But he'd made a decision the day he graduated from a private high school, thirteen years ago, to stand on his own two feet. That meant moving away from the ranks of primarily conceited snobs who called Deevy Isle home to the somewhat less ostentatious city of Crichton and taking whatever job he could get with no experience.

He'd worked at the auto plant for over a decade. And now, more often than not, he worked in the nude and relied on his dick to bring in the all-holy dollar.

The babe at the bar wouldn't know what he did. The lack of knowledge combined with her sizzling hot body, bedroom eyes, and appearance in the mostly locals-only pub made for an interesting invitation.

Nash slid his attention from her secretive smile to the other side of his table. Months had passed since Benny, a former plant coworker and current partner in Loose Screws construction company and gigolo service, joined in their Saturday evening ritual of beer and burgers at McCleary's. Still, the small wood table felt disturbingly empty. Benny's reason for staying away, because he spent all of his nonworking and sleeping hours at his fading, Alzheimer's-stricken foster mother's side, was respectable. But Nash missed and worried about him a hell of a lot.

Shaking off that worry, Nash caught Thad's eye as the other man took a last drink of his beer and set the empty bottle back on the table. Nash inclined his head toward the woman at the bar. "What do you think?"

Thad had quit the gigolo side of Loose Screws since finding himself a full-time woman, but he could still read body language as good as any man. "Cheap. Fake. Probably picks up a different guy to sleep with every other day." Amusement curved his mouth and reached into his blue eyes. "Perfect for you."

"That's what I was thinking." Nash pushed back his chair.

He grabbed the empty longnecks from the center of the table and headed for the bar.

Brenna, the nighttime bartender, hit him with a smile that showed off her snaggletooth. The short, busty redhead was married and typically not what he would consider his type, but he found her crooked tooth charming in its imperfection.

He set the empty bottles on the polished teak of the counter. She picked them up, sliding them into an empty case behind the bar. "Two more?"

"Make it three." He nodded at the skimpily dressed woman who sat a few stools down and currently faced away from him.

Brenna raised her eyebrows. "I haven't seen you pick a woman up from this place in almost a year."

"That's because most people who come in are regulars." And because using his body for profit was eating up too much of his time and energy to use it for fun.

Laughing, Brenna grabbed three bottles of Bud from the cooler behind her. She untwisted their tops and set them down in front of him. "Ah. They know all your dirty little secrets."

Not even close. Crichton might be less affected than Deevy Isle, but the bulk of the residents were conservative as hell. Outside of clients, who were required to sign silence agreements before they could touch, few knew about the woman-pleasuring side of Loose Screws. "They sure as hell don't look like her."

She gave the woman an unimpressed glance. "Maybe that's because they have the brains to wear clothes when it's barely twenty out."

It was entirely possible Brenna was accurate in the assumption the black-haired babe wasn't all that bright. Since Nash wasn't looking for a rocket scientist, just an appealing woman to have a few hours of naked fun with when money wasn't a factor, he would let her questionable taste in cold-weather clothing go.

He pushed one of the beers back toward Brenna. "Have Tiff deliver this to Thad when she gets a chance," he said of the server working their table. "Tell her to tell him to drink it, then get his ass to his woman's house. It's Saturday night for Christ's sake." He punctuated the sentence with a wink, because he knew Thad kept up their Saturday evening routine, despite preferring to spend the time with Lissa, for Nash's sake.

Tossing enough cash on the bar to cover the round of drinks and the tab and tip for their burgers and earlier beers, he grabbed the longnecks and moved down the bar.

He slid onto the empty stool next to the woman. Setting the beer in front of her, he appreciated the princess-cut diamond piercing her belly button—clearly a knockoff given its five-carat size. "So what's your excuse?"

Her head jerked around. Blue-green eyes went wide. She recovered almost immediately, lowering thick, black lashes to a seductive level. "My excuse?"

Up close, she looked different. Not fake or cheap. High cheekbones cut into an elegantly narrow face. Glossy, raven-black hair was styled chic and shoulder length. Her makeup had been applied with a heavy hand, but in a fashionable, night-out-on-the-town way. Nash had spent most of the last years away from money, but he still visited with his folks once a month or so and remembered his upbringing enough to recognize her skimpy top as fine silk. A glance back at her belly had him believing the piercing was an authentic diamond.

No doubt about it, she was a looker. Smelled damned good, like some flowery, but not sickeningly so, perfume. Her long legs encased in sheer, silver stockings and the sensual curve of her painted scarlet lips had his heart rate up and his cock stirring.

But did he really want to tangle with class?

Most nights and with most moneyed women, the answer would be an unequivocal "hell no." The truth was, with Benny not around and Thad spending so much time with Lissa, Nash was getting a little lonely. The woman's solo presence in the modest McCleary's hinted she was trying to escape her wealth for a few hours and that she might just be lonely too.

Or she might just be horny and hungry for a man with more on his mind than his finances. "This is a local's pub. Unfamiliar women don't often come in alone, looking like their fresh off the ready-to-fuck-mobile. When one does come in and starts giving me eyes that say I'm the one she's ready to fuck, I have to wonder what brought her here. So what's your excuse?"

Genevieve lifted the beer the stranger bought her to her lips. She took a long, slow pull, appreciating the crisp, simple taste she rarely had the opportunity to indulge in, as she contemplated how she was going to get away from him. And when she was going to get away from him. Before or after she confirmed his guess, that with the sexily arrogant look in his espresso-brown eyes and his untamed nearly black hair pushed back from his face and curling around his ears, he was the one she was ready to fuck.

If she were Allison, just thinking that crude word would make her feel dirty. But then, if she were her sister, she would still be at the country club, stuffing her face with finger sandwiches and making nice with relatives she'd never before met.

She wasn't Allison and, for once, she wasn't wrapped in her overgroomed web.

She was Genevieve and she was having her own private bachelorette party. A couple more drinks would cover her drunken stupidity hopes for the night. His line on her excuse could loosely work for bad humor. And if the forearms snaking out from beneath the pushed-up sleeves of his olive green sweatshirt were a sampling of the rest of his body, then he was rock hard. All she had to do was get him naked, sweaty, and dancing and her party would be in full swing.

Just her, him, and a megadose of guilt.

The same punch of shame hit her now as it had when she slid off her engagement ring and left it in the glove compartment of her Benz. It was a beautiful ring, and Tom was a great guy she'd known her entire life. She didn't want to be away from either of them permanently, or even away from her parents in the long run.

She just wanted tonight.

One night without guilt. One night to be a little bad. Nothing unforgivable, like actually sleeping with the guy. Just a small walk-on-the-wild-side prewedding gift to herself.

Genevieve set her beer on the bar and swiveled on her stool. Her knees brushed against the side of the stranger's muscular, jeans-covered thigh, and the heat of his big body filtering through to hers was pure ecstasy. Sad all it took was the brush of a male leg to get her excited. Tom was anti–sex before marriage, and so while she wasn't a virgin, it had been ages since she'd gotten anything more than felt up. "You're wrong."

The arrogance in his eyes stretched downward, curving his mouth in a cocky grin and deepening the cleft in his chin. His gaze left her face to drift along her body, touching, stroking, caressing every inch of her. "Am I?"

"I don't want to sleep with you." She pressed her thighs together against a belying rush of warmth. "I just want to watch you dance naked."

"I normally get paid for that sort of thing."

His immediate response snagged the breath in her throat. He didn't look like he was joking. Did he work as a stripper or in some similar role? Would agreeing to his monetary terms land her in a jail cell?

Genevieve took another drink of beer and watched him do the same. His lips closed around the head of the longneck, and she couldn't stop from wondering how they would feel on her bare skin, running over her sensitive belly, kissing along her inner thighs and then higher . . .

No higher. No touching her. Just dancing.

She set her beer down but didn't unwrap her fingers from the bottle. She couldn't get thrown in jail for watching him dance, not when she should have been doing the same with another guy at an actual bachelorette party. "How much?"

He finished drinking and set his bottle next to hers, skimming her knuckles with his in the process. Heat shot up her arm and reflected in his eyes. "Depends if you plan on touching."

A lump of lust settled in her throat. She swallowed it back, along with her crazy desire to say yes.

She didn't really want to touch him. It was just the need to be held, stroked, made love to, eating at her. Just over a month and Tom would do all of that for her. Probably with the same composure he did everything else. But there were a lot worse things in life than boring sex.

There were a lot better things on her mind right now.

Like watching this sexy stranger touch the areas she couldn't. It was a little naughtier than she set out to be, but still nothing more than she probably could have seen if her party went off as planned. "I don't, but you can. Touch yourself, that is."

He leaned closer toward her, just an inch or two, yet enough to set her heart to pounding. "Do you think you're up to watching me masturbate while I'm dancing around naked, yet not touching you at all?"

"I have two perfectly capable hands to get myself off with." The bold words that slipped out of Genevieve's mouth surprised her as much as they seemed to please him.

Lips curving in a full, appreciative grin, he returned his knuckles to hers, sliding back and forth lightly. Pumping wave after wave of warmth up her arm and zinging it back down again to settle between her thighs as wet heat.

He leaned a little closer, spoke in a rough voice, "Will you be dancing naked too?"

Her pussy clenched with the idea it could be filled before this night was over. Not by her own fingers or a vibrating chunk of plastic, but the warm, solid flesh of a man's cock. It wouldn't be happening, just as he wouldn't be kissing her, the way his continual descent toward her mouth suggested, but it was still blissful to think about.

The thought of her naked body jiggling all over the place—not so blissful.

She worked out several times a week and had a firm belly and arms and legs to show for it, but her butt and hips had a long way to go. "I like dancing and I like being naked, but I don't like the way my body looks when I dance naked."

He moved again, more this time, until his face was an inch from hers, his lips hovering seconds away. She could hear his breathing, see the pulse flutter at his throat. Wicked want burned in his eyes. "Do I at least get one or the other?"

"I thought I was paying you," she murmured, holding on, holding out for a kiss she could not have.

"Right. You are." He pulled back, straightening on his stool abruptly, and then stood. "I'll be at my table. Let me know when you're ready to go."

Exhaling a shaky breath, Genevieve watched the enticing play of his faded jeans across his ass as he returned to his table. Never was the right answer to when she would be ready to go somewhere and be alone with him. It was the only answer . . . if she was cloaked in her overgroomed web.

This was her bachelorette party and she was webless. Regardless, she should say no. But if she did that, if she forwent his erotic dancing show, she would never forgive herself for letting this one stolen moment of imperfection pass.

2

"I'm ready."

At the sound of the black haired babe's voice, Nash looked up to find her standing less than a foot from his table. An anxious smile lined her lips and her shimmering silver miniskirt rode teasingly high on her shapely thighs. Thad had already left the pub, and Nash had planned to do the same after finishing his cigarette.

It looked like his plans had changed.

No matter how antsy she'd seemed over the casual brush of his fingertips, she was ready to go through on her words and pay him to masturbate while he danced naked.

The smile fell from her lips. "You didn't expect me to come over here."

He took a drag on his cigarette, exhaling slowly. "I expected you to let me finish this smoke first."

She looked at the cigarette and the fresh film of smoke lingering on the air. The tip of her narrow nose crinkled. "Finish."

It was tempting to fault her response on wealth, but too many less privileged women had given him the same disapproving look. Hell, even Benny and Thad rode his ass about quitting the habit before it killed him. He'd cut back in recent months, but certain activities seemed to require indulging, namely, drinking and sex. "I know they're bad for me."

"I didn't say anything."

"You didn't have to." He snubbed the cigarette out in an ashtray and stood. "Let's go."

She lifted a black leather, ankle-length jacket from the crook of her arm. Blame it on the idea she was among the socially elite, but Nash was taking the jacket from her and helping her into it before he registered the move.

"Thanks." A fresh smile touched at her lips.

It was way too nice of a smile, not the faintest hint of seduction there. She was impressed by his behavior, probably thought he was a regular Mr. Manners. He did tend to be good about things like opening doors for women and old people, but that was just common sense.

Before she could get the crazy idea he was a gentleman, Nash pulled on his own coat and nudged her toward the pub's entrance with the blatant press of his stiff cock against her back.

She didn't withdraw, but reclined against him. She was taller than he'd guessed; the silver stilettos bringing her nearly even with his six foot one. The ankle-length coat hid her body. Even so, with the gyration of her hips, he couldn't miss that it wasn't her back rubbing against his cock, but the lushness of her ass.

Her hips moved a second time. His shaft responded with a jerk, and a soft sigh left her lips. His balls went a little tight in anticipation of her next move. Then she pulled away and headed for the door.

Nash narrowed his eyes. A tauntress he would never have guessed her for. Reminding himself she was a paying tauntress and that, with winter almost here, construction work was at an all-time low, he followed her outside. It was barely seven, but above the glow of downtown lights, the evening was already pitch black and cold enough to have his shaft going flaccid and his balls running for cover.

They would recover, just as soon as she was ogling his naked body. "Your place or mi—"

"No!" Her warm breath hung in the icy air as she swung around with a furious shake of her hair.

He knew she'd had an excuse for being in the pub alone. Whatever it was kept her from taking him home. If he was going to spend naked free time with her, as he'd first planned, he would question what that something was. She'd changed his plans, wanted to be a client, so her life beyond the next hour or two was none of his business.

"Fine. We'll go to mine." He tucked his hands into his coat pockets and started along the sidewalk, noting a handful of pedestrians milling about the snowy, downtown area.

"Wait!" she called after him. "Where do you live? My car's the other direction."

Nash stopped twenty feet later, in front of a short cement stoop leading to a green steel door in need of a new coat of paint. "No driving necessary. We're here."

She came up next to him, frowning at the aged red bricks surrounding the door. "You live here?"

"Beneath you, I take it." He didn't bother to hide his displeasure. A paying rich tease he could handle. A conceited rich snob was another story.

"I'm not my mother," she snapped out. A smile returned to her lips, curving them into the secretive one she first wore in the pub. Her gaze journeyed down his body, coming to rest on his groin. "Besides, my attention isn't going to be on your apartment."

"Right," he said smoothly, relieved she wasn't a total snob at least. "You're going to be watching me strut my stuff while I stroke my cock."

Anticipation sizzled in her eyes so hot he didn't have to

worry about relying on her ogling his naked body to get him hard. His dick forgot how cold it was and shot to instant arousal.

Nash pulled open the steel door and gestured for her to go inside. After giving him another impressed smile, she moved past him and up the bare stairwell leading to his second-floor studio apartment. He hobbled up after her. His door was the second one on the right, and he turned the knob and pushed the door in.

"You don't lock it." The words came out as a stunned statement.

He shrugged. "Someone needs something of mine so bad they're willing to risk stealing it, more power to 'em."

Admiration filled her eyes. "You said need, not want. That's respectable."

If she was at his place for free naked fun, he would take the words as a compliment. But she was here as a pleasure client, and most of them would rather have him shamefully wicked than a respectable gentleman.

To remind her why she was here and how unrespectable it was to charge for the honor of watching him shoot his wad, he flipped on the apartment lights and walked into the open living area, patting the back of the worn plaid couch. "Make yourself comfortable. If you want to take your clothes off, I can jack the heat up."

The admiration left her eyes. Her gaze skipped around his apartment, taking it in so quickly, he figured she wasn't seeing a thing but her own anxiety.

Where had the tauntress from the bar gone?

Nash considered telling her it was okay to change her mind and leave. Before he could say a word, she shrugged out of her jacket and tossed it against the back of his recliner. Smoothing the miniskirt along her thighs, she sat on the couch and crossed her legs with a graceful slide of sheer stockings.

His pulse picked up. Damn, he'd always been a sucker for stockings, loved the silky feel of them beneath his hands almost as much as he loved peeling them off his lover's legs. If she was sticking to her terms from the pub, he wouldn't be touching her stockings, or the eye-pleasing bounty beneath them. He wouldn't be touching her breasts either.

He took a lingering look at her tits anyway.

Where her hot-pink sleeveless top bared her toned, diamond-adorned belly, it covered her cleavage, leaving him to guess if her breasts were actually the size of tangerines or if a padded bra created the illusion.

A soft murmur had him lifting his gaze up to find her eyes intent on him. She still looked edgy, but beyond the nervousness was a lust that told him how bad she wanted this to happen. "Do you live far from here?"

"Not really. Why?"

"I was going to offer you another beer"—try to kill her anxiety altogether—"but if you live more than fifteen miles away, I'm not going to be able to drive you home later."

Her expression went from edgy to intrigued. "Do you have a tether?"

His cock twitched with the unexpected question. Who was this woman? Tensing up one second and teasing him the next. "Which part of me are you hoping to bind?"

"I meant on your leg. I knew a guy once who was pulled over for drinking and driving. As part of his probation, they made him wear an ankle tether that would alert the police if he went beyond the fifteen miles it took him to get to work."

"I've never gotten a DUI. The only tethers I have are the kind meant for pleasure." He glanced at the bed, draped in a navy comforter, occupying the far corner of the open apartment. Thoughts of pushing her back on it and peeling off the sexy stockings to get to the warm skin beneath bombarded him.

Would she fall back on her social standing and act sophisticated when he had her naked? Or brazenly share her fantasies, so he could make them realities?

Didn't matter. Wouldn't be happening. She just wanted to watch him get off. He could rush it and have her out of his place in ten minutes. Only, until her nerves settled, she wouldn't enjoy the show.

He looked back at her. "How about that beer?"

"I want one, but I'll pass."

Ignoring the second half of the reply, Nash crossed to the kitchenette in the corner opposite the bed. He pulled a can of beer from the fridge. He only had enough gas left in his S-10 for a thirty-mile round trip and the money in his bank account was already designated for bills, but since this had become a paying gig, if she lived farther than that, he could add the cost of gas to her tab.

Returning to the living area, he popped the can's tab and handed her the beer. "Drink up. I'll drive you home wherever you live."

"What about you?"

"I'm too busy getting naked."

Genevieve watched in silence as he began to undress. His coat came first. Then he pulled the olive green sweatshirt over his head and she nearly swallowed her tongue. He definitely had rock hard down. His torso was a study in the sculpted masculine physique, and her fingers tingled with want to run all over it.

No touching. It was her rule and it was a good one.

His fingers went to the button of his jeans, popping it open and then tackling the zipper with gusto. Warmth coiled in her belly, and her throat went dryer than sandpaper. She brought the beer to her lips, taking a long drink. Then a longer one as he pushed his jeans and black briefs down strong thighs lined with crisp, dark hair.

He toed off brown leather boots, then bent to remove his socks and kicked the clothes aside. Straightening brought his cock in line with her eyes. And what a lovely cock it was. Long. Thick. The head tinged nearly purple with his stimulation.

Her pussy pulsed with liquid excitement. She started to reach a hand toward his shaft only to catch herself. She tucked her hand back at her side.

No touching. No touching. No touching.

"What kind of dancing did you have in mind?"

Hearing the humor in his voice, she looked at his face. A grin as wolfish as it was arrogant turned up the corners of his lips. Through the years it had become second nature to hold her thoughts in. But this was her webless night, so she returned his grin and let them out. "Anything that jiggles all those stunning male parts."

He gave a low laugh and fell easily into a smooth left foot change that, for just a moment, opened his stance and displayed his balls to their best vantage.

Genevieve took another long drink, rapt in his moves. She'd expected a stripper routine. Or maybe some hip-hop type of street dancing. She didn't expect this. "Who taught you how to waltz?"

He began a promenade that bobbed his dick and made her clit itch to be stroked. "Not what you expected?"

So far not much about him was what she'd expected. It was better—his personality and his body. "No, but you're good. Have any faster moves?"

"How's a jive suit you?"

If she was the one dancing, she would look ridiculous. Bouncing around on his feet, kicking up his heels, his big, hard, beautiful body looked wild and primitive and like she wanted to wrap her own around it and feel the press of his cock with each of his fast moves.

Pre-cum emerged at the tip of his shaft. She sustained her

needy growl by taking a drink. It had been so long since she'd tasted a man's cum.... "Very nice. You said something about masturbating."

He quit dancing to stand in front of her, arms hanging loosely at his sides. He looked totally at ease with his nudity, like he danced naked for unfamiliar women on a regular basis. And, of course, he did. He'd told her as much back in the pub.

"Naked dancing's free. Masturbation will cost you." One hand went to his groin. He cradled the lower half of his cock in his cupped fingers while he rubbed the pad of his thumb over the plump head, spreading the silky fluid. "Unless you want to dance naked and masturbate with me."

She watched in jealousy of his fingers, wishing they were her own. "I told you I don't dance naked. I will masturbate, though."

She would?

Genevieve lifted the beer can to her lips only to find it empty. Guzzling it, after drinking two others in the pub, had to be the reason she was saying bold and really stupid things. It had to be the reason she wanted to follow through on those things.

It wasn't cheating so long as they didn't touch, right? Besides, this guy was a paid professional. "Do I get a discount for fingering myself?"

"A masturbation discount?" He barked out a laugh, and the absurdity of the question had her laughing along. "Tell me your name and make good on the masturbation promise and I'll waive the fee this time."

Her laughter ended. Tension pushed through her. It was do or die with yet another regret time. "Jenn," she improvised quickly, meeting his gaze with her lie. "With a J and two Ns."

"And an E in the middle?"

The humor in his eyes eased her strain. He was playing with her, teasing her like an old friend might do. An old, naked friend with his hips swiveling in the stripper move she'd first expected and his dick pumping in his hand.

Tom would never give her a moment like this. None of the straightlaced guys she'd dated before him had. This was her chance to steal a little naughty fun, and she was going to do it with her hand in her panties.

3

Nash slowed the pumping of his fingers around his cock as he watched Jenn spread her legs a few inches apart on the couch. Her hand disappeared beneath the tiny hem of her skirt. Seconds later, her eyes widened a fraction and he knew her fingers had brushed against her pussy.

Was she half as aroused as he was?

He'd never danced naked for a woman, paying client or otherwise. Why he'd shown off the years of dance lessons his mother had forced on him was a mystery. Maybe just to impress Jenn's refined tastes enough to see she used his services again, only next time she would be footing the bill.

Hell, he couldn't afford to do this for free tonight. But then, he'd planned on doing her for free before she brought up the whole dancing thing, so why not? If she did end up living more than fifteen miles away, he would just have to do some bill juggling until more money came in.

"Crap." Her hand pulled from beneath her skirt.

He lifted his attention to her face to find her frowning. "What's the matter?"

"I forgot I'm wearing nylons. I'm going to look dorky wiggling out of them."

He almost laughed over her completely unrefined language. The idea she was worried about looking dumb in front of him stopped him. She was turning out to be nothing like he'd imagined. She was also worrying way the hell too much about appearances.

Releasing his shaft, Nash went down on his knees in front of her. Close enough that he could smell her arousal mingling with her light floral scent and see up her skirt. "I can do it for you. With my teeth."

Jenn's breath caught and he grinned. She might be playing a you-can't-touch-me hand, but she definitely wanted him to.

"I've got it," she said after a few seconds, her voice thick. "But don't expect me to use my teeth. I'm not quite that talented."

She bent to remove the stilettos. Slipping a hand beneath either side of her skirt, she grabbed hold of the waist of the stockings. She lifted her butt an inch off the couch and slowly squirmed free. Her panties clung to the stockings, pulling away from her body and flashing a glimpse of damp black pubic hair before she hurried to right them.

His cock throbbed, more caught up in the artless flash than any true teasing could have accomplished. "Something tells me you're a lot more talented than you give yourself credit for."

"Thank you." The words whispered from between her lips.

Nash nearly whispered them right back when she spread her legs a little farther and dipped her fingers beneath the crotch of her panties.

She wore gray panties. Simple cotton that didn't go with her risqué outfit and suggested she had no plans of ending up in a scenario like this tonight. He liked that he'd somehow made her change her mind and he liked the way the cotton revealed her wetness even more.

He took his cock back in his hand, stroking idly as he absorbed the carnal sound of her pussy sucking at her fingers. It should have been enough, but he wanted more, wanted to watch her fingers disappear inside her sheath. See her creaming around them. "When I said I'd waive the fee if you masturbated, I meant so I could see what you were doing. I can tell you're finger fucking your pussy, but I can't see how much your pussy likes the treatment."

Jenn's fingers went still. When she didn't respond after a few seconds, he looked up at her face. She was back to looking anxious, her blue-green eyes wide with uncertainty. Then all at once a slow, sensual smile crept across her mouth.

Long, slim fingers latched onto the sides of her panties. She stripped them quickly down her legs. Relaxing back, she parted her thighs wide. "Better?"

"Much." Now he could see her pink folds were dripping with desire and eager to take him inside. His cock pulsed savagely.

Despite his easy handling, he was already too damned close to coming. He needed a temporary distraction, something to sharpen her pleasure while maintaining his own. "You're not wet enough."

"I'm not?"

"Nope." He stood. "You need help."

"You can't touch me." She sounded half afraid he would, half afraid he wouldn't.

"I don't plan to." Nash went to the bedroom area, moving between the bed and the side wall to reach his dresser. He opened the bottom drawer, which was filled with sex toys and stimulation aids.

The elegant red rosebud-tipped black mini-flogger had appealed to him since he picked it up from an online vendor, but he'd yet to come across the right woman to use it on. With her contradicting mix of naughty and nice, Jenn was a perfect fit.

Holding the flogger's short handle, he fisted the twisted rope tails and returned to the living area. She looked up when he was a couple feet away and he let the tails fly out of his hand to crack against the air.

She jumped on the couch. Surprise and excitement flashed in her eyes.

He held the mini-flogger out to her. The thought of using it on her personally held far greater appeal, but he would have to settle for playing voyeur. "Use this."

She eyed it suspiciously. "Whose is it?"

"Mine. In my line of work, you need toys to cover every imaginable fantasy." He hadn't told her what his line of work was, just hinted, and he could see the unasked question in her eyes. Payment was no longer an issue, so neither were specifics. "Run the roses around the mouth of your cunt. Slip them into your pussy and tease your clit."

She looked wary another few seconds, but then sat back on the couch and relaxed again. Taking the flogger by the handle, she trailed the rosebuds down the length of her slit. Her eyes narrowed. The breath pushed slowly from her lips. She brought the rosebuds racing back up, burying them partway inside her sex, letting out a wail caught between a moan and a sigh.

Nash's cock jerked with the primal sound. He took his shaft back in hand, spreading pre-cum from the weeping tip along the length of it. "Part your lips. Make the rosebuds go deeper. Feel the tails inside you."

Nodding, Jenn brought her bare feet up on the edge of the couch and used her free hand to spread her labia. The rosebuds journeyed back downward, caressing her clit. Pink flared into her cheeks and her hips shot forward.

"Oh my . . ." Juices sluiced from her sex.

Blood pumping hot, he tightened his fingers around his dick. The dampness of his shaft within his hand alluded to the way her cunt would feel milking him, but it could never be the same.

She pulled the rosebuds from her folds and then sank them inside again. Panted out, "Don't you want a toy?"

He was struck by the consideration in her words. That she would give such thought to his pleasure on the verge of finding her own release told him exactly what kind of woman she was. Not pretentious or snobby, not a typical Deevy Isle girl at all.

Maybe she wasn't from Deevy Isle. Maybe she wasn't even wealthy.

Who she was and how much money she had really didn't matter. All that was important was seeing she was left happy enough to seek out his services again. "Not if you want me to last longer than a few more seconds."

Obviously she didn't. Her smile came quickly and naughtily. She lifted her fingers from her labia to dip one into her sheath and coat it with her juices. She brought the finger to her mouth, trailing it along her swollen scarlet lips before flicking her tongue out and lapping at her essence.

"Yum," she breathed huskily. "I taste good."

His balls drew tight and he pumped his cock harder. A throaty moan accompanied the next lash of her tongue. Her chest heaved with enough force to jerk his attention from her mouth. Her pelvis rolled forward, bringing his gaze lower. She whimpered once. Again. The rosebuds pulled hard from her pussy.

Jenn's hips bucked up, cream gushed from her sex. She uttered mindless, illogical words that still managed to sound sexy as hell. Then dipped a finger into the flood and brought it back to her mouth, licking greedily at her salty, warm cum.

Nash groaned at the erotic display. Tension chased up his legs to ball at his lower spine. His hand worked faster, stroking along his length until a furious release took hold. Locking his thighs, he pumped the cum from his body. It jettisoned from his cock, plastering her bare stomach and the shimmering diamond in her navel.

She stopped licking her fingers to look down at her belly. The tip of her nose scrunched up, annoyance flickering in her eyes. He reconsidered every thought he'd had about her. Became convinced she was a Deevy Isle snob to the core, destined to show her class by getting pissy about the mess he'd made.

Then she coated her finger with his seed and brought it to her mouth.

No licking this time, just sucking it between her lips and savoring with a murmur. Playfulness took over the annoyance in her eyes. She went back for a second fingerful and pulled it between her lips. "Mmm . . . You taste good too."

Hell, he hadn't seen that coming. And he really wished she hadn't done it . . . because the free naked fun was over and he was more eager than ever to touch.

"You know people who live out this way?" Genevieve winced over her snooty tone. Nash didn't deserve her bad attitude. It wasn't his fault she had to return to her world of pretense and perfection after stepping into his world of freedom for a couple hours and finding hedonistic delight.

He glanced over, his face lit in the dark night by the green glow of the S-10's dashboard lights. "Why?"

The cleft in his chin appeared deeper in the lighting, and her tongue ran over her teeth with the urge to dip into it. But that wouldn't be happening. Her bachelorette party was over. It should have been over long before she tasted his cum.

Shame and annoyance rolled through her, as it had when she'd first given in to the reckless urge. She concentrated back on the snow-cleared, cobblestone streets. "The snowplow took out the one-way sign last week and there have been a lot of people driving the wrong way since. You turned off right before it became one way."

"Sometimes I get bored and go for drives."

His response sounded as edgy as she felt. Asking about his

tone would be moot. Asking anything about him and his actions would be a waste of his time and hers. Besides, they'd already crossed the covered bridge connecting the mainland with the island. Tia's house and an inevitable grill session were less than a minute away. Along with the news of how badly Genevieve's mother had taken her leaving.

Nash turned onto Tia's street. Hulking, multilevel homes and currently closed-up summer vacation properties rose up around them.

"One of these yours?" he asked.

He'd sounded displeased earlier tonight, when he suggested she found his apartment beneath her. He sounded even more displeased now. Obviously, he didn't hold the wealthy in high regard. She couldn't blame him where most of her uppity neighbors were concerned. "I don't live on this street, but my girlfriend Tia does and I was planning on spending the night with her."

"Guess that explains the no-touching rule."

Frowning, she looked over at him. "What does?"

"Your preference for women."

The idea went so far against the beliefs of the conformist residents of the island, she laughed out loud. "I don't mean girlfriend like that. Tia has been my best friend since we were ten, when she spent the summer here on the island with her grandparents. From time to time we still have sleepovers."

"That's nice. Most people lose track of their friends through the years."

He sounded surprised yet sincere in a way that tugged at her heart. Tom thought her and Tia's gab-session sleepovers were juvenile. Her parents and sister had never thought much good about her friend at all. Truthfully, the only reason most of Deevy Isle put up with Tia—a recent permanent transplant, and therefore a should-be outcast, to the island—was her grandfather's part in the establishment of the elite community.

Genevieve sighed. Just thinking about her family and fiancé had the veil of exhaustion falling back on her shoulders.

Tia's corner estate home appeared a block ahead. With the Thanksgiving holiday newly past, she'd kept to her late grandfather's tradition and already put out her Christmas decorations. Thousands of miniature white lights were strung in the front trees, illuminating the yard.

Those lights were like the worst kind of beacon, signaling it was time to face reality, by crawling back into her overgroomed web. Her belly tightened. "You want the white place on the corner with all the lights."

"Trust me," Nash said dryly, "I don't want it."

The censure was exactly what she needed. Her weariness lifted with her short laugh of agreement. "It's way too big and not even close to Tia's style. Her grandfather left it to her when he passed away, and she promised to keep the house occupied by family the bulk of the year, so she's stuck living there for the time being."

He pulled into the plowed driveway seconds later. Nerves rose up as she unbuckled her seat belt. How was she supposed to say good-bye to the guy she'd spent the evening masturbating with?

She looked over to find him watching her expectantly. He was barely smiling yet gave off an arrogant charm she acknowledged was the reason he first appealed to her. Now she knew she liked him for that and many more reasons.

Genevieve leaned across the seat to brush his mouth with a quick kiss. "Thanks for the ride." She slid back to her side of the truck and opened the door, triggering the interior lights and letting in a blast of icy cold air. Dropping down onto the shoveled sidewalk, she let the memory of the rest of the night heat her through. She smiled. "And the freebie."

"My pleasure."

She'd started to close the door, when he said, "Jenn?"

She stuck her head back inside the truck's heat. "Yeah?"

He held out his hand, a white business card with blue and black text wedged between his fingertips. His smile turned to a sexy grin that tingled want deep within her. "Here's my card. Next time won't be free, but if you're ever in the need of a masturbating naked dancer, you'll know where to reach me."

She glanced at the card. No last name. Just an unusual first name and beneath it the words Loose Screws and a telephone and fax number. "Nash?"

"It's an old family nickname." He nodded past her shoulder. "Tia's waiting for you."

Genevieve's wonder over his name disappeared as the tight sensation returned to her belly. She turned to see Tia standing in the opened doorway of the estate house. Her face was lit up beneath the porch light, revealing a mixture of concern and irritation.

Really, what had Genevieve expected after disappearing the way she had—a pat on the back and a "You go, girl!"?

With a last good-bye to Nash, she tucked his card inside the pocket of her jacket and headed up the shoveled stone walkway to face the potentially dire consequences of ditching her so-called bachelorette party.

"Your mother is livid," Tia said the moment Genevieve stepped inside her friend's grossly massive house—ten of Nash's apartments would fit inside it.

Genevieve leaned back against the double French doors and closed her eyes, granting herself a few more seconds of freedom. Opening her eyes, she stepped into the gray marble-floored foyer and unzipped her coat. "Allison must be thrilled."

Tia waved a dismissive hand in the air. "Allison is Allison. Tom is concerned."

"Mother called him already? It hasn't even been three hours."

Rolling her eyes, Tia crossed to the winding staircase that

led to the open second floor. She sat down on the off-white carpeted bottom step and hugged her arms around her knees. "You missed your bachelorette party, what did you expect?"

Genevieve eyed Tia's black sweatpants and gray sweatshirt longingly. The only time she got to dress so comfortably was during these sleepovers.

With Tia's inherited staff on paid vacation while she adjusted to life on the island, Genevieve hung up her own jacket in the nearly concealed wall closet. She crossed to the stairs. "That was *not* a bachelorette party. But you're right—I did expect her to call him." She gave her friend an apologetic look. "I'm sorry I left you to take the rap and to worry about me."

The carefree Tia she knew and loved emerged, intrigue lighting her hazel eyes. "Forget that, who's the stud and where's your car?"

Genevieve nodded up the stairs. Tia stood and they started up. "I had a few beers and Nash didn't want me driving, so he brought me home." End of story. Yeah right.

"What kind of name is Nash?"

"What kind of name is Tia?"

"Good point." They cleared the top of the staircase. "So who is he?"

"No one important. Just a guy I met at the bar."

"Liar. If he was no one important, you would still be wearing pantyhose." Tia's breath sucked in. "What the hell did you do, Gen?"

Genevieve kept walking, passing several bedroom doors before her own came into sight. She sighed. Comfort was less than a minute away. "I did meet him at the bar—a pub actually—and I didn't do anything close to what you're thinking."

Just enough to make her feel damned guilty in hindsight.

Shame reared up again, tensing her from head to toe as she entered her temporary bedroom. Pulling the bulky white sweatshirt from the foot of the bed and over her skimpy top eased her anxiety a little. "I wanted a real bachelorette party"—she sat on the side of the mattress and took off the stilettos—"so I asked him if he would dance naked for me and he said he usually gets paid for that sort of thing. So I said I would pay, but then he said if I masturbated for him, he would waive the fee."

From where she leaned against the door frame with her arms crossed, Tia snorted out a laugh. "Imagine that."

"No. It wasn't like that. He'd already agreed to masturbate for me at that point." Realizing how much the admission didn't help her situation, Genevieve crossed to the wardrobe armoire and squatted to pull gray sweater socks from one of the low drawers.

"Exactly how many beers did you have?"

"It was innocent fun." After tossing the socks on the bed, she eased the miniskirt down her legs and then the oversized, white fleece pajama pants back up them. "We didn't even touch each other."

Tia smiled astutely. "You just wanted to."

"No." Genevieve let the lie linger long enough to sit back down on the bed and pull on the first sock, then admitted, "Okay, yes. But I would never cheat on Tom."

"He might say you already did."

"I know." Particularly if he knew the full details. "I needed to get away from it all. It was a one-time deal. Now I can get married and be the perfect Stepford Wife and he'll never have to worry about me straying to see what it's like to leave tighty-whiteys behind." Her belly knotted with the thought of what a truly perfect wife she would be expected to be. Really, it ought to be easy, given her parents had spent the last twenty-seven years grooming her for the role.

"I can hardly wait to hear him say I do." Unintentional sarcasm filled her words.

"Sounds to me like you'd be better off if he said I don't."

"No, I wouldn't." Genevieve pulled on the other sock, cautious to keep her voice even. "I love Tom. He's a good man. My parents and I have known him his whole life."

"Why do your parents get top billing?"

"That was etiquette talking." *Was it?* "It isn't nice to put yourself first."

"It isn't nice to masturbate for a stranger when you're engaged either, but you did that."

Genevieve winced. She opened her mouth to come up with some excuse that would never be enough to justify her behavior.

Tia held up a hand, keeping her from wasting the effort. "I'm not saying it was wrong, Gen. I think it was a sign. This is your chance to move on and become someone other than Mrs. Tom Granger." She said his name like it was a sentence of lifelong boredom. "He's all wrong for you and marrying him would be a huge mistake. You need to spread your wings, play the field a bit. Be your own woman."

"My mother is livid about my going AWOL for three hours. What exactly do you think she's going to do when I leave Tom so I can spread my wings and play the field?"

"That's where the being your own woman part comes in. You learn to accept that what your mother, and father for that matter, want doesn't have to be what you want."

That part sounded good, Genevieve had to admit, but unrealistic. She truly enjoyed her job as the head of administration at the estate collections company and was eager to take her place as president when her father retired. That wouldn't happen if she routinely acted against her parents' wishes. "It's easy for you to say that."

"Because my parents are dead," Tia said sarcastically. "Wow, lucky me."

Groaning over her own stupid mouth, Genevieve pushed off the bed. She went to her friend and pulled her into a hug. "I'm sorry. I didn't mean that to sound the way it did." Stepping back, she smiled. "I'm happy, Tia. Really. Tom can be boring and even selfish at times, but in general he's a great guy and I love him. That's all that matters."

Genevieve peered out the narrow, vertical window lining Tia's double French doors. Tom stepped from his maroon Expedition, resplendent in suit and tie, his neat blond hair never budging an inch in the crisp morning breeze.

Butterflies somersaulted in her belly. She'd tried to tell herself what she said to Tia two nights ago was true. But it wasn't.

She wasn't happy, damn it.

The episode with Nash wasn't to blame—she hadn't been happy long before he showed her how incredibly good being imperfect felt. If anything, that episode and Tia's candid words had given her the courage to see a truth that had existed for months and voice her feelings on it, accepting all unfavorable outcomes.

Tom reached the door and flashed a flawless smile at her through the window. Then, like the total stuffed shirt he was, he rang the doorbell.

Genevieve opened the door. He stepped inside, wiping his shoes on the entry mat before kissing her quickly on the cheek. She tried to curb her disappointment over his lack of anything remotely like passion, but that was hard to do. He hadn't seen her in four days, she'd gone missing for three hours during that time and he claimed to her mother he'd been very concerned about her absence, and all she got was a little buss on the cheek?

Some fiancé.

"We need to talk," she said seriously.

His smile never faltered. "If this is about your disappearing from your party Saturday night, I told you on the phone yesterday I forgive you. The prospect of marriage is intimidating for a lot of people."

He *was* stuffy and lacking in the enthusiasm arena where anything other than work was concerned, but he was also a great guy. If they were to end up together, then he deserved to know her heart was with him 100 percent. Not just enough for her parents' affection for him and their ability to lord over her to sway her into marriage.

Genevieve pushed her hands into the pockets of the navy tailored slacks she put on, along with a white Angora sweater, specifically for his arrival. That she felt the need to dress up for him was probably, in itself, a sign of how wrong they were together. "Then you'll understand when I say I need some time off before we take our vows?"

His smile wobbled. "What is 'time off'?"

"A couple weeks to spread my wings. Be my own woman." She sucked in a breath, letting it out quickly. "See others."

Red fanned up Tom's neck from the collar of his white dress shirt. His smile vanished. "We're supposed to be married in less than a month and you want to see *others*?" The words roared from his mouth.

She took exception to his shouting. He was hurt, but he would be hurt even more if she allowed him to enter into a marriage based on one-sided love. "I want to be sure I'm doing the right thing. I want to know if we marry, it's going to last forever."

"*If*?" He snorted. "Tia put you up to this, didn't she?"

Aversion for her friend, which he'd never before let show, heated his words and faded her sympathy for him. "This isn't her doing."

"You know how I feel about your lying to me, Genevieve."

The usage of her whole name killed the rest of her sympathy while setting her teeth on edge. They'd known each other their whole lives, the last two years they'd been a couple, and he still insisted on referring to her so formally. "I'm not lying. I shared my feelings with Tia. All she did was summarize them for me."

"Did you ever think there's a reason Tia is single?" he asked mockingly.

"I don't have to think about it." She mimicked his tone. "I know there's a reason. Up until five weeks ago, she spent every day of her adult life caring for her ailing grandfather. That doesn't leave a lot of time for other men."

"I never thought being engaged left time for other men either, but apparently you do."

Blame slammed Genevieve in the gut. The fight drained out of her because he was right. She gave him a repentant smile. "I'm sorry, but I can't change the way I feel."

"I'm sorry too," Tom said sternly, his smile nowhere to be found. "Take your time off, Genevieve."

"Will you tell my parents?"

"We work with your father. Your office is right next to his. Don't you think he's going to wonder when I don't show up at your door like a faithful dog to take you out to lunch on Wednesday, the way I have for over a year and a half now?"

Is that how she made him feel? Like a dog? Was it possible he wasn't happy with their relationship either? No. He wouldn't be acting so upset if that was the case. "I already took this week and next off, which is why I'm not at the office this morning. After what happened Saturday night, Mother decided I'm overstressed with wedding preparations and made the suggestion."

He didn't respond, just held out his hand. "Give me your ring."

She frowned at his open palm. "*What?* Why?"

"I don't want a symbol of my love for you being forgotten on some one-night stand's dresser."

Genevieve's mouth went agog. She snapped it shut. "I never said I wanted to sleep with—"

"Give me the ring," he snapped.

She worked the ring from her finger and held it out to him. He jerked it up and stalked the handful of feet to the door, turning back when he reached it. His mouth opened. She thought he might have changed his mind. Then he said, "See you in two weeks. Try not to get knocked up between now and then."

4

"Loose Screws. How may I help you?" Nash winced at the formality of his words. Spending time with Jenn the other night obviously had old habits rearing their head. Not that the time they'd spent together had involved much sophistication. Just raw, unadulterated fun that left her intruding on his thoughts.

"Be my boyfriend," came from the other end of the phone line.

He frowned over the words as the caller's identity became clear by the slight aristocratic edge in Jenn's voice unique to those who called Deevy Isle home. It had taken the better part of a year to work that edge from his own voice.

Grabbing the remote control from next to his hip on the couch, he turned off the television to concentrate on the conversation. "As intriguing as the offer sounds, my job and a girlfriend don't mix."

"What do you do? Dance naked for money, but what else?"

"For the right amount, just about anything."

"How does ten thousand sound?"

Damned appealing. "What are we talking about?"

"You being my boyfriend for the next week and a half and me paying you ten grand for your effort. Five up front. Five on the morning of the last day."

She wanted to pay him ten grand to spend ten days kissing and touching every inch of her nude body, the way he'd wanted to do three nights ago for free? There had to be a catch. "I don't do the socially elite scene."

"Thank God," Jenn sighed into the phone line.

Nash's take on her personality had been flip-flopping from the moment they met. Now the truth came out. "Don't want your friends catching us together?" he asked snidely.

"No, I don't." She hurried to qualify, "But not for the reason you think. I want to see what it feels like to have a relationship with someone who isn't perfect, but I don't want to do it with all of Deevy Isle breathing down my neck."

Hell, he could understand that logic. He could also hear the tension in her voice and knew she hadn't meant to insult him. In an amused voice, he asked, "So you thought of imperfection and my name popped up first thing?"

She laughed tightly. "I don't mean imperfect like flawed. I mean imperfect in the sense you aren't afraid to get dirty, or let your passion out for the sake of passion alone. Or be completely unpolitically correct by waltzing naked while stroking your cock."

His shaft stirred with the memory. So she liked his impromptu moves enough to have it stay with her, huh?

Nash caught himself grinning like an idiot and flattened his lips. What they were talking about here was a simple business proposition decked out to look like something more for the sake of a client. "I have another job. I can't just forget about it to dedicate twenty-four hours a day to you."

"Shockingly, I have a job of my own . . . though I took off this week and next so I could get away completely. I wouldn't expect you to do the same."

"Gets old being rich."

"I'm sure it's hard for you to believe," Jenn said dryly, "but, yes, it does."

That had been an automatic observation on his part, but it was for the best she took it as sarcasm. "Let me check with my partners, see what the schedule looks like. If I can't do it right now—"

"After next week, it will be too late."

Why? And why did she suddenly sound so grim? Did it have to do with whatever kept her from taking him home with her the other night?

The answers didn't matter. She was offering him ten grand to be her boyfriend. Regardless of the noise he made about working his other job, Loose Screws didn't have any current construction work to worry about. Even if there had been construction work to be done, he knew he would still take her up on her proposition.

For Benny's sake and for Nash's own reasons, he would risk the odds of spending the next ten days grinning like an idiot over nothing more than a business transaction.

Nash stabbed the doorbell of Benny's mother's house. Technically, Benny's house, since he'd been living in the yellow two-story for over a year and the odds of his mother ever coming back to live in it herself were next to nil.

Benny opened the door a half minute later. His blond hair was matted against the side of his head and orange lettering was pressed into the skin just right of his gateau, suggesting he'd slept with a magazine for a pillow again. The guy spent too much time running himself into the ground and often only made it to the couch before crashing for the night.

Benny blinked at him. "What the hell are you doing here? It's not even light yet."

Nash knew he would be out the door to make money by

whatever means possible the second the sun rose. So while he didn't enjoy waking him up early, he figured it his best chance at catching him. "You're taking this week off," he ordered. "Spending the entire time with your mom. No isn't an option."

Benny scrubbed a hand over his mustache—probably thought he was still dreaming for Nash to be talking this way. "You know damned well I can't afford it. Mom doesn't have insurance and I already told you I'm not taking a loan from you."

"I'm not offering you a loan." Nash pulled a folded stack of hundreds from his coat pocket. "Just giving you your cut from weekly business a few days early."

Benny came instantly awake. "What'd you do? Rob a bank, or hit up your dad?"

"Got a good-paying, several-day gig with a Deevy Isle babe." To make certain he didn't do anything asinine, like offer to not accept her money at the end of the ten days, Nash had met Jenn at the bank last night. She'd given him the promised cash up front and signed the Loose Screws silence agreement. And he'd given her an openmouthed "see you in the morning" kiss that had his cock solid and her squirming against him so blatantly the security guard had asked them to leave. "She's paying the rest after the fact, so you can afford to take off next week too."

"I can't take your—"

"We agreed to split all profits the day we started up Loose Screws," Nash reminded him before Benny could finish his objection. "With Thad sitting out the woman-pleasuring side these days, your fair cut is half."

"We agreed to put in a reasonable amount of time each week, and I won't be doing that if I'm sitting in a nursing home."

"Your mom's dying, Benny." He hated stating the facts so plainly. Feared that combining them with Benny's overworked, overstressed mind could be enough to remerge the harmful, potentially dangerous habits of his youth. But right now, the facts appeared the only option. "Do you really want to look back a year from now and think you didn't spend as much time with her as you could have because you were too much of a stubborn ass to sit out work a couple weeks?"

A good fifteen seconds of silence passed and Nash thought he might have to take Benny inside the house and kick his ass to get him to accept the money, but then he finally nodded and took it. "Thanks."

Curiosity entered Benny's eyes as he fisted the bills. "This woman must really be something to have you looking past where she comes from. You thinking about playing a Thad and getting personal with her?"

"Jenn's after a change of pace from the moneyed scene, wants someone to show her how the other half lives. Once she put ten grand on the table, I could hardly tell her I wasn't technically the other half. But, no, I'm not playing a Thad. She seems decent enough, but there's no way in hell I'm getting myself wrapped up with the Deevy Isle set on a permanent basis again."

Judging by the stricken look on Nash's face and the fact he wasn't letting her come out of the sparse second-floor hallway and into his studio apartment, Genevieve had done something wrong. "I thought you said to come by at ten this morning?"

"I did." His gaze fell on her suitcase. "You never said anything about living together."

After how quickly their kiss had gotten out of hand at the bank last night, she wasn't so sure it was a good idea to do so—Nash obviously got the supply of passion Tom had missed out on. But if she didn't live with him, where would she live? Tia's house was always open, but people knew to find her there.

Now that she'd found the courage to step away from her overgroomed web for more than a couple hours, she didn't want anyone from her day-to-day life, aside from maybe Tia, dropping in on her. "How else am I going to get away completely?"

He considered her suitcase a few more seconds before meeting her eyes. "Ten days and you're out?"

"Yes. That's what we agreed on."

"All right." The arrogantly amused smile he'd given her at the bank emerged. Then it had her damp, and now it did too. He came forward to take the tow bar of the suitcase from her and pulled the burgundy case inside. "It ought to make for a great sex life."

The breath snagged in Genevieve's throat. She halted with one foot inside the door, gaping at his broad back cloaked in a black T-shirt. "I never said anything about sex."

Nash turned around to give her a disbelieving look. "What the hell kind of relationship doesn't have sex in it?"

Apparently, just hers. "I've had them."

"If they were any good, you wouldn't be here now."

That much was true. And Tom had basically said he expected her to sleep with other guys with his snarky comment about her getting knocked up. Then there was the reality she all but dry humped Nash at the bank last night. Still... "I don't know that I'm ready to sleep with another man."

"Obviously your past men have been serious slouches in the sack that you even have to question something like that."

"My last boyfriend and I never slept together," she confessed before she could stop herself.

He narrowed his eyes, looking more stricken over the idea than he had of her living with him. "How long did you date?"

"Almost two years."

"He's a eunuch?"

He's a gentleman, was Genevieve's first thought. Then she recalled the way Nash had helped her into her coat and opened the doors for her the other night. How he had her suitcase in his hand right now. They were both gentlemen, just in different ways. "He doesn't believe in sex before marriage."

"Do you?"

She could say no and explain away her reason for not wanting him to touch her on Saturday night and ensure he kept his hands off her these next days in the meanwhile. But she wasn't so sure she wanted him to keep his hands off her. In truth, the more she thought about him sliding those big hands over her naked body the way he'd so skillfully moved them over his cock the other night, the more she was certain she wanted that very thing.

Her heart beating harder with the reminder of him climaxing on her belly and her fingering up and swallowing back his cum, she risked stepping the rest of the way inside the apartment and closing the door. "I'm not a virgin."

"Dildos don't count."

"I know. I've been with men. It's just been"—*three and a half long, horny years*—"awhile."

Nash released her suitcase. He retraced his steps to the door, until he was less than a foot away and looking at her with some serious heat in his potent brown eyes. "Are you afraid of my touching you, Jenn?"

Yes. But only of how uncontrollably she might respond. "No. I'm just not sure I'm ready for it. That doesn't mean I won't be ready in a day or two." Or an hour or two, if the throbbing ache in her pussy his mere proximity caused was a sign.

"So what do we do until then?"

"Whatever couples do." And whatever involved him removing his too-temping body from arm's reach. He wore the kind of simple gray sweats she adored and hardly ever got to wear, and his T-shirt clung to every hard, virile inch of his torso.

"I always thought they had sex."

"We could play a game." Anything to get him to stop using the s-e-x word. "Your choice," Genevieve said too brightly. She brushed past him and retrieved her suitcase. "I'll get moved in while you decide."

Since she'd only brought the essentials, it took less than ten minutes to move her clothes into the dresser drawer Nash emptied out for her and her few toiletries into the bathroom. Thank God her period wasn't due until the day after their time together was up. He'd given her pink razor such a revolted look that moving tampons into his space would have probably sent him into shock.

While she was in the bathroom, she changed out of her slacks and sweater and into sweats. Not only was she comfortable, but the chance of him being attracted to her and therefore wanting sex while she was dressed in such baggy attire was slim.

Just in case he *was* into the baggy look, Genevieve played it safe when she returned to the living area by sitting down on the recliner a good five feet from his position on the middle of the couch. "What's it going to be?"

"Why doesn't my girlfriend want to sit by me?"

"I'm in the mood to rock," she improvised. Then felt like a total idiot when she attempted to rock only to realize the chair was a stationary unit.

Humor lit Nash's eyes, suggesting he knew exactly what a load of bullshit that was, but he let it go. "Twenty questions. I figure it's the best way to get to know each other."

She tried not to react. But, crap, that game could put a serious crimp in her plans for the next ten days. Right about the time he asked her when things with Tom had ended and she proved she couldn't pull off a lie by admitting they hadn't officially. "Do we get an opt-out question?"

"Only if we agree the other nineteen have to be answered truthfully."

"Deal."

Nash stood from the couch. "I'll get us a drink."

Good idea, Genevieve thought as she watched his tight, yummy ass move into the kitchen area. Get some alcohol in her system, so she was loosened up enough they could have a repeat duo masturbation session.

"Are you into froufrou drinks?" He turned around, leaving her to stare at his groin.

The thing about sweatpants was while they were baggy in most places they had a way of molding to certain others. The outline of his shaft was evident against his inner right thigh. It wouldn't be so defined if he wore briefs, as he had the other night. Which meant he had on either boxers beneath his sweats . . . or nothing at all.

Cheeks warming with the prospect, she pulled her attention to his face. "I don't like girly drinks, but sometimes I drink them anyway."

"Why?"

"Only if that's question number one."

He pulled two beers from the refrigerator and opened them. Coming back into the living area, he handed her a bottle. "It is."

Genevieve took a drink as she watched him settle on the end of the couch nearest her. Just two short feet away. Close enough she could touch the bulge in his sweats by simply extending her leg.

God, how tempting. "It's expected of me."

"Do you always do what you're expected to do?"

The answer to that question—she had until last Saturday—was an immediate arousal killer.

Why had she let others rule her life for so long?

Because she felt obligated to do so. But she wouldn't anymore. Her parents had given her a lot through the years, and she'd done everything she could to give right back in return. They were officially even. If she chose to marry Tom—which was seeming more unlikely by the second—it would be for her sake alone.

Holding the beer bottle between her thighs, she flushed thoughts of her fiancé from her mind. "It's my turn. When did you decide to sell your body for profit?"

Nash took a pull from his beer. Fingers loose around the base, he rested the bottom of the bottle on his thigh. "Eight months ago."

"Obviously I'm rusty at this game. I should have asked, why?"

"Because I love sex." A taunting grin tugged at the corners of his mouth. "And I don't believe in waiting for marriage to enjoy it."

It was a crack at Tom and, while she really didn't want to think about him, she couldn't stop her snicker. Sobering, she asked, "That's the only reason? Doesn't it make you feel cheap?"

"That counts as two questions. The answer is no to both."

Genevieve frowned. "It seems like for ten grand I should get more than a no."

Wiggling his eyebrows, he looked at the length of her. His gaze lingered on her breasts, his pupils darkening to near black as they moved to her groin and stayed there. "You show me yours, I'll show you mine."

Clearly, sweats were no defense against him. Her sex fluttered under his scrutiny, her pussy heating so quickly she gave serious thought to moving her beer up a few inches in an attempt to cool things off. "We already saw each other's."

"Doesn't mean I don't want to see yours again. Run my hands over it." Nash's fingers tightened around his beer bottle, coasting suggestively upward and back down again. "My lips." He brought the bottle to his mouth, running his lips along its damp sides. "Stick my tongue in it." The tip of his tongue came between his lips to penetrate the mouth of the bottle with short, teasing thrusts.

White hot desire stabbed deep in her cunt. She gave into her urge and shifted the bottle up her thighs, pressing its cool side against her quickly swelling sex. "I think it's my turn. Do you—" His free hand went to his groin, stroking the bulge of his cock through his sweats, and the words stilled in her throat.

"Whatever it is, I'm sure I do."

"I meant to say where. Where did you learn to dance?" And why was he fondling himself?

"From an instructor at an academy."

Genevieve looked up at his face with the unexpected response. She'd guessed him to be living day to day, by the aged furnishings in his apartment and the older style of his truck. But obviously that hadn't always been the case. Or maybe he'd pinched pennies to save up for lessons. "Is it a passion you have?"

"Only when I'm erect and naked and you're eyeing me up."

A second jolt of desire pushed through her, dampening her panties. She sighed. The man had a one-track mind and made her own mind follow the exact same route. At least with Nash, she would never have to worry he lacked in the passion arena.

She shifted the bottle against her slit as covertly as possible, hoping to ease her sensual ache. "Why did you learn?"

He looked up from her crotch. "My mom made me do it."

"Are you close with her?" That he respected her was a given by his serious tone.

"We get along. Same with my old man. What about you? What are your folks like?"

"What you'd expect."

He smirked. "Conceited rich snobs."

"Maybe not conceited, but snobby." Or maybe conceited and snobby.

"Would sticking my tongue in your pussy count as sex?"

"No. Yes. Maybe. I'm not sure." Genevieve stopped rambling to suck in a hasty breath. What was he thinking, changing topics so quickly and drastically?

Nash's smirk turned to a cocky grin. He stood. "You think about it while I get us a snack."

He crossed in front of the recliner, and the side of his leg rubbed against hers. Warmth zinged up to gather more wetness in her sex. Just that easily she wanted to say a vehement "No—sticking your tongue in my pussy would most definitely not count as sex."

He came back too fast to give her heated body a reprieve. Brushing his leg up against hers again was nearly enough to have her coming on the spot. She was seriously springloaded for a man-supplied orgasm.

Sitting on the edge of the couch, he held out an open bag of salt and vinegar potato chips. Typically, the mere thought of indulging in something so bad for her would have her jamming her hand in the bag. Right now, she was so keyed up with the want to get physical, she was liable to forget to chew and end up choking to death.

He sat back and grabbed a chip out of the bag, watching her watching him as he chewed it. The man had every right to his self-conceit—even the way he ate potato chips was somehow sexy. "What do you think of the women who pay you to get naked and do things for them?"

He shrugged. "Depends on the woman. Most of them I don't think about at all."

"So you don't think they're easy or slutty or unfaithful?"

"I'm hardly in the position to be calling a woman easy or slutty. What do you mean by unfaithful?"

Like sleeping with one guy when she was sort of still engaged to another. But Tom had indicated he expected her to do as much, Genevieve comforted herself, and the wedding was all but off. "You must get married women calling you up."

"From time to time, though most women don't tell me their marital status and I don't run a background check. So long as they consent to the terms and sign the silence agreement, they generally get what they want." Nash sat forward suddenly, his body noticeably tense and his expression stone serious. "You're married?"

"I'm not married." Even if she was, seeing how badly he took the idea, she probably would have attempted to lie about it. Since she wasn't married and hardly even engaged, she lowered her lashes and gave in to a naughty smile. "I'm not easy either, but I do want your tongue in my pussy."

5

Nash had slept with married women before, though he hadn't found out about their husbands until after the fact. The thought of Jenn having a husband whose existence had kept her from taking Nash home with her turned his gut.

Only, she didn't have a husband. And he had a green light to eat her out.

Setting his half-drank beer and the bag of potato chips on the floor, he went down on his knees and crawled in front of the recliner. He nudged her legs apart with his shoulders and used his lips to lift the beer bottle away from her crotch. If he was feeling patient, he would rub it against her sex a little more. The color that flared into her high cheekbones when she tried to discreetly grind the bottle against her pussy told him just how much she liked the sensation.

He wasn't feeling patient. He'd been thinking about burying his tongue inside her for four nights, and it was time to make those thoughts a reality.

After placing her beer on the floor, he brought his mouth to her sex and nipped at her pussy lips through her sweatpants and panties. Jenn let out a low cry and bucked her pelvis up against his face. He nipped at her a second time. She moaned and latched her fingers onto his shoulders.

The heady scent of her arousal lifted through the layers of cotton to grab hold of his senses and take them on a reckless, need-to-get-naked-fast ride.

"Time to lose these." Nash tugged at the waist of her sweatpants.

Her fingers lifted from his shoulders to cover his hands, halting them. "Maybe we should wait. This *is* only our first day together. We could start out slow, do some naked cuddling."

He looked up at her face to find her smile had lost its naughty edge. Need still sizzled in her eyes, turning them almost completely green, but beyond that was tension.

Disappointment kicked through him. Then eased up a good deal with the thought of spooning against her warm, naked body. He never cuddled with a client more than the requisite minute or two, and it had been too damned long since he held a real lover in his arms. Jenn was a client, but given how they'd met, she also felt like a real, short-term lover and a prime candidate to keep him from feeling lonely for a while.

Coming to his feet, he warned her, "You do realize my dick will be prodding you in the ass the whole time, right?"

Her tension visibly drained away as her smile became one of gratitude and anticipation. "That sounds really good."

He held out a hand to help her up. "Then let's get naked and in bed."

She took his hand and stood. She didn't immediately let his hand go as he'd intended, but moved toward the bed, pulling him along with her. The intimate gesture made her seem far more a real lover and far less a client.

Nash went with the moment and let her have the lead. She stopped at the foot of the bed. Turning back, she released his hand. Her smile became demure, revealing remnants of her anxiety still existed, as she pulled her sweatshirt over her head and unhooked the back clasp of a blue bra.

There wasn't any illusion to his thought her tits were the size of tangerines. They were pale, perfect globes and he had to stop himself from taking them into his hands.

She nodded at his chest, the upturned ends of her silky raven hair whispering over her bare shoulders. "We're both going to be naked, right?"

Hell, yeah. Though having his cock that close to her bare behind was bound to be a life lesson in self-control. Not to mention have him feening for a smoke. He'd been good the last few days, hadn't reached for a single cigarette despite the now-and-again craving. He would like to keep it that way.

Reaching to the tail of his T-shirt, Nash yanked it up and whipped it over his head. He dragged the sweatpants down his legs, remembering with 3D clarity he hadn't bothered with underwear, when his shaft sprang up rock solid and leaking pre-cum.

Jenn's eyes widened. She licked her lips. Was she hoping for another taste of his cum? If so, he would be happy to oblige.

"Even better than I remembered," she uttered, then went fast to work on removing her socks. The sweats and blue panties quickly followed to expose the stimulated plumpness of her pussy peeking through her damp black curls.

Her skirt had camouflaged her hips the other night. Now, he could see they were wide and lush and, as she turned and moved to the head of the bed, he noted her stunning ass was the same. "What don't you like about your body to make you avoid dancing naked?"

She tossed back the faded navy comforter and 1250 thread count top sheet—his one snooty indulgence—and climbed into bed, patting the mattress on his side. "How round it is between my waist and thighs. I exercise every weekday morning, but certain parts don't want to cooperate."

Nash climbed into bed. She rolled onto her side facing away from him. He came up behind her and, as he'd forewarned, his dick prodded her in the backside. "Would one of those parts happen to be the amazing ass my cock is attempting to find its way into right now?"

She tensed, and he slid an arm around her middle and stroked his thumb across her navel. "I wasn't planning on doing it—hey, you took off your diamond."

Jenn's stomach muscles tightened even more beneath his palm. "*What?*"

He feathered his fingers over her belly and around her upper thighs, attempting to relieve her tension. "The other night you were wearing a diamond stud in your belly button."

"Oh." One of his fingers moved higher than intended, brushing against her mound. Her breath hitched in. "It, uh, was a fake."

He brought his fingers along her lower belly. She squirmed against him, hitching her body up higher, like she was trying to get his fingers inside her. Just in case that was only wishful thinking, he took a test run, trailing a lone fingertip through her pubic curls and lightly down her slit.

She sighed and canted her hips upward again. "I hate pain. Even the temporary kind that comes from piercing a hole in my navel."

Giving her mound a gentle, whimper-inducing swat, Nash dropped his lips to her ear. "Guess that means using the rosebud flogger as it was intended is out."

Jenn turned her head far enough to meet his eyes. "You like whipping women?"

She might claim to hate pain, but she wasn't looking any too upset about the idea of being whipped. If anything, she appeared eager to give it a try. "I like making them feel the most extreme pleasure imaginable. For some that means whipping.

For others, all it takes to reach their peak is a little public exposure."

"I know it's pathetic to admit, but I've never had sex outside of the bedroom."

"I'd be happy to remedy that for you." He sounded more than happy to do so. He sounded like he wanted to take her out on his crappy little balcony, which overlooked Crichton's millpond park, to fuck her this very second. "I know you're not ready for that yet, just wanted to plant the idea as a potential for later in the week."

"I'll think about it." She looked away from him. Her hips shifted, her pelvis rising up to brush her mound against his fingertips. "For now, you could finger me."

Nash's cock twitched against her backside with the words. They weren't spoken in a low, uncertain voice riddled with anxiety or an uppity, pompous tone. But a loud, positive voice rich with lust.

Apparently, Jenn was ready to bridge the gap from nice to a little naughty. "So soon?"

Her pelvis retreated. "You're right. I shouldn't have—"

"I was teasing." He slipped a finger inside her wet folds, rocking it deep in her core. "It's not too soon. If anything it's four days too late."

Her thighs fell apart on a throaty sigh. She tossed her head back, giving his mouth full access to her neck. He closed his lips over her pulse point, sucking and nibbling as he slid a second finger into the slick walls of her pussy.

She shivered, taunting his cock with the press of her ass. Her hips joined in on the rhythm of his fingers, then took the pace up several notches. "That feels so good."

"It gets better." Much better would involve planting his face between her thighs. Since that wasn't liable to go over, he used his thumb to increase her pleasure.

Continuing to milk her cunt with his fingers, he applied pressure to her clit with the pad of his thumb. He circled the tip over the swollen nub just barely, just enough to drive her wild.

"Oh yes. It's—oooh . . ." Jenn's head tipped to the side.

Nash broke the contact with her neck to slant his mouth over hers. Her lips parted. He slid his tongue inside, met hers, and mimicked her frantic strokes as the muscles of her sex clenched around his fingers.

Cream drenched his hand. Her tongue stilled and he felt the hot puff of her breath into his mouth. She went a little wild then, darting her tongue around in his mouth, sucking at his forcefully as her hips canted hard and she rode out her release.

He lifted from her lips, and she said in a breathy voice, "Thank you. I needed that." Her gaze came up to his. Concern entered her luminous eyes. "What about you?"

"I'm good just feeling your ass rubbing against me. Tomorrow's liable to be a different story." All right, he wasn't good just feeling her ass, but he was as good as he was going to be without making her give in to something she wasn't ready for.

A slow smile curved her lips. "I can hardly wait for tomorrow."

Nash wasn't aware of falling asleep after fingering Jenn to climax. But he was damned aware he'd just woken up to find her on all fours with her parted lips poised above his hard cock. One hand lifted off the bed to curl around the base of his shaft.

He groaned. "What are you doing?"

Her gaze shot up to his face. Pink settled over her cheeks, making it clear she hadn't planned to wake him for whatever she was about to do.

"It's tomorrow in some countries." The damp, pink tip of her tongue came from between her lips. "Just a taste."

Eyes trained on his, she swept her tongue along the head of his cock. Salty fluid beaded up. She licked it away with a moan.

Then she made herself a liar and him one damned happy man by opening her mouth wide and taking his cock inside.

A lot of women had given him blow jobs, but Jenn clearly hadn't given them to a lot of men. There was no finesse to the erratic swipe of her tongue along his shaft and the greedy sucking of her lips. No purposeful timing of the pumping of her fingers around his upper cock.

She just licked and sucked and pumped and hummed in the back of her throat... and made him come so damned fast he didn't have time to offer to pull out.

Nash dug his fingers into the sheet beneath him as his cum slammed into the back of her throat. Inexperience obviously was a huge bonus where giving head was concerned, because he'd never experienced such an intense orgasm over a mouth job.

Jenn pulled her mouth from his cock. She rolled onto her back beside him. "Sorry. I didn't mean to do that." She sounded embarrassed. "I got carried away."

He came up on an elbow to give her an incredulous look. "You just gave me the best blow job of my life and you're apologizing?"

"Thanks, but I know it was pretty awful. It's not something I do on a regular basis... or at all in years."

He frowned at her self-contempt. His first instinct upon discovering she was moneyed was to believe she would be conceited. If anything, the opposite appeared true. She needed to beef up on her arrogance. "I was serious."

"Oh. Okay." She didn't sound or look like she meant the words.

"You know, there's nothing wrong with a little pride."

"I've been pleasing others for so long, I'm not sure I know what pride is." The admission came in a quiet voice. Jenn climbed out of bed, moving to the end of it to pull her sweatshirt on.

She bent for her panties and Nash's gut tightened. Had she

inadvertently progressed things too fast and now planned to call an early end to their arrangement? No, she couldn't do that. She was the first wealthy person, outside of his folks, he liked in ages. And, besides, he was counting on her company. "Where are you going?"

She slid the panties up her legs, then stooped back down for her bra and sweatpants. He breathed a little easier when she didn't make a move to put them on. He couldn't see her running out of his apartment half dressed.

"To get cleaned up and make lunch."

"You can cook?" Yeah, he definitely liked her and her endless surprises.

"Watch and see." She started toward the bathroom, only to turn back halfway across the room to flash an impish smile. "You like peanut butter and jelly, right?"

"For ten grand, you deserve to go somewhere a hell of a lot nicer."

Genevieve smiled around a mouthful of French fry. After swallowing down the salty, greasy, golden indulgence, she looked around the fast-food restaurant. They sat in a brown plastic booth in the rear of the place, and this early in the afternoon were two of only a dozen diners. "I go somewhere nicer all the time. The only time I get to eat at Burger King is when Tia and I escape without my family's knowledge."

Nash frowned. "You let them rule you."

"I used to, but not anymore. I'm being my own woman. Spreading my wings. Seeing others." His frown moved into his eyes, and she realized what she said. "It's a figure of speech."

From across the booth, he studied her face. His gaze was measuring in a way that reminded her of her father just before he told her how disappointed he was with her behavior. Nash might be disappointed, but he wasn't her father. For one thing, her father would never be caught dead in a fast-food joint. For another, his scrutiny wouldn't give way to a playful grin, the way Nash's did.

"Up for a game?" he asked.

Pleasurable sensation washed through Genevieve. She should be ashamed for allowing him to finger her and then giving him a blow job in return—things with Tom might be over, but he didn't know that for sure. Still she wasn't ashamed. Not when Nash made her feel better about herself with a simple smile than Tom had ever been able to pull off with all the stuffy compliments in his vocabulary.

Dipping a fry into the pool of ketchup he'd squeezed from tiny packets for her, she returned his grin. "We never finished twenty questions."

Wicked heat entered his eyes. "I had something else in mind."

Her feminine muscles clenched with the sensual promise in his words. "It's dirty, isn't it?"

"It doesn't involve us having sex."

Well, damn. She wasn't positive she was ready for public exposure sex or full-out sex of any kind with him, but the idea had her wet to at least give it a try. "I wasn't worried about that."

His mouth curved higher with amusement, intensifying the delectable cleft in his chin. "We just try to make each other want sex. Whoever begs the other person to stop tormenting them first loses."

Genevieve's heartbeat picked up. Warmth licked at her lower belly. She was going to lose and quite possibly make a huge scene in Burger King, but so what? Their antics weren't liable to make the paper. And if they did and it got back to her family and Tom, it would probably be the best thing to ever happen to her. "What does the winner get?"

"Name your stakes."

Popping the ketchup-soaked fry into her mouth, she considered. There were so many wonderfully naughty things she would love to do to him, with him, how could she ever narrow it down? "Whoever wins can pick their prize later. Just so long as it's not totally outrageous like making me dance naked around the millpond."

"You really don't like your butt and hips, do you?"

"No."

"Funny, because I happen to love them." Nash's voice dropped to just above a rough whisper. "Thinking about wrapping my hands around your beautiful hips and pounding into your dripping pussy has my cock hard and aching to take you right there in the booth. You already know my dick has a thing for your luscious ass. Of course, he can't just come across the table and slide right inside. First, my fingers get to fuck your asshole, get it all good and wet, so your heart's galloping in your chest and your pussy's so heavy with cum you feel like you're going to climax before I even get inside you."

Genevieve swallowed hard. Yep, she knew she was going to lose. He'd barely even started the game and already her body was following his command: her heart galloping in her chest and her pussy heavy with cream.

Squeezing her thighs together, she sank down in the booth an inch to take pressure off her sex. "I don't think I'm going to win this game."

"Would it help if I took off my shoe and rubbed your cunt with my toes?" His foot was in her lap in the next instant, his sock-covered toes nudging at her mound. "Spread your legs a few inches," he quietly commanded.

His toes nudged a second time. Shock waves of carnal sensation rippled through her. She was finished with following commands, unspoken or otherwise. Commands that were for the sake of *another's* welfare. Nash's command was centered on her pleasure, and she eagerly obeyed, letting her legs fall open.

His big toe pushed against the crotch of her jeans, pumping into her clit and pulling a whimper up the back of her throat and out her mouth.

His smile was pure male ego. "Your clit's at the perfect angle for optimum pleasure. I bet you'll be the first person to ever cum while eating at Burger King."

Instinct had her wanting to look around, to see if anyone was nearby enough to hear her whimper, to see what was happening beneath the table. Genevieve was sick to death of going with instinct and caring too much what other people thought of her actions and not nearly enough of what she thought of them.

What *she* thought was that she wanted Nash so badly her pussy felt liable to explode with the next brush of his toe.

As if on cue, his toe started into a circling rhythm around her clit. Heat spiked up her chest, puckering her nipples and quickening her breath. Closing her eyes, she wrapped her fingers around the front edge of the booth.

Then she snapped her eyes right back open. Right on the sexy, hard-bodied man sitting across from her, wearing a sinful smile that reached well into his espresso-brown eyes.

She wanted *Nash*. Not his toe. Not his tongue. She wanted his cock inside her, delivering her to orgasm in a way she hadn't experienced in years. In a way she could guess she'd never experienced, given how completely passionate he was and how incompletely passionate her few past lovers had been.

Her fingers released from the edge of the booth with the urge to run through his untamed hair. "Nash—"

"Do you want me to forget the toes and use my tongue? We could act like you dropped ketchup on your jeans and need help cleaning it up. Everyone would think I was being a gentleman, while the whole time I'd be eating you out." He lifted a French fry off his tray. "We should save some of these to take home, just in case you decide it's okay for me to stick my tongue in your pussy. Once you're good and creamy, I can dip these babies in and have my own special sauce."

The muscles of her sex clenched tight. Juices welled in her

panties. The game was officially over. It was time for the real fun to begin.

Genevieve pushed her tray of half-eaten food to the side and sat up straighter in the booth. "I don't want to play anymore."

"That doesn't sound like begging to me."

She caught the displeasure in his voice and smiled. As much as she didn't want to remember she was paying him for his time and actions, the reality was she had paid him. His displeasure now made it seem he might want her for reasons beyond his job. "I'm not telling you to stop. I'm telling you to take me home and do me the right way."

Surprise flickered in his eyes . . . quickly masked with burning anticipation as he slid from the booth. "I've got a better idea."

Nash emptied their trays into the nearest trash bin. He returned to the table and held out a hand to her. She looked at his open palm, expecting to feel guilt over the decision to take the final step toward severing romantic ties with Tom.

There was no guilt as she placed her hand in Nash's. Locking her fingers with his and letting him guide her out to the parking lot was as natural as breathing.

The icy cold air barely touched her heated body. The snow crunching beneath her tennis shoes was hardly a consideration. And when he opened the passenger's door of his truck and she climbed in and he climbed in right after her, pressing her against the bench seat back with the weight of his chest upon hers, she didn't notice the weather at all.

His palms planted on the seat back at either side of her shoulders, and he brought his mouth over hers. Teasing. Testing. Taking her senses on a glorious ride that wasn't nearly wild enough for her keyed-up state.

Genevieve curled her fingers in the front of his coat. She kissed him hard, deep, wet, until they were both breathless and she was pretty sure she had her point across. Just in case he was still unclear, she pulled her mouth back to pant, "I want to fuck."

The relief in Nash's eyes was almost tangible. He came up on his knees as far as the truck's ceiling would allow and moved his hand into the tight space between his ass and the dashboard. Tugging the wallet from the back pocket of his jeans, he opened it to lift out a foil square. "Lucky for you I carry a condom in my wallet."

Yeah, lucky for her. Because if they had sex without one and she got knocked up, Tom would never let her live it down. Not to mention the unholy fit her parents would throw.

He tossed the wallet on the seat behind the steering wheel, then looked back at her. His eyes narrowed. "You still with me?"

"Yeah."

"Then why the frown?"

Because she was an idiot, letting the guilt come now. Tom was history, at least as a fiancé. Her parents would never learn to accept she was less than perfect. Nash was here and real and rock hard, as evidenced by the impressive erection rubbing against her belly. "Dumb thoughts. They're gone. I want you inside me. I want imperfection."

He chuckled. "That your way of saying you want it dirty and passionate?"

Genevieve's laughter was automatic and uplifting. All trace of guilt left her. "You can hardly waltz naked in a truck, now can you?"

He nodded toward the frosted window behind her head. "That's what the bed's for. This time of year, it's probably so iced over we'd fall and bust our asses trying to dance. Come spring, it'll be another story."

The only problem with that, of course, was that spring was a lot further away than two weeks, and she didn't have eighty grand to buy his time until then. Her parents were loaded. She, personally, only had a few thousand left in savings after paying for his services and a handful of untouchable savings bonds and stock certificates gifted to her or acquired through the years.

It was best not to think about spring. It was best to focus on getting him naked and getting her naked and getting their naked bodies joined together.

Genevieve reached for the zipper on his coat. As if it was all the incentive he required, Nash's hands shot to life. She hadn't bothered to do up her jacket for the short trip outside, and his hands quickly found their way beneath the sides and under her sweatshirt.

His fingers skimmed over her sensitive belly en route to fondling her breasts through the thin cotton of her bra. He twisted at her nipples, and she sucked in a breath, freeing it as she worked the sides of his coat apart and lifted the hem of his T-shirt to get her hands on his bare, muscled torso.

His body was hot beneath her fingertips, hard, male. She needed more hardness, more maleness. Needed all of him now.

"Change positions." She barked out the order.

"Should have figured you'd prefer it on top." Teasing glinted in his eyes.

That had to be a flippant shot at what he believed to be her wealth. Even if it was, she wasn't going to correct him. She was going to push him aside, so they could both get half naked.

Only, she didn't have to push him aside. Nash was already in the center of the bench seat, yanking down his pants and freeing his hard cock to the cool lick of the air.

Her mouth watered as he rolled a condom onto the long, luscious length of his shaft. Her pussy pulsed wildly. Her fingers shook as she attempted to undo her jeans button without success. She tried again and then once more before it finally gave way. The zipper came down much easier. Lifting her butt off the seat an inch, Genevieve worked the jeans down her legs, not caring if she looked dorky or even if someone might be passing by the truck, peering in.

All that mattered was getting him inside her.

The jeans cleared her feet and she threw herself onto his lap. His hands grabbed hold of her hips and he surged up to meet her landing, impaling her with a thrust that brought tears of exquisite pleasure to her eyes.

My God, it had been so long. *Too* long.

"I needed this," she moaned, taking hold of his shoulders, arching her hips and bending her knees to plant him farther inside her slick folds.

Nash's thrusting stilled. "Why do you always say that like you have to defend your actions? You deserve to have sex. It's your right. Take pride in it."

"You're right. It is. I can. I will." Moving her fingers into his hair, she held on to the long, thick, nearly black strands and silenced any additional observations with the push of her tongue into his warm, damp mouth.

His tongue met hers in a wild dance of hunger and urgency. His hips rose up, driving his dick upward with each downward slide of her pelvis. The fingers lifted from her hips to stroke over her ass, petting the soft center where her cheeks met.

He couldn't get his fingers inside her asshole with the way they were positioned in the close quarters of the truck, but she knew from his earlier words he would like to touch her there. Take her there. Her ass was pure virgin territory and the thought of his cock pushing inside of it had her pussy vibrating with blissful tremors.

Moving his free hand beneath her sweatshirt and then the underwire of her bra, he found a stiff nipple and pulled on it hard enough to make her squeak. She told him she wasn't into pain, but this sort of light pleasure pain wasn't what she had in mind. This pain she liked incredibly much.

He coasted his tongue over her gums, along the ridges of her teeth and back to furiously lick at hers as he pulled on her nipple again and again, adding a twist at the end of each tug. Liquid heat charged from the red, aching tip to her throbbing core. Release barreled almost to the pinnacle.

Digging her fingers into his shoulders, Genevieve ground her clit against the hard edge of his shaft . . . and, with just a few pumps, brought orgasm screaming to its crest.

Delicious waves of intense pleasure tore through her, flooding her cream all around his driving cock. She pulled her mouth from his to cry out, "Oh. Oh *yes*. I needed that!" Crap, she had to quit saying that. But it was the truth. "I really did need it," she wailed as mini-waves continued to ripple through her. "I deserved it, damn it!"

The amusement in Nash's grin registered for an instant and then she couldn't see it anymore, as his mouth was on the side of her neck. Nipping at her flesh. Stinging little bites that zinged fresh desire directly to her core.

Her cunt clenched, hypersensitive from the last orgasm and already eager for another.

She picked up the pace, concentrating on the play of her pussy lips. On clasping her feminine muscles around his hard sex with each pull of his cock nearly from her body.

The sudden tensing of his shaft inside her was breathtaking. The unstoppable suspension of his lips on her neck empowering. The utter look of ecstasy on his face—heart-stopping. The veins in his neck corded and the muscles beneath her hands went taut as he gave in to his release. A release she'd caused. In a truck. Without caring who watched. Because making herself happy, and admittedly him, too, was what mattered most for one of the very first times in her life.

He wanted to see her pride and Genevieve was feeling smug enough to show it. She tried on a cocky grin. "I was good."

Nash laughed out loud, the rumble working its way through

his chest and shifting his cock inside her to stimulate her aroused body into wanting more, more, more. "So good I'm going to take you home and let you do me again."

She rose up on her knees, and the slide of his pubic bone against her clit was sheer rapture. She repeated the move, elating as shivers racked through her. "Sounds perfect . . . right after I give you a little more special sauce for your fries."

6

The bathroom door *snicked* open a few inches. Nash stopped flipping through television channels to look in that direction, anticipating Jenn's emergence through the door and the moment when she would lie down on the couch with him.

He'd always known once he found the right woman he would be the king of coupling. He loved playing the bad boy and sleeping with a different woman whenever it appealed to him—making money off the deal was even sweeter. But he loved having one good woman to kiss, touch, hold, and talk with even more.

The last few days with Jenn had been remarkable, filled with easy banter as much as amazing sex. Days he'd spent proving how much he found every inch of her body sizzling hot, particularly her lush hips and rear end. And days where she learned to accept having pride, and even a little selfishness at times, was a good thing.

Nash snorted. That he had to give ego-pumping lessons to someone from Deevy Isle was damned ironic. Either that or people had changed a lot in the years since he'd moved to the mainland. Only, he knew they hadn't. His mother kept him up on the community, assuring him in not-quite-so-crude words that the bulk of the island population still had their heads stuck up their asses.

The bathroom door opened the rest of the way. Jenn stepped out wearing his old Detroit Red Wings jersey and white fleece pants. Her easy smile told him exactly how much she appreciated the comfortable attire. She was definitely not among the snobby island set. She was also definitely damned appealing in all that soft, worn cotton.

He could barely make out the shape of her breasts beneath the oversized shirt, and thus was the basis of her appeal. He didn't like to compare his pleasure clients, but the reality was most of them fit into a mold. They wore skimpy clothes or nothing at all. Carefully applied makeup accentuated the positive. They wanted him to be bad and badder still. Expected to climax at least a couple times every pleasure session and for him not to expect to climax at all unless they gave permission.

Jenn broke the mold. Traipsing around in sweats with her elegantly narrow face free of makeup. Seeing to his pleasure as completely as he saw to hers.

Regardless of her atypical behavior, she was still a client. Not the *right* woman, but one who would be gone from his life in another week.

Unless she paid for more of his time.

No. Even if she made the offer, Nash wouldn't take her up on it. He was getting as much as, if not more than she was, out of their arrangement. He should pay back the money she'd already given him, but he needed it. Benny needed it even more.

Jenn wasn't the *right* woman, but she was still his pretend girlfriend, and so the coupling and intimacy had to continue.

"What do you want to do?" he asked as she moved to the bedroom area, placing the clothes she'd changed out of on the foot of his bed. "Watch a movie? Go for a walk—"

"Have balcony sex." Her lips curved seductively at the corners.

Every other time she flashed that smile his cock hardened, his blood humming with the want to get her naked fast. Now, it and her words ate his gut, by confirming exactly what he was to her: an imperfect guy to fuck.

"But not until after we watch a movie," she added. "I'll make the popcorn and get the drinks. You see what's playing on cable."

Nash sighed. The tension on his gut let up. Maybe he was more to her than a sex object. Not that it mattered. Like he told her, his job and girlfriends didn't mix. Until construction business picked up, with luck by early spring, he had no choice but to continue pleasuring women for profit.

Suddenly not too thrilled of the job he'd always found great satisfaction in, he clicked through the pay-per-view movie channels. The buzz of the microwave and the ensuing popping of corn felt homey. The soft sound of Jenn's stocking feet falling against the kitchenette tile was heartwarming. It all felt too damned good.

But it wasn't good. That was just a façade.

Even if he didn't need his woman-pleasuring job, he wouldn't get wrapped up with her beyond the next week. She might not be conceited, but she was normally surrounded by those who were. She called Deevy Isle home. She worked for a company headquartered on the island, owned by her rich, pompous father, no less.

Dating her would mean immersing himself back in the pretentious environment to a level that roiled his gut. She wasn't worth it. No woman was.

The microwave dinged. Two bottles of beer dangling from the fingers of one hand and a large wooden bowl of popcorn in the other, Jenn came into the living area. After handing him an open beer, she put her own and the popcorn down in front of the couch, within arm's reach. Then she sat down on the edge of the couch and continued to lie back, sprawling her warm body against the front of his. Snuggling her backside tight to his groin. Bringing her silky raven hair inches from his nose.

Inhaling her light floral scent, Nash brought an arm around her middle. He had to keep up the pretense he'd agreed to put on when he signed her contract, so he held her tighter and kissed the side of her temple . . . and knew damned well the moves had nothing to do with pretense and everything to do with a want he shouldn't have.

"How about this one? Tia saw it in the theater and gave it two thumbs-up."

He brought his attention back to the TV and glimpsed at the movie title without putting any thought into what it was about. "Sounds great."

He clicked on the purchase tab and the movie started up. Jenn's soft snoring followed less than five minutes later. He smiled at the far from genteel sound—one she made every night when she first fell asleep. It was just another imperfect facet of her personality. Just another way she'd gotten under his skin so quickly.

For the next two hours, Nash focused on the movie—a drama about which Tia's positive opinion ended up holding true. Jenn roused as the closing credits began to roll, shifting her shapely bottom against his groin.

"Oops," she said in a sleepy voice. "I missed the ending."

He laughed. "You missed the beginning."

"I'm not used to so much physical activity."

"But you're enjoying it?"

Her backside shifted against him again, this time with purposeful pressure that stirred his cock to hardness. Turning in his arms, she nipped at his chin and ground her sex along his, sighing with the contact. "Mmm. . . . You can't tell?"

"Yeah, but I wanted to hear it from you."

"I'm enjoying it. I'm going to be enjoying *you* on the balcony in about ten seconds." Her mouth slanted over his, kissing him long and deep and wet while her pussy continued its grinding game along his shaft.

Her lips lifted from his. Flashing a smile loaded with sensual promise, she glided from the couch and raced to the sliding glass door.

The door hissed open and shut, depositing her onto the small, snowy terrace overlooking the frozen millpond. This time of year the park was mainly used for cross-country skiing and by a few hardy joggers and walkers who didn't mind the bitter temperatures. Before five on a weekday, the odds of anyone being out there were slim. Still, the thought of burying his dick inside of Jenn when there was the potential to be caught was enough to engage his mind in things as much as his body.

Nash started for the sliding glass door. He veered off to the bedroom area last minute and yanked open the sex toy drawer of his dresser. She'd changed her mind about letting him stick his tongue in her pussy, so it was also possible she'd changed it about wanting him to use the rosebud mini-flogger on her as it was intended.

Genevieve leaned against the railing of Nash's balcony, taking in the pristine snow and iced-over millpond below while trying to forget she was freezing.

Maybe sex out here wasn't such a good idea.

She hadn't planned on having time to get cold, figured he would be right out after her. Dragging her pants down and pushing into her from behind.

Was he already bored with her? Ready to bring an end to their deal so he could move on to clients who were sexual divas from the start?

The sliding glass door hissed open behind her. Relief swept through her, along with a healthy dose of warmth. She wanted to turn around, move into his arms, greedily capture his mouth and never let go. But she wouldn't worry him that way by making it seem she was after more than the next week.

Not yet anyway.

"I wouldn't trust that railing." Nash's voice was low, raspy. "It looks sturdy beneath all the snow, but it needs as much repairing as the rest of this place." One of his arms came around her waist from behind to pull her against him.

The solid length of his cock cradled along her ass. Her breath puffed out, fogging the air. "I like this place just how it is."

Her first take on his apartment building had been that it was small and run-down. Now, Genevieve saw its rustic charm and how small spaces were conducive to growing a relationship. Even a feigned one. Or at least one that was feigned until she convinced him to make it authentic.

Nash's hand slipped beneath her fleece pants to stroke her backside. The heat of his palm made her forget all about his apartment and what they were or weren't to each other. His fingers moved lower, brushing against her feminine lips from behind. Then something coarse was pressed between her butt cheeks. Whatever that something was moved, sliding along her crack, creating erotic friction like she'd never experienced.

Her breath caught. Juices leaked from her sex. She squirmed back against it, wanting it deeper inside her, the friction increased. "What *is* that?"

"Your friendly flogger." His voice was rough as one of the twisted leather tails of the flogger retraced its path, until it was dipping inside her slit. "Why don't you lean up against the door and let me use it on you."

That wasn't a question, no matter how he worded it. Rather, 100 percent demand. Genevieve's heart kicked with excitement even as her belly tightened. "You know I don't like pain."

The tail jerked up the length of her crack, flying free of her pants. She gasped with the hasty retreat. Then gasped even louder when Nash grabbed hold of her hips and pushed her face forward up against the glass door, with her palms bracing her weight. "You'll like this. It's good pain."

Her pants were jerked down her legs, her panties coming along with them. Quickly, he worked her clothes around a tennis shoe and free of one foot. His foot moved between hers then, pushing them apart, spreading her thighs and bringing her naked ass up in the air, exposing her pussy to anyone in viewing distance.

One of his fingers speared into her from behind, pushing deep into her sheath. Genevieve shuddered. She'd never had a man act this way toward her.

Recklessly. Violently. So passionately it was beyond awesome.

In the sliding glass door, she caught the reflection of his hand as he brought the rosebud-tipped flogger up and cracked it into the air. Her body hummed. Her blood sizzled. There wasn't room for tension in the wake of her anticipation.

"Yeah," she panted out, trembling for the first swat. "I think I will like it."

His hand rose up again. She clenched her butt cheeks, waiting, waiting. The tails of the flogger swatted across her ass. The rosebuds pelted her skin, nipping into her flesh like a dozen bee stingers. "Oh." She bit her lip with the pain.

"Okay?" Nash's fingers rubbed over her throbbing behind. His touch wasn't rough like his voice, but gentle, soothing.

"Stings." But it would get better. He'd been too nice to her to turn into a monster who got off on hurting women now.

"Give it a few swats." He stroked her ass a few more seconds, the tender touch reassuring her it would be okay.

Then the flogger rose into the air again. She closed her eyes against the reflection, curled her fingers into fists against the glass. The twisted tails lashed against her bottom. Her eyes watered and pain licked through every inch of her.

Another swat fell.

Her ass tingled. Her pussy burned. Not for relief, but for release.

Holy crap, she was actually getting into it.

"Do it again." The fevered words left her mouth without thought.

"Push your ass out more. Let me get a better look at your hot cunt."

She obeyed eagerly. Rewarded when his left hand came around to her mound. His index finger pushed into her slick folds, pressing against her swollen clit with the next of the rosebuds' assaults.

Cream dribbled along her inner thighs, the scent of it rising thick on the air.

"There's a guy running on the walkway."

Genevieve stiffened with Nash's observation. "There is?"

"Sure is." Two of his fingers spread her pussy lips. In the glass, she saw the flogger arc up. It changed course at the last minute, the rosebuds bypassing her cheeks to slap against the rear of her blood-reddened labia.

Pleasure pain spiraled through her, slamming her eyes closed with the incomparable sensation. She moaned loud and long.

"He definitely heard that." Nash's fingers moved against her parted sex. "He's looking up here. You ought to see his face. Doesn't know whether to report us to the cops or pull down his pants and jerk off."

Genevieve's pussy clamped. Her clit pulsed.

The tails of the flogger returned to her body, this time not to swat but to bury between her folds. She opened her eyes and looked down. One of his hands held the rosebuds at the front of her sex and the other held the handle of the flogger behind her.

He moved the leather tails against her pussy, brushing them back and forth across her clit. The pressure built a little more with each pass. With the idea there was a guy one story below, eyeing her bare, wet cunt. "Wha-what's he doing now?"

"Watching." He released the rosebuds and gave the handle of the flogger a hard tug. The roses jetted along her folds, chafing her clit.

She gasped out a rapturous cry.

"That did it." The rosebuds pushed back inside her, filling up her hole. "He's got his hand on his cock. He's stroking himself through his pants."

He pulled on the end of the flogger and the roses jerked partway out of her. She sucked in a breath. "Is he going to come?"

"Not until you do."

The rosebuds yanked hard from her pussy, abrading her clit. Raw sensation poured through her, pulling her into its grasp and pushing her into a mind-spinning orgasm.

"I'm coming!" The shout was moot given the juices streaming down her thighs, but it felt incredibly good.

Nash dropped the flogger. One strong arm came around her middle, holding her in place when it felt her legs would give away. He pulled her back against him, providing warmth she hadn't realized had been missing. "Baby, you made him blow it." His lips tickled her ear. "How's he ever going to go home and explain his cum-filled shorts to his wife?"

Genevieve tipped her head back, inviting his mouth to do more than just tease. Then curiosity got the better of her, and she turned far enough to see the millpond. See that there wasn't a person in sight. "There's no guy down there."

Letting out a hoarse laugh, he kissed the shell of her ear. "Yeah, but it got you off thinking there was."

She turned in his arm the remainder of the way. His features were tight with restraint, as if denying his own release while she had hers had been a matter of epic control. She would see that he got his, but first he had to understand one thing. "I liked the idea of being watched. But you're the one who brought me to climax. You're the one whose hands I wanted on my body. The one I trusted not to hurt me."

"I would never hurt you on purpose, Jenn."

The sincerity in Nash's eyes tugged at her heart. She rose up to meet his mouth. Gone was the demanding man who'd pushed her up against the door. His kiss was gentle, unhurried.

Dare she believe caring?

A phone rang inside his apartment. He lifted his mouth from hers. "That's my cell. I need to get it."

Stealing his warmth away, he slid open the balcony door and went into the apartment. Heat blasted Genevieve as she followed him inside, almost painful in its intensity after being out in the cold half dressed.

More painful, though, was the idea of who waited on the other end of the phone.

Another client. Some woman who would pay to share his bed and time after this week was over.

The thought twisted her belly. In case her feelings were clear on her face, she averted it from Nash by bending down to work her panties and pants back over the foot he'd freed them from. "It's your work phone?"

"Yeah. But that's not why I need to get it. I told you I have another job. I own a construction company with a couple friends. One of the guy's moms is dying and, when she does go, he's not liable to take it too well."

Feeling like the worst kind of bitch over the relief that sighed through her, she pulled her pants up and watched him answer the cell phone.

"Loose Screws. This is Nash." A few seconds passed and he said "Just a minute" and held the phone out to her. "It's Tia."

The twisting started back up in her belly as she took the phone and brought it to her ear. "Hi. What's going on?"

"The jig's up," Tia said in her straightforward "life's a bitch, deal with it" voice. "Your parents found out you haven't been staying at my place and are on the hunt to find you and bring you home."

Genevieve winced. Damn it. This couldn't be happening. She still had almost a whole week left with Nash. "Tom told them?"

"Allison."

"Crap." She had the worst sister ever.

"How are things on your end?" Tia asked in a brighter voice.

She looked over to find Nash smiling at her. She smiled back, wanting to end this call and pretend it never happened. In fact, she would. "Too good. Thanks for calling, Tia. See you soon."

She pushed the End button and handed his cell phone back to him. His smile wavered as he took it. "Who's Tom?"

"A friend I've known my whole life. He's like a brother to me." The words rushed out defensively, but they were the truth, Genevieve recognized. Tom really was like a brother to her. It was the reason they had no sexual chemistry between them. The reason he would soon thank her for ending things.

"I take it Tia said something good?"

"Not really. Why?"

Amusement entered Nash's eyes. "You're smiling like you just had a French fry dipped into you."

As he had a way of doing, he made her laugh and eased her troubled mind. "Turns out I'm really into pleasurable pain." She crossed the few feet to him and did what she wanted to do back on the terrace—tugged him into her arms and attacked his mouth with no plans to release it, or his big hard body, anytime soon.

Pretending the phone call from Tia had never taken place worked for almost two days. After that Genevieve couldn't ignore it. She had to go to Tom and end things between them 100 percent. Then if her parents tracked her down at Nash's, she at least wouldn't have to feel like a cheater on top of being a failure in their eyes.

Pulling her Benz up to the curb in front of her soon-to-be-ex-fiancé's two-story home, with its wraparound deck overlooking the currently ice-covered Lake Erie, she considered her approach. They'd been some form of friends her entire life and she never wanted to lose that. But no matter how she broke the news, Tom was going to be hurt. He would need time to heal. To understand she loved him too much as a friend to become his wife and hate him for it.

She would simply say that. Lay the truth out there and hope for the best.

Gusting wind laden with snowflakes whipped around her as she stepped from the car. She hugged her arms around her body and made her way up the sidewalk. A girl in her early teens was finishing up with clearing the sidewalk of snow. Genevieve smiled at her as she passed by, and the girl smiled back.

How sad was it that the girl's actions and expression were all it took to tell Genevieve she wasn't from the island?

She didn't just want away from Tom on an intimate level, Genevieve realized. She wanted off Deevy Isle. Away from the job she did impeccably but still owed to her father for giving her. Though it wasn't clear on this island, the economy was rotten right now and the odds of her finding employment in a nearby city slim. If worse came to worst, she could always go Nash's route and sell her body.

Laughing, because she knew damned well she would never have the guts to do it, she reached Tom's door. She turned the knob and pushed the door in . . . and saw a side of her sister she never cared to see—her bare behind.

Genevieve's mouth fell open. "Oh. My. God."

Allison jerked up from the living room floor. Off of Tom's nude body to expose his hard, glistening penis.

Genevieve blinked. No sex before marriage, her ass.

Shock crossed her sister's face. With a squeal, Allison jumped behind the couch and hid from sight.

Tom leaped to his feet. He yanked tan slacks from a pile of tossed-aside clothes on the floor and hurried into them. Guilt slid into his eyes. "Christ, Gen. I never meant for you to find out this way."

Since when did he say Christ, not to mention call her Gen?

Allison poked her head out from behind the couch. Her cheeks were stained with furious pink as she met Genevieve's eyes. Her sister looked at Tom and affection replaced her embarrassment.

It hit Genevieve just how well the two of them went together. "It's perfect."

"You said to see others and while I never actually planned to—" Tom stopped short to frown. "Did you say 'it's perfect'?"

"Yes. You two are perfect for each other." Genevieve started backing toward the door. "I'm thrilled for you. Honestly."

"I've loved him for years, Gen," Allison admitted, and then blurted out, "Since we couldn't wait to be together and neither of us believes in hindering procreation by using protection, we plan to marry next Saturday."

Genevieve stopped backing up to raise an eyebrow at Tom. Had he planned to tell her their engagement was off before he married her sister?

Tom swore again. She dismissed him and the irony of her sister's potentially knocked-up state as the meaning behind Allison's words registered.

Genevieve looked at her sister. "He's the reason you've been even bitchier to me than usual the last couple years?" Here she'd been ready to tell Allison the presidency spot at the collections estate company was hers whenever their father retired, and here it seemed her sister might not even want it. Tom could have it. Or whomever else their father found worthy.

Allison smiled sheepishly. "I'm sorry."

"Don't worry about it. You can pay me back by telling Mother and Father my wedding's off because you slept with my fiancé."

Allison gasped. Tom looked stricken. Genevieve left, enjoying a laugh over their expressions when she got in her car.

Her mood grew increasingly better as she drove back across the covered bridge to the mainland. She was grinning like a mad woman by the time she reached Nash's apartment. Then she nearly broke out in tears when she stepped from her car to find her parents parallel parked behind her, getting out of their own vehicle with matching looks of disappointment on their faces.

They probably caught her leaving Tom's place and tailed her to Nash's without even knowing where she was headed. Just in case they did somehow know about Nash, she held up a hand to halt their certain lecture. "Save your breath. There's still going to be a wedding. In fact, it's been moved up to next weekend."

"Is Tom the lucky man?"

The question was Nash's, edged with an icy chill that turned Genevieve's belly and took away nearly all of her hope for a genuine relationship with him.

7

Jenn spun around to give Nash an apologetic look. "I swear it's not how it sounds."

"It doesn't matter how it is." At least, it shouldn't matter.

Despite what he told himself about her not being worth immersing himself back into the Deevy Isle society for, he'd started to believe otherwise. Started to think he was going to do as Benny mentioned and pull a Thad by giving up his woman-pleasuring ways to pursue a real relationship with Jenn.

Hell, he'd even considered going to his old man for a loan in order to make ends meet while he waited for the economy to rebound and the construction company to take off. All for a woman who was already in a relationship.

Her engaged status sure as hell explained why she hadn't wanted to take him home with her that first night in the pub. "I've slept with married women before," he said for his own benefit as much as hers. "Engaged women aren't much different."

"Genevieve!" The prissy-looking woman he assumed to be Jenn's mother, by their matching hair color and style, wailed.

The prissy-looking gray-haired man next to the woman

eyed Jenn like she was the equivalent of street scum. "Good God, Genevieve. You're going to be married in a week and you've been sleeping with this—this man?"

"He's not just a man. He's—"

"I don't have time for this." Nash cut off what promised to be a lame excuse that would end with Jenn kowtowing to her parents. He thought she'd gotten over that weakness and learned to be her own woman, the way she'd claimed, but he'd been mistaken about her on that front as well.

His gut churned. The need for a smoke clawed at him. He didn't have time to acknowledge either. Didn't have another second to stand here while her folks looked at him like he wasn't fit to do their lawns, let alone their Deevy Isle princess.

He hurried around the corner of the building and into the alley leading to tenant parking. Jenn followed him, grabbing hold of his arm when he stopped long enough to pull the driver's door of the S-10 open. "Nash, please. Just listen—"

"I'm needed elsewhere." The words growled out.

Behind him he heard her indrawn breath. She released his arm, and he got in the truck and slammed the door. The defrosters shot to life with the starting of the engine, but they were going to take way too damned long. If he let them clear the ice from the windows alone, it might be too late to stop Benny from hurting himself.

Nash grabbed the scraper from underneath the driver's side of the bench seat and pushed the door open, prepared to do battle with Jenn. But she was already gone.

He attacked the windows of the truck, his concern for Benny and his fury over allowing Jenn to get to him on a level beyond the physical egging him on.

With the windows cleared enough to stop him from getting pulled over, Nash jumped in the truck and zipped out of the parking lot toward Benny's place. His friend had called fifteen minutes ago, piss-ass drunk. Nash had gotten out of him that his foster mother had died in her sleep and that Benny was considering easing the pain of her loss by reverting to the harmful ways of his youth and cutting himself.

As sick as the woman had been, her passing was a blessing. Benny would see that in time. For now, all he could see was the kindhearted woman who had taken him in as a twelve-year-old runaway from a family of mentally abusive drunks was gone.

Nash pulled into Benny's subdivision ten minutes later to find Thad's vehicle already in his driveway. He shut off the truck and hurried to the front door. That Thad was inside was a good thing. Still, as easygoing as Benny usually was, when he was upset he could be one damned big, mean handful.

Crashing erupted from inside the house, followed by swearing. Nash pushed the door in to find Thad sitting in the middle of the floor, with one highly pissed-off Benny on his stomach beneath him, kicking like a bull with its nuts in a cinch and swearing up a storm.

"Just ignore him." Thad's voice was casual, but his expression was pure concern. "He's talking out his ass."

Nash focused on Benny's arms. They were bare beneath the short sleeves of his T-shirt, but the only marks on them were decades old. "Is he okay otherwise?"

Benny lifted his head to glare through red-rimmed eyes. "I didn't shoot my fucking head off if that's what you're thinking. Hell, I didn't even take a blade to my arm yet."

"Told you," Thad said dryly. "Talking out his ass."

Only, they all knew he wasn't talking out his ass. But venting a long-subdued desire he was liable to give in to the moment Thad released him.

Benny gave another kick, attempting to buck Thad off his back. His nostrils flared when the other man didn't budge. "What the fuck are you two assholes doing here? You have women to be with. Goddamned parents who think your shit don't stink."

Thad looked at Nash. "Since when do you have a woman?"

The last person Nash wanted to think about now was Jenn, but it seemed she wouldn't be ignored. "I don't. She's marrying someone else."

Disbelief entered Thad's eyes. "You're just gonna let that happen?"

"Candy ass," Benny put in. He managed to catch Thad off guard then. Bucking Thad off his back, Benny scrambled to his knees.

Nash pounced, toppling him back onto his belly. Resorting to dirty moves wasn't his style, but this situation seemed to require it. He shoved his knee between Benny's thighs and up against his balls through the man's clearly slept-in jeans. "Move and I break them."

"Like I give a goddamn, you candy ass." Benny jerked his chin up on the carpet to smirk at Thad. "You know why he's going to let her marry someone else? Because he's a chickenshit afraid of big, ol' nasty Deevy Isle."

From where he moved to sit vigilant from the edge of the couch, Thad looked to Nash for confirmation. "She's got money?"

Nash shrugged. "She's got a fiancé."

"Yeah, but what about the money? That doesn't bother you?"

"Jenn's not like most of Deevy Isle." Nash gave a bitter laugh as the reality of what she was really like reared up. "At least, I didn't think she was. Turns out I was wrong."

Benny jerked beneath him. The move pressed Nash's knee tighter against his balls, and he gave up the fight on a pained-sounding grunt. "Hey, I got an idea," he said in a deceptively calm voice. "Why don't you two head over to McCleary's and share some tears and beers? I'll join you in a few."

Thad snorted out a laugh. "Bullshit you will. You'll go back to drinking and cutting."

Rage flared back up in Benny's eyes. He gritted his teeth. "I didn't cut myself."

"Nah," Nash said, "you just called us both up and implied you wanted to. Your mom's gone, Benny. She's been sick for a long time. Now, she's finally at peace."

Benny sneered. "You should get a job with Hallmark."

"I'm serious."

Thad squatted down on the floor in front of Benny. "You know what, you sorry bastard, you got the two of us. So don't even start on this 'I'm all alone' shit." He looked to Nash. "Is this the woman from the pub the other night? The one we thought was a cheap, easy fuck?"

Hell, did they have to keep going back to Jenn? "Yep."

"Don't you wonder what she was doing alone, dressed the way she was and making it clear she wanted to fuck you, if she's about to be happily married?"

"It's crossed my mind a time or two." More like a dozen times a day from the moment they'd met.

"You didn't ask her?"

Nash had asked her why she was in the pub that first night. But then, she'd wanted to become a client, so it hadn't seemed his place to ask. He gave Thad an amused look. "Lissa got you thinking rationally? Damn man, I didn't know that was possible."

"Blow me, and when you get done think about what I'm saying. If she was happy, she wouldn't be screwing around with you so close to the wedding."

"She was living with me for the last week." Thad's eyebrows raised and Nash clarified, "She paid for the honor."

"Even as a paying customer, you think she'd be doing something like that if she was excited about becoming the next Mrs. Deevy Isle?"

"I don't know what the hell I think about her anymore."

* * *

She couldn't handle this.

She. Could. Not. Handle. This.

Genevieve had to get out of here, both the godforsaken froufrou bridesmaid dress and the church as a whole, before she got nauseous from pastel overload.

The entire place was done up in pink and purple. Obviously their mother hadn't found out about what happened between Allison and Tom, or her sister's wedding gown would be a shade of pastel instead of pristine white.

When the day came that Genevieve got married, her parents would probably demand she wear scarlet they thought she was such a sex-ruled hussy. Imagine their faces if she told them how much she'd enjoyed being whipped, how incredibly good Nash's toe felt rubbing against her crotch in Burger King.

Hell, if they even knew she'd gone to Burger King.

She snorted out a laugh. The red-haired girl standing up in the wedding next to her—one of Allison's stuffy friends—elbowed her. Their mother glared at her from the end of the first row of pews.

For her sister and Tom's sake, Genevieve put on her perfectly fake smile. She'd worn it twenty-seven years, so what were a few more hours?

That theory probably would have played out fine if she didn't reflect on her thought of Nash toeing her in Burger King. Of him doing so much more with her. Having sex with her, yes, but also making her laugh, making her feel good about herself. Making her see she could be her own woman, let her true personality shine through, and still have a man like her.

Only, he didn't like her.

If he did, he would have given her a chance to explain herself. Or maybe he wouldn't have. Really, how would she feel learning he was engaged? It was hard enough just knowing he'd spent the last days sleeping with other women. Clients, sure, but still other women.

Genevieve sighed. The bridesmaid next to her elbowed her again, harder. She considered elbowing her back and knocking her on her butt while she was at it. Then she caught her mother's glare and put the stupid, perfectly fake smile back on.

Allison recited her vows. Tom started in on his own. Genevieve held her breath in anticipation of the "I do" part. Just a few minutes after that and she could escape this pastel hell. Of course, the reception hall would probably be decorated in the same fashion.

"I do," Tom finally said.

"Shit. I'm too late," another man's voice echoed from the back of the church.

Gasps sounded throughout the pews. Heads turned.

She narrowed her eyes on the guy standing in the center of the last row of pews.

Nash wore jeans and a sweatshirt. Frustration and regret warred on his face as he eyed the bride and groom, and he still looked better than any other man she'd ever known.

"Who are you?" someone asked.

"A jilted lover," another suggested, sending tongues to wagging.

Genevieve started down the aisle toward him before her brain could tell her what a huge scene she was making.

"Genevieve!" her mother wailed.

"What are you doing?" Allison shrieked.

Nash's gaze jerked from the bride and groom to Genevieve's face. Confusion entered his eyes. "Jenn? I thought *you* were getting married."

"My sister slept with my fiancé, so I let her have him."

"Allison!" Their mother's gasp of horror filled the church.

Genevieve bit her tongue. "Oops."

"Genevieve, do you mind?" Tom snapped.

Not at all, because she'd finally reached Nash. She looked back to give her sister and Tom an apologetic smile. "Sorry."

"Me too." Nash started to turn to leave. "I'll just—"

"Wait." Sliding into the empty last pew, she grabbed his hand. "Sit down. For just a few minutes until we can talk. Please."

He hesitated, but then sat down beside her. She held fast to his hand as the priest told Tom to kiss his bride before there were any more interruptions. Tom did as suggested, and the newly married couple was introduced as husband and wife. The wedding party moved back down the aisle sans one bridesmaid. People filed out of the main cathedral and into the receiving area.

Just when it seemed they would be alone, Genevieve's parents appeared. Her father glowered at Nash. "I didn't like you the first time I saw you and I still don't like you. What do you say you leave now, son? We wouldn't want things to get any uglier."

Nash came to his feet, towering a good three inches over her father. "You don't know who you're talking to."

"You're right. And, frankly, I don't care to."

Shame filled Genevieve for her father's behavior. Her mother wasn't any better, standing there, looking down her nose at Nash. It was no wonder he disliked the wealthy so much. She wasn't any too fond of this snobby, rich couple herself, and they were her parents.

"I'd just watch what I say if I were you," Nash warned, his voice steely, his eyes filled with loathing and something else she couldn't place.

Her father's lips twisted into a belittling smile. "You need to learn to respect your elders, son."

"I'm not your goddamned—"

"Nash. Let me handle this. Please." Genevieve slid from the pew to stand in front of him. She didn't want to make him feel less of a man by taking things over, but then he shouldn't have to be subject to her parents' ridicule in the first place.

Facing her parents, she did something she hated, by mimicking her mother and looking down her nose at her father. "You might not like him, but I do. As a matter of fact, I like him one hell of a lot more than I like you. He's a gentleman. He's fair and he doesn't treat people like dirt just because they aren't rich."

Her mother gave a patronizing sniff. "He doesn't know what it's like to have money."

"Actually, I do." Nash placed a supportive hand on Genevieve's arm. "It makes people greedy and conceited. It makes them blind to the rest of the world. They can't even see an equal when they're standing in front of them."

"Nash, you aren't their equal." She turned to retake his hand. "You're way better. Let's go."

"My name's Nathaniel." He looked at her parents. "That would be Nathaniel Graham the fourth for those of you who judge a man by his name."

Her father's sneer melted to shock and then dread, as it sank in how entirely he'd insulted the son of a major figure in the Deevy Isle community. Her mother looked ready to blow a gasket. Genevieve was a little surprised but not really shocked to learn Nash came from parents who were benevolent and caring yet had more money than her own parents would ever see. It just made sense.

She felt a little guilty leaving the church without wishing Allison and Tom well, but they would surely understand. And thank her for it, given the way she'd interrupted their nuptials.

Proudly holding Nash's hand and her head up high, she walked down the church steps and past the milling wedding guests, most of whom were eyeing them with disapproval.

When they were out in the parking lot, she looked over at him and, for the first time, let her feelings for him come through in her smile. "My parents are going to be spending the next year kissing your parents' butts. Actually, I expect them to kiss ours pretty thoroughly too."

The way Jenn felt about him was clear in her eyes, and Nash wanted to tell her he felt the same. He hadn't known he had, even upon accepting that Benny was accurate—Nash had been acting like a candy ass—and making the decision to tell her marrying another man was wrong, because she clearly didn't love that man. He hadn't known that he loved her until he foolishly ran out of gas on the way to the church and had to hoof it the rest of the way on foot.

The thought he would be too late had eaten at his gut. Arriving to find he really had been too late had torn at his heart. And then realizing he hadn't been too late, because Jenn wasn't the one getting married, had mended his heart, made him feel whole, made him feel he would never be lonely again.

Only, maybe he would.

The way she made a huge scene in the church and then stood up for him in front of her parents suggested she was through with the island set. But was she ready to accept being poor, or at least having a relationship with a poor man?

He stopped walking. Their joined hands pulled her to a halt as well, and she turned to face him. "I don't like being rich, Jenn. It's hard. Damned hard."

Her smile faded a little, but she nodded. "I agree. I want to move back in with you." Her smile disappeared the rest of the way as regret filled her eyes. "I was engaged the night we met, which is why I wouldn't let you touch me. But after that, when I asked you to be my boyfriend, I'd already started to leave Tom behind. He was never right for me."

Pausing for a breath, she pulled her hand from his and hugged her arms around her body. He'd been so wrapped up in how she felt about him, Nash hadn't considered how little she wore. Actually, the gaudy pink dress was pretty damned big, but it bared her shoulders and arms to the icy afternoon air.

He shrugged out of his coat and wrapped it around her shoulders. Jenn shook visibly, and he pulled her into his arms, hugged her tight to his body, relished the press of her soft curves against him. "We should go back inside."

"I'd rather freeze to death." She mumbled the words against his chest, and still he could hear her loathing for the mostly pretentious pricks in the church and loved her all the more for it.

She tipped her head back to meet his eyes. "I'm quitting my job with my father's company. I want to earn my way somewhere that family ties and social standing aren't an issue. I don't expect that to be easy, but it will be worth it."

"Will it be worth living in a cardboard box in an alley and eating out of dumpsters?" Nash asked seriously.

She frowned. "What do you mean?"

"You're not going to have a job, and I can't see you going for the idea of my bringing pleasure clients home to share my body and our bed, so I'm guessing you're going to want me to give that job up. I don't expect to see any construction work for at least another few months. No income means no way to make rent, pay bills, eat."

Jenn's smile returned, edging into her blue-green eyes. "Money won't be an issue. I have the other half of your fee in my purse and another three grand in savings. That should get us by quite nicely until I find a job and your construction work comes through."

For a few seconds, he got caught up in the idea she had five grand lying around in her purse, where anyone could steal it. Then he forgot about the money to smile at the amazingly imperfect woman in his arms. "There's nothing snooty about you, Genevieve."

She winced. "That name alone is snooty. I prefer Gen, with a G and one N."

"And an E in the middle?"

Humor filled her eyes, then ever so slowly melted to lust. She rubbed her mouth and body against his. "We could do it in the cab of your truck again and really give everyone something to talk about."

Nash's cock was hard from her first wiggle. If his truck was anywhere nearby, he might have grabbed her up and done exactly as she suggested. But it wasn't nearby, and they both deserved better than to have her parents' prying eyes and those of many from Deevy Isle cheapening their sex life anyway. "We could, but it would mean walking a mile. I ran out of gas on the way here. I thought I wasn't going to make it in time. I thought I was going to lose you."

Gen's eyes softened. Sliding her hands from between their bodies, she wrapped them around him and moved her mouth against his in a tender kiss. "You weren't a second too late. In fact, you were just early enough to stop me from making what would have been the biggest mistake of my life." She looked across the parking lot to the church. "I'll risk going back inside to get my jacket and my purse, which has my car keys in it, but only if you promise to take me home and make love to me."

"We could do that, though I was actually hoping for a naked waltz for four."

Her gaze jerked back to his. "*Four?*"

Grinning, he slid his hands down to cup her butt through the layers of her dress. He pumped his hips against hers. "You, me, and your dynamite hips and ass."

She laughed. "They are pretty amazing, aren't they?"

They were, but not nearly so much as their owner.

Watching Benny struggle with coming to terms with the loss of his mother in a healthy manner these last days had shown Nash how easy he had it in simply having to move past his cigarette cravings. Moving past his Gen cravings, however, wasn't nearly so easy.

He'd ached for her body, her touch, her tongue.

He got every one of those things now, as he slanted his mouth over hers and her lips opened to him on a sigh.

Their tongues glided together, their hands moved over each other's bodies through their clothes, remembering each curve, each angle. He savored her intoxicating taste, the velvety softness of her tongue, the needy grinding of her sex against his. And she savored him right back, until they were both pulling away, smiling but breathless.

"I needed that," Gen said in a throaty voice. She seemed to recall their earlier conversation and clarified in an assertive voice, "No, I deserved it. I expect you to do it at least a hundred times a day for the rest of our lives."

Chuckling, Nash moved his tongue back between her lips and started to work on fulfilling her expectations, kiss by soul-searing kiss.

THIRD TIME'S A CHARM

1

What was she thinking, taking her cousin Tia's advice?

Holly Daringer considered her cousin as intelligent as she was forthright. But it didn't feel any too intelligent to be sitting in her car in the driveway of a stranger's two-story subdivision home, with plans to go inside and sleep with him.

Tia called it sexual healing. A chance for Holly to cleanse her mind of everything, including the guilty thoughts that had plagued her for months now. Holly called it shelling out five hundred bucks to screw some guy she didn't know a thing about. Five hundred bucks she shouldn't be spending, given how quickly her savings was disappearing.

You wouldn't need to dip into your savings if you were earning a paycheck, a little voice niggled from the back of her mind.

She gave that little voice the mental finger.

Then she accepted the voice was right. She needed to go back to work. Not just so she could afford to live once her savings was depleted in another few weeks, but because she loved being a mental health therapist.

At least, she would love it if she ever managed to keep a client around and alive.

Holly had taken on her first solo client last year. She thought things were going well, right up until the moment she got news that the woman wouldn't be in for any more appointments because she'd taken a bath with a running blow dryer.

It wasn't easy to stomach, her first solo client killing herself. Holly eventually chalked it up to beginner's bad luck and gave a second client a try. And he'd sneaked into her office in the middle of the night and slit his wrists with her envelope opener, leaving a note so she'd know it was her counseling that drove him to suicide.

She hadn't been able to ignore that note. And she couldn't ignore the guilt engulfing her again, now, over the idea she'd been responsible for his death.

"I didn't kill him," Holly vented into her otherwise silent sedan.

She knew it was the truth. Knew she was a great therapist. A woman who listened with an open mind, ready support and as-needed guidance. Somewhere in her head, she knew all of that. Just right now it was buried beneath the damned guilt.

Focusing out the windshield at the recently cut, lush green grass surrounding the yellow two-story, she pulled in a deep breath and then another, urging the guilt aside.

It would have been really great if it went away. But it didn't. It just stayed in place, clinging to her shoulders and eating at her belly like the worst kind of acid.

Holly looked to the front door of the house. Somewhere behind it was a man awaiting her arrival. A man with a body and hands so gifted women shelled out half of a grand for the pleasure of a single hour of his company. A man Tia said a friend of hers spent time with several months back, when the woman hadn't been able to get her mind off a problem she was having at the office, and he effectively and permanently lifted each one of her worries away.

Was there a chance of it working for Holly?

Hell, the odds were so slim. The idea all but ridiculous. She had to give it a try anyway.

Without this guy, she might never convince herself she wasn't the devil disguised as a therapist and might never give a third client a chance. With him, well she probably still wouldn't, but at least she would be sexually fulfilled along with unemployed.

Mind made up, she grabbed her purse from the passenger's seat and slid from the car. Nerves flared as she made her way up the short walk to the front door.

What kind of man was named Benny? It sounded mousy, juvenile. Then there was the color of his house—yellow was hardly masculine.

She reached the door and lifted her hand to knock. Before she could make contact, the door opened to reveal a guy nowhere close to mousy or juvenile. As for masculinity—it poured off his nearly naked body in waves.

Swallowing past a suddenly parched throat, Holly took in his big, hard body, towering a good eight inches over her average, five foot six frame.

Curls on a man had never been her thing, but even with his blond hair wet, he wore them in a manner so unruly and defiant, her fingers itched to slide into them. Or coast up the length of his legs. The same blond curls covered him from ankles to calves to powerful thighs that disappeared far too quickly beneath a low-slung gray towel.

Her gaze moved upward, to the bulge straining beneath the towel. From all perceivable accounts, his cock was well proportioned with the rest of his body.

It was big. And she was wet.

"Holly?" Her name rolled out of his mouth, dark and enticing.

She caught herself growing damper with his deep voice. Bringing her attention up to the grooves cut into his hips, only attained by rigorous exercise, spiked her heart rate. His ripped abs and honed torso and pecs were utterly mouthwatering. His mustache and gateau a potentially thrilling backdrop for lips that looked soft yet firm.

Benny's body was a female playground. The idea of shelling out five hundred for her turn on his flagpole no longer seemed outrageous.

She wanted to reach out and unwrap his towel, get a complete look at what her money would be buying. But Tia told her, despite his job's potentially smarmy front, he was 100 percent the professional. Before Holly got to touch, she would need to fill out some minor paperwork and lay down the cash that would take them from fly-by lovers to business associates.

"Yes. I'm Holly." She extended her hand in the same way she offered it up to a new colleague or client.

He was no colleague or client, and he didn't react by sliding his fingers into hers and shaking. No, he slid his fingers into hers and used them to jerk her up against him.

Her breasts pressed into his warm, naked chest. Her bare belly brushed against his groin. Gasping, she dropped her purse and flattened her palms against his chest.

And he lowered his head and devoured her mouth.

His hands moved down her back to grab hold of her ass and lift her up his body. Where her belly had only been able to identify the existence of his shaft against it, her pussy could tell he was huge and hard . . . and risking the confines of his towel.

His tongue moved with hers, wicked, wild, making Holly want until she ached from the inside out.

She wriggled against him, and the towel fell to the floor with a glorious swish. She'd had no idea what to wear for this adventure. She'd gone with simple white cotton shorts and an orange and white tee that freed her sun-baked belly and molded to her small, firm breasts. What a choice decision that was. Her shorts and panties were so thin she could feel each twitch of his cock against her stimulated sex.

Benny's mouth lifted from hers. "Where do you want it?"

Anywhere he wanted to put it. Only, weren't there some preliminaries to get out of the way? "Don't I have to sign some forms first?"

"Your friend handled everything." Holding her legs around his waist, he backed her into a good-sized living room. He unfolded her legs from his middle and set her on the back of a flowered couch. Sinful heat flashed in his golden brown eyes. "All you have to do is let me know when the pleasure becomes too much to bear."

He stepped back from the couch, just a few inches, just far enough for her to finally get a full look at his body. His cock jutted out long and thick, the head deep pink and already seeping silky fluid. The same blond curls lining the rest of his body surrounded his member, thicker here, darker. Her view disappeared then, as he returned to the vee of her thighs.

One hand moved to her back, cupping her lower spine, pinning her in place. The other grabbed hold of the side of her shorts and panties.

Holly's heart knocked against her chest. She held her breath in anticipation.

She didn't have to wait long.

Muscles corded in Benny's forearms as he yanked the clothes from the lower half of her body with a single, smooth tug. Her sandals thudded against the beige carpet. Her clothes slipped from his fingers, barely registering a sound as they joined her shoes. Then he reoccupied his fingers by placing both of his hands upon her thighs and spreading them wide.

His head bent toward her sex in a flash. The breath wheezed out of her mouth as he closed his lips over her exposed folds and suckled.

His tongue pushed inside her body, lapping at her with forceful pressure. She cried out and arched up, nearly tipping backward off the couch. Before she could lose her balance completely, his hands shot around to cup her ass, steadying her and spreading her butt cheeks all at once. Her thighs spread farther apart in tandem, opening her pussy to the limit. His tongue slipped deeper inside her, bringing the coarse hairs of his gateau into direct contact with her clit.

Holly grabbed hold of his shoulders and shrieked as sensation after erotic sensation zinged through her. Then he twisted his lips around her labia, corkscrewing his tongue inside her sheath, and she came with a strength that left her dizzy.

She clung to his shoulders as he lazily licked at her cum, as if he couldn't get enough of it. The man was definitely worth his pay. "Do you always greet clients this way?" The words came out as shaky as she felt.

Tipping back his head, Benny looked up at her with his tongue still buried partway inside her. He retracted his tongue slowly, trailing her cream in its wake. "Only if they're prepaid."

How watching his tongue pull from her body could be more intimate than actually having it inside of her, she had no idea, but the heat of fresh arousal burned her cheeks.

She looked away from his face. His muscled arms had brought her pleasure on sighting, so she picked them as a focal point . . . and felt her heart constrict in her chest.

When she ogled his body at the door, her mind had obviously been on sex alone. Otherwise she would never have missed the multitude of little scars crossing the insides of his upper and lower arm. She looked at his other arm and found it in the same condition.

This pleasure session—as Tia had called it—was supposed to take Holly's thoughts away from everything, particularly her therapy work. Instead it had her mind racing with the need to console. "Cutting is a great form of temporary stress relief."

Benny stiffened with the words he never expected to hear from a pleasure client. Never wanted to hear from anyone.

Hell, he'd known this job wasn't going to be easy from the moment her friend Tia called up and pleaded with him to help fix Holly. She wasn't broken in regards to sex. She was broken in regards to being able to verbally open up enough with her lovers to enjoy sex to its fullest and potentially have it become something more than physical gratification.

Considering he didn't know a damned thing beyond the physical these days, he'd doubted his agreement to help. Now, he doubted it a hell of a lot more.

A glance across the living room, to the open kitchen door and the stack of bills on the counter, was all it took to remind him he needed this weeklong job. He'd skimmed the surface of the medical bills left behind when his foster mother passed away, but that was eight months ago and he needed to accomplish more than skimming if he was ever going to get the creditors off his back.

Benny moved from the cradle of Holly's thighs, easing her onto her feet. He took a step back, and then another.

Most people assumed his scars were from an accident or something else beyond his control. For her to know the truth of their origin suggested she had insider experience. "You some kind of advocate for self-injury?"

"No." She met his gaze. "But I've been around people who do it, and I can see how much better they feel afterward."

Understanding filled her eyes and turned his gut. She was supposed to be aroused, not telling him it was okay to use himself for a human cutting board. "I haven't done it since I was twelve, so you can check me off the list."

"You've never been tempted over the years?"

Fuck no, was the answer he wanted to give. Tell her he hadn't been tempted to hurt himself in any way, shape, or form since leaving behind his shitty blood ties. But in the drunken days following his foster mother's passing, he had been tempted. Enough to let the idea rule his mind and drive away all semblance of friendship. Removing Thad and Nash from his life meant giving up not only his closest friends, but his stake in Loose Screws, the construction company they'd started up together and what had served as the springboard for his woman-pleasuring services.

Those services fueled Benny now. So long as he was having sex on a regular basis, all negative thought remained in the recesses of his mind. So long as he whored his body out to every woman in the area, he would be just fine.

Holly frowned. "Forget I asked." She bent to grab her panties from the floor and started them up her legs.

She obviously sensed the foul shift in his mood and planned to leave. As much as he wanted to let her go, he couldn't. She was opening up to him—about an off-limits topic, but opening up all the same. Learning to be more vocal was the reason she'd come to him and the reason he had to take her suggestion and forget she asked.

Watching her wriggle back into her panties proved an instant mood lifter. They settled into place, but the sheer white cotton didn't begin to conceal the tangle of dark, moist curls at her mound. "Cold?"

"No." She bent back down to work the legs of her shorts over her feet.

His cock had started to soften with her observation on his scars. It returned to full hardness now, as he appreciated the roundness of her ass. She had a nice-looking face to go with it, big blue eyes and soft warm lips. He'd yet to see her breasts out of the snug-fitting top, but from what he could tell, they were the perfect size to keep his hands happy without having a lot of excess going to waste.

If he could keep their conversation off his personal life, they could have themselves a mighty fine time this week. "Then why are you getting dressed? Your friend paid for three hours a day and I intend to see you get her money's worth."

Holly's hands halted with her shorts pulled to mid-thigh. Her head snapped up, sending tawny hair across her face. She brushed the wavy strands aside, so they fell partway down her back. "How many days?"

"Seven."

Her eyes went wide. "We're going to have sex for three hours a day for the next week?"

"You and your friend didn't discuss the particulars?"

"I thought so, but apparently not clearly enough. This was supposed to be a one-hour, one-time deal."

What difference did the amount of time they would spend together make, once they had sex the first time? Unless it was his arms worrying her. Now that she'd seen his body wasn't perfect, the way Benny worked endlessly to make it appear on first sighting, she was turned off.

Nah, he wouldn't believe that. Not when she acted supportive of the bad habits of his youth. She probably just realized she was opening up to him and started freaking out as a side effect. "You trust your friend?"

"Tia's my cousin, but, yes, I trust her."

"She trusted me with seeing to your pleasure, so why don't you come over here and let that happen?" He wasn't much for coddling these days, but for the sake of the job, he reached a reassuring hand out to her.

Holly looked at his hand. She pulled her shorts up the rest of the way, as if removing the potential tripping hazard so she could close the distance between them. Only, she didn't move. Just stood there, staring at his hand.

"Want me to come over there and get you?"

Her eyes lifted to his. The hesitation in hers was strong enough to suggest she had no plans to budge anytime soon. Standing and staring at him wasn't doing either of them any favors, so Benny answered his own question, eating up the space between them in a single, quick stride.

He grabbed hold of her around the middle and lifted her up, planting his shoulder into her stomach. The behemoth move was for the sake of pulling her out of her silent stupor as much as allowing him to safely take the stairs.

Gasping, she clamped her hands onto his back. "What are you doing?"

"Taking you to bed. My room's on the second floor."

She didn't make another sound until he reached his bedroom, and then it was a squeak as he dropped her down on the bed without thought to gentleness. Most of his clients preferred it rough. The glint of rekindled desire in Holly's eyes suggested she liked it that way, too, even if she couldn't work up the words to say so.

Tomorrow, once he had a chance to put on a better game face in expectation of her making further comments on his scars, he would worry about getting her to open up to him vocally. Today, he would focus on her physical responsiveness.

Benny dropped down onto the end of the bed on his knees. She lifted her head off the mattress an inch, eyeing his face and chest appreciatively before sliding her gaze to his groin. His cock jerked toward her, and an eager smile curved her lips.

He caught an ankle in each hand and spread her legs apart. Excitement danced through her eyes with the first stroke of his fingertips along the insides of her calves. "Tia said you're up for anything, but I always start new clients out in bed."

He circled the sensitive skin behind her knees. She sighed and her head lolled back on the mattress. "I thought we already started downstairs."

"That was foreplay." He ran his fingers up along her inner thighs. She tensed, but he wasn't sure if it was a good response in reaction to his touch or a bad one in reaction to his words. Some women held oral sex more intimate than full consummation. Given Holly's communication issues, it was entirely possible she was among that group. "You don't like foreplay?"

"I like it." He dropped his mouth to the cuff of her shorts and nibbled at the skin there. Her hands went to the bed, her fingers curling in the covers. "I've just never had a guy give me an oral sex orgasm and then tell me he still plans to give me real sex."

Surprised she said that much, he lifted his mouth to the crotch of her shorts and nipped at her pussy through her clothes.

Her breath caught, hips surging up beneath him. He shifted his body over hers, nudging the tip of his cock against the inside of her leg. Pre-cum beaded up with the press, and his shaft throbbed.

The response was predictable, easy. A rush of sexual adrenaline and a tension reliever he relied on.

The smell of her juices seeped through her clothes. Wetness emerged with his next nuzzle. The question seemed moot now, but he asked anyway. "You want real sex, right?"

"Yes. I do."

There was shock in her voice. Enough to have Benny lifting his mouth to look up at her face. Anger tensed his body with the discovery she wasn't watching him eat at her through her clothes but was back to staring at his arms.

Fuck. He might not be capable of pulling this job off after all.

"It's shocking you could be attracted to me?" Aversion bled into his words.

"Of course not!" Holly's gaze zipped to his. "I don't have sex as much as you do, or make a profit off it, but I've been attracted to and have slept with plenty of men I barely knew at the time."

The heat in her eyes and the misunderstanding of his question told him while her gaze had been turned away, her mind had been completely focused on what he was doing to her. He was the only one still thinking about his arms.

But he could stop thinking about them, now that he knew for certain she wasn't.

Now he could get back to being the mind-numbing lover he was developing a reputation as, despite his attempts to keep his name from circulating among the mostly conservative residents of Crichton.

Benny's anger died away. His body eased back into the moment.

Moving up on the bed beside her, he reached a hand out to lazily caress her bare belly. He smoothed his fingers along the skin just above the waistband of her shorts and then slowly took his fingers lower, dipping beneath her panties.

He fanned his fingers out, brushing her mound with the tip of his index finger. Holly's breath sucked in. Her hands returned to balling in the covers. He fisted his hand and spread it open again, teasing a finger past her mound and lightly into her slit.

Juices gushed out to meet him. Her eyes blinked closed. She whimpered and arched her back, taking his finger deeper inside her wet channel.

He pulled his finger out again, brought it back to her belly, and toyed with her soft skin. Her eyes snapped open and she huffed. And he pushed his hand back into her shorts and gave her what he knew she craved, pumping his finger deep into her pussy.

"Yes." The word whispered from her lips and soothed along his spine.

He rewarded the small advance in verbalization by adding a second finger and moving them together inside her.

With each push of his fingers, her breasts rose and fell beneath her tight shirt, distractingly, enticingly. Too temptingly to ignore a second longer.

He pushed his free hand beneath the snug material and found her tits unfettered. Taking one in his hand, he squeezed and massaged the small mound, while he fucked her cunt until her muscles started to clench around his fingertips.

Benny jerked his fingers from beneath her clothes. He removed her shorts and panties with a unified tug. He moved back up to do the same with her shirt, but she'd already yanked it over her head and tossed it aside.

Holly's smile was lusty and encouraging. Her eyes deep blue and heavily lidded. He'd had hundreds of women look at him the same way, like they were deep in heat and dying to have his dick buried inside them. Knowing she was looking at him that way when she knew the truth of his scars made him feel different than he'd ever felt with a sex partner, paying or otherwise.

For once, he didn't feel at peace with his thoughts.

His body hummed with electric need. His cock pulsed with raw desperation.

He felt alive for the first time in too damned long.

Taunting her had been the game plan. Drawing out her pleasure until she was insensate with her want to explode. The game plan was changing, because the need to lose himself in her was pulling at him with a commanding hunger.

Benny grabbed a condom from the supply he kept in the nightstand drawer. He ripped the package open and rolled the rubber on. Lying back on the bed, he took her hips in his hands and lifted her up over him, guiding her opening to the tip of his cock. Slowly, he started her down his length.

Holly looked into his eyes, gripped his arms, and touched his scars with her fingertips . . . and didn't even shudder a little bit in revulsion.

Only, then she did shudder.

A shuddering gasp of pleasure as he slipped deep inside her warm, wet sheath.

With her cloudy gaze trained on his, she rocked back, placing his dick inside her at an angle so intense ecstasy burned at the backs of his eyes. Bringing one hand up to pull at a hard, dusky nipple, she moved the other to his balls.

What she lacked vocally, she more than made up for physically.

Stroking his balls and perineum, fondling her breasts in turn, she rode him fast and hard, like he was her prized bull and she was long overdue for more than an eight-second ride. That was how she made him feel, with each grind of her pussy against his shaft, like an animal who'd been left caged too long and now it was out and kicking.

Her butt cheeks pressed down on his balls, capturing tender, hypersensitized skin between them, and the furor of that animal slammed into him.

Spinning them around on the bed, he flattened her onto her back. Her breasts rubbed against his sweaty chest as he pushed his cock into her again and again. Tension knotted at his heels and splintered up the backs of his legs to his ass. He found her mouth with his and attacked it with openmouthed kisses. She kissed him back frantically, urgently, like she understood his wild need, which was damned ironic considering he didn't fully understand it himself.

Benny didn't get the extent of the whys, but he sure as hell got the when.

Right now, her pussy was milking him, clenching tight and soaking him with her orgasm. Right now, he was giving back to her, gripping the ends of her hair in his hands as he pumped into her and found a violent release.

Holly's mouth pulled from his in the midst of the mind-bending climax. She panted beneath him and he panted right back. Riding out the intensity of his release, he buried his face in the crook of her neck.

Damn, she smelled good. Felt soft.

So did a lot of the other women he fucked this month. But those others didn't make him feel alive. Alive, and whatever else it was that had made him lose control. Whatever else it was that made him think beyond the physical for the first time in eight long months. And then made him wish she'd decide to go with her original idea and only employ his services for a single hour and a single pleasure session.

A week of out-of-control sex with her, when verbal communication would be a must, was liable to be more than Benny could handle while remaining "just fine."

2

Holly bypassed the doorbell and pounded on the door of Tia's inherited Deevy Isle estate house. Along with acquiring the massive home from her late grandfather, her cousin had been passed down his staff. Even so, Tia's roots were grounded in less privileged living and she answered the door herself most of the time.

Today was no exception. Tia opened the door barefoot, wearing faded jeans and a boob-tube-style halter top the same reddish orange as her cropped hair, and so unlike the formal attire of most of the residents of the island.

Glaring, Holly stepped into the spacious, marble-floored foyer. "You never said anything about seven days of sex."

When she wasn't putting on a show for the sake of keeping her grandparents' name respected in the island community, Tia didn't bother to waste energy on sugar coating. She didn't even bother to bat an eyelash now. "Did you really think a single hour with Benny would be enough to cleanse your mind?"

"A whole week with Benny isn't going to be enough to

cleanse my mind of therapy matters. He's a cutter, Tia. How did your friend fail to notice *that?*"

Lifting a slim, bare shoulder in a shrug, Tia crossed the foyer and dropped down on a gray and gold fainting couch—a recent addition to the foyer that was her cousin's style yet enough of an antique to be considered chic by her island peers. "She isn't a shrink. Neither am I, and I also have no clue what you're talking about."

Holly sighed. She wished she could relax enough to sit down.

How had so many women managed to miss the truth in Benny's scars? Or had they just not cared? Maybe they even liked them, thought they added to his rebel-without-a-care appeal. "He cuts himself to relieve emotional tension, because he doesn't know how to get it out any other way. At least, I'm guessing that's why. I didn't ask for specifics, considering how unimpressed he seemed when I mentioned it at all."

Tia raised a skeptical eyebrow. "This guy has cuts all over his body and yet he manages to bring in five hundred plus an hour?"

"His body is unharmed and totally gorgeous." Not to mention a machine made for making a woman climax in short order.

Heat zinged from Holly's belly to her core. The way he could get a woman wet with the mere thought of him probably explained how so many had been blind to the reality of his scars.

"The cuts are just on the insides of his arms. Only, they aren't cuts. They're scars. He says he hasn't taken a blade to himself since he was twelve, but I think he's wanted to do so." Call it therapist intuition, but the way he tuned out on her and then got that scowl on his face following her inquiry if he hadn't been tempted suggested his lack of response was equitable to a yes.

Tia waved the words away with a flick of her hand. "It's only seven days, six now. If he hasn't succumbed to temptation in well over a decade, why are you worried he'll do so this week?"

"I feel the need to console him, and I don't think I'm capable of keeping my mouth shut about it. I was so afraid of saying something to encourage him to talk about his scars that I barely said a word from the time I noticed them."

"Actually, that's a good thing." A sheepish look crossed Tia's face, so uncharacteristic it quickened Holly's heart. "He thinks you're seeing him for the sake of learning how to open up better with your lovers from a verbal standpoint."

"He *what?*"

"I didn't think you wanted me to tell him the real reason—because you can't stop feeling guilty about killing off your clients."

Holly gasped. For once, she didn't feel guilt over the idea but fury her cousin would dare to suggest such. "You bitch, I didn't kill anyone."

Teasing filled Tia's hazel eyes. She gave a short laugh. "We both know you couldn't hurt a fly. But he doesn't know that, and I didn't want to give him any reason to assume it. The sex was good?"

Tia shifted gears so fast it took Holly a few seconds to catch up. Then every red hot detail of the three hours she'd spent with Benny yesterday afternoon filled her head. After taking a few minutes to recharge following their in-bed liaison, he'd taken her down to his kitchen and made her dinner, literally.

Her pussy tingled with the memory of his fingers coating her sex with cheese spread and then licking her clean. "The sex was great."

"Enough so to clear your mind while you were having it?"

"Definitely." When his hands were on her body—or his tongue, or most any other part of him—thoughts of healing him had taken a backseat to pleasure.

"Then remember your favorite cousin shelled out a bundle to

see you happy, and keep your mouth shut and enjoy him. The worst that's going to happen is you spend the next six days having multiple orgasms. The best is you get to have all those orgasms and a mind cleansed of everything negative, including guilt."

Benny flipped the burgers on his back porch grill in preparation of Holly's arrival. That it was Saturday evening, the night he used to meet with Nash and Thad for burgers and beer at McCleary's, wasn't lost on him. But hell, sitting in the pub with the guys, while they attempted to gauge his emotional well-being like a couple of pansy asses, wasn't worth it.

It was bad enough he let his emotions come into play yesterday, with Holly.

It had taken him awhile to figure out that the rising of his long-subdued emotions was to blame for his losing control so quickly and completely. He'd let her get to him with her knowledge of what—or rather who—caused his scars. Benny had spent the hours after Holly left thinking it best to phone Tia and tell her the deal was off. She could have her money back so long as her cousin stayed the hell out of his head.

Today, he realized he wanted Holly in his head, just not from an emotional standpoint.

He'd never gone to therapy as a kid, for all the shit that plagued him while living with his natural, more-often-than-not drunk parents. His troubles had disappeared on their own from nearly the moment his foster mother took him in and showed him life didn't have to suck.

Since her death, those troubles had been rearing up again. While sex seemed to combat his more harmful urges, he didn't want to be relying on the vice when he was seventy. With his need to get her to communicate better and her knowledge of those who injured themselves, he could get Holly to school him on the subject without having to ask outright and make it seem he cared.

"Whatever you're making smells great." Holly's cheerful voice came from inside the house. She emerged through the kitchen screen door a few seconds later, ponytail swaying behind her head and an inviting smile curving her lips.

Her outfit was casual yet as appealing as yesterday's had been. Cutoff jean shorts hugged her hips and thighs and a midriff-baring black tank top clung to her breasts. The tented shape of her tits beneath the top told him she hadn't bothered with a bra again. Typically, Benny would consider that a good thing—all he had to do was stuff a hand under her shirt to get a breast in it. Right now, though, he hadn't planned on moving straight to sex, so the hardening effect it had on his cock wasn't ideal.

He returned her smile, his lips feeling awkward in the all-but-foreign position. "Just cheeseburgers. But I did use my special seasoning salt on them." He nodded toward the cooler on the bench seat of the wood picnic table a few feet from where he grilled. "There's beer in the cooler if you want one."

"I'd love one." Holly frowned. "On second thought, maybe I shouldn't. My lips tend to get loose when I drink."

"Isn't that what you're after here?"

"Right. I am." She didn't sound too sure of herself, but she grabbed a beer from the cooler. Screwing off the bottle top, she sat down at the picnic table.

Then she didn't say a word, just drank her beer and watched him grill. Surprisingly the silence wasn't uncomfortable the way he would have guessed. Even so, one of them needed to get talking if she was going to learn to be more vocal.

"Nice day." Benny sneered at the cheese melting on the burgers. Damn he was rusty at nonsexual interaction to be relying on the weather as a conversation piece.

"It's beautiful out. Not too hot. Not too cold." She laughed. "Not exactly a wonder with words, am I?"

He pulled the cheeseburgers and the butter-toasted buns off

the grill and put them onto a serving plate. Setting the plate on the condiment-laden table between them, he slid onto the bench seat across from her. "You're doing fine. Eat up, and after we'll work on your ability to tell your lover exactly what it is you want him to do."

Holly set a bun on her plate. Squeezing ketchup and mustard onto the top half, she asked, "Exactly?"

Nerves tinged the question. He gave her a chance to relax, fixing his own burger and taking a bite before responding. "Guys like dirty talk. So do most women."

She lifted her burger to her mouth and eyed him over the top edge of the bun. "You think I will?"

Hell, she was even more nervous than Benny thought to be hiding behind a cheeseburger. That was bound to change the moment she realized the arousal to be had in explicit talk. "Does it get your pussy wet when I talk about bending you over the table and sliding my cock into your dripping cunt from behind?"

Above the edge of the bun, she blinked. "Will you do that?"

She spoke softly, quietly, clearly all she thought she could manage. She would have to try harder if she wanted him to fuck her. "Do what?"

"Bend me over and . . . do me."

Not hard enough. He shook his head. "I'm not touching you at all until you ask for it the right way."

Holly stuffed the burger into her mouth. Keeping quiet on the way she truly wanted to respond to his verbal taunting was even more difficult than she guessed it would be. His roughly spoken words about bending her over and sliding into her cunt from behind had her mind empty of all thought but that of her damp sex and her body's burning desire to do something about it.

She couldn't blow her cover. She *could* eat fast.

After downing the cheeseburger in record time, she slammed

the rest of her beer and slapped the bottle back on the table. "That hit the spot. Thanks."

Benny looked up from his half-eaten burger. His astonished gaze went from her empty plate to the portion of her stomach visible above the picnic table, like he was trying to figure out where her food had gone. His eyes returned to hers and she gave him her most seductive smile; after all it wasn't physical communication she was supposed to have a problem with.

That did the trick.

Comprehension flashed in his eyes. "You bet." The heat of arousal took over the understanding. He set his burger down and pushed his plate aside. "Anything else sound good to you?"

Holly shivered as his deep voice coasted along her spine, sizzling heat throughout her. She struggled to keep her tone coy. "Like dessert?" At his nod, she looked down at the table. "Would it be offensive if I said I wanted to suck the cream from your cock for my dessert?"

His breath dragged in audibly, and she had to fight off an amused smile. "If you were looking at my face, you'd already know the answer."

Catching her lower lip in her teeth, she slowly met his eyes. She released her lip to utter, "I don't know how much is too much."

"There can never be too much of a good thing."

"Okay. Just don't laugh if I say something stupid."

Aware laughter would be the last thing on his mind, Holly slid off the bench seat to the floor of the patio. Concrete abraded her bare knees as she crawled under the table and grabbed hold of Benny's thighs through his black board shorts. A few minor scrapes were more than worth feeling his powerful muscles tense beneath her hands.

She released his thighs and tugged at the string holding the front of his shorts together. The string gave away. He lifted his hips off the seat an inch, encouraging her exploration.

Pulse racing, she dragged the shorts down his hair-lined thighs and took his solid staff in her hand. Moisture pearled at the dark pink tip. She licked her lips. "I'm going to do you with my mouth." Anticipation made her voice quiver.

"Did you say something?"

"I'm going to take your cock in my mouth and suck on it," she clarified in the naughty words and voice she knew he wanted to hear.

Only, the silky bead of moisture was too tempting to take him between her lips all at once. She flicked her tongue out, licking up the glistening pre-cum and pulling it back into her mouth to savor his salty essence.

His thighs went taut. His hips surged toward her tongue. "Doesn't feel like sucking to me," he said in a sedate voice totally at odds with his moves.

"I wanted to see what your pre-seminal fluid tastes like." The words were so textbook, Holly almost laughed out loud. Dipping her tongue into the tiny slit at the head of his cock kept her silent ... until his sex pulsed under her touch. Then she couldn't stop her blissful moan. "It's good." Playing with the seeping hole, she ran her fingers the length of his shaft. "You— I mean, your cock feels hot, velvety."

"What about my balls?" Benny shifted back on the bench seat, opening his thighs and giving her full access to his testicles.

She took them in her hand, cupping them, feathering her fingers against their heavy weight. "Soft yet tight." Smiling, she brought her mouth to the sensitive sac holding his balls and lightly brushed her lips against it. "Can I suck them?"

He groaned, the sedate show he'd put on a thing of the past. "You can do whatever you want, so long as you keep talking."

"I don't think I'll be able to talk much when your balls are in my mouth."

A chuckle rumbled through his big body. "How about we say when your mouth's full, you're excused?"

For the sake of pretense, she told him not to laugh at her. Given the reason he was laughing and how the deep, delicious sound had her pussy clenching tight, she let the oversight pass.

Carefully, Holly fed one of his testicles into her mouth. She sucked at the tender nut, running her tongue all around it as she mumbled her agreement, "Mmhhmhm."

She moved her mouth to its mate, pulling it between her lips and increasing the strength of her slurps. Benny's ass muscles tightened, lifting him higher on the seat. His fingers dove into the top of her hair, gripping the strands near the roots. "Oh fuck."

She freed her mouth of his balls to ask in a shy voice, "That was bad?"

"That was damned good."

Moisture welled in her core with his rough response. As good as teasing his testicles was, she wanted more. "Okay, well I'm done sucking on your balls for now. I'm going to swallow your dick to the back of my throat and fuck you with my lips." She sounded far too self-assured, so she added a low, "Is that okay to say?"

"That's damned okay to say." His pelvis pushed toward her face in the next instant, his cock seeking out and finding her mouth.

Fisting his shaft down low, she parted her lips and took his steely flesh inside.

His taste was clean, warm, pure male. She explored his sex with her tongue and the soft suction of her lips until there was no more left to learn. Then she did as promised and took him deep, swallowing his dick until the head nearly caressed the back of her throat.

Stroking the base of his cock, she pumped his throbbing member with her mouth, fluttering her tongue out again and again. The pull of his fingers in her hair increased with each of her mouth fucks until he was clenching the locks so tight shards of pain shot through her skull. That pain arrowed down, past her tented nipples to her wet cunt and became keen, burning pleasure.

She sucked him harder, with a strength she'd never before known, took him deeper, until his tip really was nudging at the back of her throat and Benny was bellowing out a shout of release.

The first spurts of his cum were hot, silky, unforgettable. His seed poured into her mouth then, and she held it there, memorizing his flavor, letting the sharp taste turn the fiery aching between her thighs unbearable.

Still holding him between her lips, she brought her fingers to her crotch. She slid them beneath the edge of her shorts and panties, and with a single, simple, swirling press against her clit let free her own, powerful orgasm.

Holly swallowed his cum as delectable tremors racked through her. When her pussy was no longer pulsing, she slipped his cock from her lips. Breathing hard, she crawled out from under the picnic table and moved onto the bench seat beside him.

His own breathing labored, he sat with his eyes closed and a replete look on his face. Not a smiling replete look, though. She had yet to see him smile in a manner that didn't look painfully forced, but she could guess he might have done so when he chuckled.

"You laughed at me," she accused.

His eyes opened and he glanced over.

Taking the tip of his softening cock between her fingers, she gently stroked. "It's all right, because I was trying to be funny."

Benny looked down at her hand but didn't comment about the potentially overintimate touch. "You did good. Real good. I'm not so sure you need me to give you lessons in being more vocal. I think you already know how to be that way, your lovers just aren't encouraging you to do it."

"It was the beer talking," she assured him quickly. Then before he could point out that she only had one, said, "Can I ask you something?"

"Uh-huh."

"Why is your house sunshine yellow and your couch and the wallpaper in the kitchen and bathroom flowered? It doesn't seem to fit you." With his amazing physique, she would expect to find a full weight room and pages from *Muscle & Fitness* posted throughout the place. At the very least, some bold masculine paint or design in place of the flowered wallpaper.

His sated look vanished. Mouth pushing into a hard line beneath his mustache, he closed his hand over her fingers and pulled them from his shaft. "My mother did the decorating." The words snapped out, and he stood and tugged up his shorts, tying the string in a fierce knot. "She's dead."

Holly tensed with his dramatic mood shift. The reality of the situation, what they were to one another, came back to her in a flash. She'd gotten carried away, let him invade her mind until her thoughts were of pleasure alone. It was what Tia paid him to accomplish. An incredibly good thing.

She still felt damned guilty about it.

From the moment Benny had started talking dirty to her, she'd forgotten his scars existed. With his anger now, she remembered them and the mental anguish that likely accompanied them. She couldn't stop her comforting words, "My mother is alive and well and one of my best friends. My—"

"Isn't that hunky-dory for you." Sneering, he grabbed an armload of condiments from the table. "I need to take this shit inside."

Holly stared at his back as he pounded across the patio and jerked open the screen door. The last time she'd tried to console him, he'd ended their conversation before she could explain that while cutting was a great form of temporary stress relief, it was also dangerous and one of the worst ways to relieve compounded stress in the long run. Now he hadn't let her finish either. This time, though, she wouldn't let him change the subject.

Whether he liked it or not, the therapist in her could see he wasn't fine, the way he pretended. Regardless that it probably wasn't a smart thing to do, the therapist had her mind set on seeing him healed. That meant making him talk about things he didn't want to voice and potentially pissing him off in the meanwhile.

3

"I lost my father years ago."

Benny stilled with his fingers on the screen door. He wanted to ignore the tender emotion in Holly's voice, get inside and the hell away from her personal questions and too-intimate touches. But she was opening up to him—the way he'd been paid to make happen—and he could hardly let the opportunity pass.

He moved inside the house. Setting the condiments on the kitchen table, he drew in a few calming breaths. Some of the tension drained from his body, enough that he didn't feel like he would buckle under the weight, and he went back outside.

She wasn't watching for his return as he expected, but kicked back on one of the white plastic patio chaises, drinking a fresh beer with her eyes closed.

A second chaise sat not far from hers. He wasn't up to being so close to another person right now, so he slid back onto the bench seat of the picnic table. After pulling in another calming breath, he asked, "How did he die?"

"He's not lost in the sense that he's dead." Without opening her eyes, Holly spoke in a quiet voice thick with emotion so raw it hurt his chest. "He's just gone to me and Mom. My father is bipolar. We tried to get him help for years, but he wouldn't have anything to do with it. Then one night when I was fourteen he disappeared. I haven't seen him since, but his leaving still affects me. He's the reason I went into the field of work I did." Her eyes snapped open. She gave him a look that said she was surprised she'd admitted so much.

Benny was just as surprised. He needed to keep her talking and keep himself stable enough to learn from her admissions. "Is your father the one who cut himself?"

"No. Someone else close to me."

He grabbed a beer out of the cooler and took a drink. When enough time had passed to make it seem he wasn't desperate for insight, he asked, "Has your friend stopped cutting?"

Holly mimicked his move, taking a long drink before responding. "The desire's dormant most of the time. Then something bad will happen and the urge returns, hovering over her huge and unyielding."

He understood what she was saying so completely he nodded without thinking. Recognizing the move and what it might say about him, he shrugged her words away.

But they wouldn't stay gone. He had to know more.

Benny moved to the chaise next to her. It was risky, but at the same time, putting himself so close to her while asking these questions would have to give the impression the conversation wasn't making him uneasy. "Is there a way to control the urge?"

She rolled to her side. Her face was less than a foot from his. Her gaze far too probing, like she was seeing inside him, seeing every one of his demons. "You can control the urges by learning to direct your emotions elsewhere."

Rage funneled through him with the personal attack, pushing pain into his temples. Impressions went to hell. He jumped up from the chaise, sending the legs skittering toward hers. "We're not talking about *my* goddamned emotions. I'm *fine*."

Holly didn't flinch. She just looked at him with sympathy filling her eyes. "I didn't mean your emotions as in yours personally. I meant that as all encompassing."

He ran a shaking hand across his mustache. Was she being sincere? Shit, probably. Maybe not.

Who the hell knew? Who the hell cared?

Not him.

Benny dropped back down on his chaise. Channeling his anger into a wicked grin, he came up on an elbow and took the easy way out. "Ready to fuck on a lawn chair?"

At Benny's skilled and completely thrilling hands, Holly's thoughts were coming clean of the guilt over what happened with her previous clients. But with only a couple days left to go in the week, she had yet to break through his walls and get him talking about his personal demons enough to help heal him.

With that goal in mind, she arrived at his house almost an hour after the time they agreed to meet tonight. Initially, she hadn't wanted to spend more than a single hour with him. Now, she hated to cut their time together even shorter than it already was, but it would be worth it if her tardiness paid off.

As he had the first day, Benny opened his front door before she could knock. Frustration poured from the rigid lines of his body. She wanted to touch his face, stroke his cheek, soothe him. But that wouldn't be enough.

"You're late," he clipped out.

Holly breezed past him into the house. Letting out an exaggerated sigh, she dropped down on his living room couch. "God, I'm sorry. My friend who's into self-injury caught her boyfriend doing another woman and instead of wanting to hurt him—the way most people would react—she wanted to hurt herself. She called me up in a panic, desperate for other outlets to help relieve her pain." She sighed again as she looked up at him. "Sex was the last thing on my mind."

The need to hear more was alive in the depths of Benny's eyes. He looked away but remained standing in front of her. Several long seconds passed and he asked, "What did you tell her?"

"To unload on me. She keeps her emotions trapped inside. Then all at once they get to be too much and she feels like she wants to explode from the tension. Confiding in a friend is one of the easiest ways to get rid of emotional pain."

"What if you don't have any friends?"

Though he'd yet to look back at her, she could tell by his low, scratchy voice she'd struck a nerve. Carefully, she offered, "You can tell me."

Finally, he looked at her, glaring. "This isn't about *me*. This is about getting *you* to talk with *your* lovers."

The retort was expected, but it didn't hold as much heat as his response had when he took her words personally earlier in the week. Maybe she'd gotten to him a little bit. Regardless, before this night was through, Holly was determined to reach him.

"There are actually a lot of things to try. Deep breathing, going for a walk, writing down how the person feels in a journal. Crying it out." Skepticism played across his face, and she knew she'd gone too far by implying he, or any man, would go to the extreme of shedding tears over anything less than tragic. "Sex is always a good way to channel emotions. When trust is a factor in a relationship, it works even better."

His skepticism gave way to sensual interest. The rigidity of his stance lessened. "How are you with trust?"

"How do you mean that?"

"Do you trust me enough to let me tie you up and blindfold you?"

After all the ways he'd touched her this week, she trusted him explicitly, grew wet just thinking about the idea of being helpless to his wild urges. But would sex ever be enough to get through to him? Even sex that involved trust and had the potential to stir emotions?

It was what he wanted, so for now, she went with it. "Okay."

He frowned. "You don't sound too sure."

She came to her feet and took his hands in hers, squeezing. "I trust you, Benny."

He glanced at their joined hands and his frown deepened. Then he shook free one hand and used the other to lead her across the room. "Do you want a safe word?"

"Isn't that for bondage?" she asked as he opened a door off the living room she'd assumed was a closet.

Benny flipped a light switch, illuminating a stairwell. He started down, pulling her along with him. "Can be. Doesn't have to."

"I'm fine without one."

A small basement was at the bottom of the stairs. The exercise equipment she knew he had to have, given the scrumptiously hard state of his body, filled up the area. What he planned to bind her to down here was as intriguing as it was exciting.

He released her hand. "Take off your clothes and lay back on the weight bench."

It was an order. He'd given her plenty this week, and each time she heard his dark, deep voice issuing a command she got a little bigger thrill out of following it.

Holly went to the weight bench, imagining how he planned to lay her body out. He was across the room, searching for something in a tall, double-door cabinet, so she didn't bother putting on a show as she undressed.

Naked, she lay back.

The cool black material of the incline and flat benches rippled waves of erotic sensation through her heated body. The rippling became a torrent of pleasure when Benny returned to her, ropes in his hands and demand alive in his golden brown eyes. "Hang on to the bar and hook your feet under the leg curl pads."

Reaching for the bare weight bar over her head, she slipped her feet beneath the pads. He grunted and spread her feet as far apart as her height and the pads allowed. He did the same with her hands, arching her back off the bench with the pull of her limbs.

Ropes were wrapped around her ankles and wrists, binding her in place. Placing one big hand upon her inner thigh, he pushed her legs as wide they could go, opening her sex completely.

His eyes went to her pussy, penetrating her with the intensity of his gaze and making her shudder. His hand moved up her thigh, the thumb dipping into her center, circling over her swollen clit.

Ecstasy ripped through her. Cream gushed forth.

Crying out, Holly bucked up on the bench. She needed more of his touch, now, but the bindings kept her from moving more than an inch. Kept her from taking his thumb deeper inside her. Kept her from keeping him by her side at all.

Benny crossed the room, back to the cabinet. He rifled through whatever was inside, taking his sweet time finding whatever he sought. While she powerlessly remained on the bench, her pussy lips spread wide, filled with juice from one simple touch. Aching for so much more.

"Come back." She was pleading, something she'd never been big on, but if she was going to do it with any man, then it would be this one.

"Why?" he asked, without turning around.

She wanted to scream. Had she not shown him enough times this week she had verbal communication down just fine? "Because my pussy is on fire and I need you to fuck it."

He turned back, came over to her. Opened up his hands. One held what looked like the handle from a jump rope. The other held a sweatband, which he brought over her head and down to her eyes, blocking her vision almost entirely.

Beneath the edge of the sweatband, Holly could still see out a bit. Just enough to see him take the end of the jump rope handle and coast it up her inner thigh.

Her belly tightened as he moved it higher. Her sex fluttered. He was going to use it on her, use it to screw her.

Even before he teased the handle up her thigh and made contact with her labia, she was squirming in her bindings. Even before he ran the handle the length of her slit, she was so juicy wet it was as if she had already come. Even before he dipped the handle shallowly inside her pussy, she was lifting her hips up that one sweet inch of freedom she had and silently begging for him to push it inside her completely.

"I can see the handle inside of me," she panted, pointlessly wriggling, attempting to take the handle deeper. "I want it all the way in my pussy."

"Too bad." His voice was callous, ruthless. "Because I want it in your mouth."

She opened her mouth in surprise. The handle jerked from her body and was shoved between her lips. She whimpered as the hot taste of her cream overtook her senses.

Benny pumped the handle between her lips, fucking her mouth with it. She wrapped her lips tight around the smooth length, fervently licking at her salty sweet juices. Need built, pitching through her higher and higher.

One of his fingers shoved into her cunt without warning. But it didn't move, just stayed there, partway inside her, lifeless, taunting. Making her sex throb for release.

She clenched her vaginal muscles and writhed against his hand but still couldn't take him any farther inside. She tugged at her wrist bindings, but they wouldn't give way. She tried to cry out for more, but she couldn't speak.

Couldn't even beg with her eyes, when they were almost entirely covered.

Please. Give me more.

Soundlessly, she pleaded. Soundlessly, he responded.

The finger within her moved, mimicking the pace of the handle in her mouth, pumping into her pussy with the same violent thrusting demand. Another finger joined in, sliding together inside her, bringing her to the trembling edge of release.

And then pulling out.

She wanted to scream. Cry. Hate him.

Then his thighs came down on hers, hot, hard, muscled. Bare. In one solid thrust, his cock pushed into her. Filled her. Took her over.

Orgasm sliced through her as a razor edge of ecstasy, stealing her thoughts and breath. But not her hearing.

She could hear Benny as he pounded into her creaming cunt. Hear him as he slapped his balls against her ass with the force of his pummeling. Hear him as he came, crying out, "You make me feel so goddamned alive."

It was an accusation laced with anger. And it brought a smile of elation to Holly's face even after her orgasm subsided.

She was reaching him. The techniques may not be altogether orthodox, but slowly, with her words and actions, she was reaching him.

Only, a slow approach was no longer an option. Their time together was nearly up, and so she had to step up the pace. Had to push his limits in a way he couldn't escape.

His body lifted off hers. She looked down, through the crack left beneath the sweatband, in time to see his sheathed cock pulling from her body. He was so big, so strong, and yet in many ways so weak.

But she would fix that. She wouldn't lose another person she'd set out to help. To suicide, or simply the emotional trappings of their own mind.

His face a stoic mask, Benny removed the sweatband from her eyes and the ropes binding her ankles and wrists.

Holly stood, took the ropes into her own hands, and cast a meaningful look at the weight bench. "Do *you* trust *me* enough to let me tie you up and blindfold you?"

4

Benny's emotions felt ripped raw from Holly's unconditional trust and how completely she gave her body over to him. Lying back on the weight bench and yielding control to her could only tear at those emotions more.

But how could he tell her no when she moved past her verbal weakness to ask?

He cast a wary look at the weight bench, then back at her naked body, flushed with arousal, sweaty from his rough handling. "Have you ever done it before?"

"I've shackled a man, but not when he was wearing a blindfold. I've never worn a blindfold before today either. Not being able to see heightens the need for trust."

"You've never trusted a guy enough?"

Her eyes narrowed in thought. After a few seconds, she admitted, "Not until today."

The confession had his blood running faster and convincing him to give in.

This felt like an attempt to get him to open up to her. But, in reality, it was her opening up to him, letting wants and needs come out she never before felt comfortable showing. "All right. You can do it."

His gut knotted as he laid back, the incline and flat benches still warm from her body. The musky scent of their screwing was thick in the air.

Holly moved up next to the weight bench. She set the sweatband beside his head. Her eyes fell on his, seeking, searching out something. Maybe the assurance he was really okay with doing this. "Do you want a safe word?"

Not convinced he really was okay with it, Benny brought his hands up to the bare weight bar and hooked his feet beneath the leg curl pads. "I trust you to know when it's too much."

She spread his limbs as far apart as his height and the exercise equipment allowed, the same way he'd done to her, then she looped the ropes around his wrists and ankles. She checked the bindings for security. Not once, but several times, like she feared he might escape.

Like she had a reason to fear such.

His stomach muscles clenched. Tension barreled through him.

What the fuck was she up to?

Moving back beside him, she smoothed her fingertips across his chest. For just a moment she smiled at him, hot, sultry, so damned sexy it started his cock to hardening. Then her smile disappeared and she asked, "What if I want to push your trust?"

The tension grew. Pain shot up his spine, splintering through his temples.

Shit, shit, *shit*. Why had he allowed her to bind him?

Benny yanked at his wrists. The bindings didn't budge. Bile rose up in the back of his throat. He swallowed it down.

He could do this. He could be brave. He could let her try to break him and not fall apart.

"Do you?" The words trembled from his mouth.

Empathy entered Holly's big blue eyes, and then she slipped

the sweatband over his head and he couldn't see her face anymore. "You'll find out, won't you?"

It was dark beneath the sweatband. Too damned dark. Just a ray of light cast beneath its edge, just a glimpse of his groin was visible.

Fear pummeled him in the gut. The bile rose back up. His heart slammed into his ribs.

Darkness enveloped him entirely.

He was ten again, locked in the pitch-black storage closet. His drunken parents shouting at him through the door, telling him how worthless he was, laughing when he tried to defend himself. Laughing when he cried.

Then he didn't cry anymore.

He found salvation in other ways. Found the carpenter knife his father had hidden in the closet, so he had an excuse not to do the repair work his mother kept screaming about, and he took the blade to his arm.

Sweet release slid through him. Sweet relief.

Their angry shouts faded to nothingness. Their laughter was gone. He was fine. He was fine.

"Tell me how this feels."

The female voice wasn't his mother's belittling one, but Holly's sensual one.

Pulled back into the moment, to the pain and fear, Benny opened his eyes, not even sure when he'd closed them. Not even sure when he'd let the memories of his youth enter into his mind.

He looked down, past the sweatband, and her hand came into view. Her fingers eased over his cock, stroking gently. So tenderly.

She didn't want to hurt him, didn't want to break him. She just wanted to pleasure. "Incredible."

Closing his eyes again, he gave himself over to the hypnotic caress of her fingertips, the easy joy in her touch.

The pain between his temples abated. The tension moved down his body, gathering in his hips and ass, hardening his cock fully, stringing his testicles tight.

Warm wetness enveloped his shaft. He opened his eyes and peered beneath the sweatband, found her lips moving along his length, sucking him.

So simple. So sweet. So much better than cutting himself had ever felt.

Her tongue joined in, licking against his hard flesh. Her mouth worked faster. The ends of her tawny hair slipped between his spread thighs, tormenting his balls. She smiled around his dick, lifted her eyes to him, and he saw that her smile was in them too.

Reassuring. Caring.

Resurging every one of his emotions. Pushing them to a terrifyingly tremendous pinnacle.

He was conscious of his every ragged breath, every sensual move she made. Every last bit of the control he relinquished to her as the emotions burst beyond the pinnacle, crashing over him violently, spilling his seed into her mouth recklessly. Leaving him shaking and breathless and needful for the comfort of another person's arms, in a way he hadn't known in months, if ever.

Holly's mouth lifted from his cock. As if she could read the thoughts he wouldn't share, she came down over him, laid her cheek against his bare, sweaty chest and hugged herself to him.

"The guy I shackled"—she spoke quietly, her warm breath whispering against his hot skin—"ended up being an asshole. Right after I took off the cuffs, he used them on me. I wouldn't have minded, if he'd touched me the way you touched me. But he didn't. He made sure I was wet enough to get inside and then saw to his own pleasure."

Benny's fingers curled above his bindings. The tension he'd only just released returned. But this time it didn't take him over.

Didn't make him want to lock it away. This time he wanted to use it to beat the shit out of the guy who'd handled her so poorly. "You're right. He's an asshole. What did you do when he let you go?"

"Went into the bathroom and screamed at the top of my lungs. It's one of the ways I blow off steam. How do you blow off steam?"

"I don't have steam to blow off." *Big fucking liar.*

Why? What was the point of it? He'd shown her time and again this week, when he snapped at her for no reason, he had more steam than he knew how to handle.

Holly's head lifted from his chest. She looked up at him. The reassurance was still in her eyes. The caring.

She eased the sweatband up to his forehead. "This is about trust, Benny. So how do you blow off steam?"

The urge to buck her off his body hit him. But he ignored it. He could do this. He could share. He wouldn't even see her again after tomorrow.

Pain started back up between his temples with the thought. Ignoring it, he admitted, "Have sex."

Smiling softly, she brought her cheek back to his chest. "It's a good vice, but you can't sleep with someone every time your emotions build up."

"Why not?"

She didn't answer. Didn't say anything for almost a full minute. The pain ebbed and flowed but didn't grow any worse. Not until she asked, "You were close with your mother?"

Benny's body pulled taut. Tension shot through him, lashing out like the razor-edged blade he'd first found in the pitch-black storage closet. Cutting into his soul. "I hate my bitch of a mother."

Her fingers moved to his sides, stroking gently, somehow managing to lessen the fury eating at him. "Then why did you leave her house yellow and filled with flowers?"

He focused on calming his voice, taming his anger back into his head. "You're talking about my foster mother. And, yeah, we were close."

"Did you tell her stuff? Did it make you feel better afterward?"

Thoughts of the woman who'd taken him in when he'd been ready to accept his life was shit and nothing could fix it bombarded him, pulling his anger right back out again, leaking it into his words. "She suffered from Alzheimer's the last few years before she died. I talked to her, sure, but not that she remembered." He jerked at his bindings, but Holly had checked them and checked them again, and they didn't give a millimeter. "What is this? Some kind of therapy bullshit?"

She tipped her head back again, meeting his eyes with the silent but chilling demand he listen in her own. "When your foster mother was alive, you talked to her. Told her things that were happening in your life. She might not have remembered, but it didn't matter, because you got them off your chest. Out of your head. You didn't have all the emotions holed up inside of you, the way you do right now." Warmth and worry took over her gaze. "You've got to get them out, Benny, or you're going to end up hurting yourself again. Maybe this time in a way that will do more than leave scars."

"I don't fucking have—"

The slide of her breasts over his mouth cut off his lie. She didn't silence him by stuffing a tit between his lips. But moved higher up, to his arms.

To his scars.

Her lips feathered over the faded marks, kissing them, accepting them.

The tension moved through his body, pooling into the backs of his eyes. He tugged at the damned wrist bindings again, pointlessly, then gave up and looked away. The tension grew, stung him out. Turned to salty moisture.

He hadn't cried since he was ten. He would not cry now like some goddamned pansy ass.

Hot tears burned his eyes. He blinked, but they kept coming. Leaking out onto his cheeks, streaming down his face.

Fuck. Fuck.

Then her mouth was there, catching his tears on her lips, licking them away. Her mouth moved over his, her tongue dipped inside, laving his, loving his. Her tongue retreated and she brushed her lips against his, softly, gently. "I won't say anything else. Just let me love you."

Did she love him? Was that why she could make him feel alive and bring him to his knees, within seconds of each other and sometimes in unison?

Probably not. Probably she was just an incredible mind fuck.

Even if she was, Benny relented to her, let her remove his bindings and pull him to his feet and into her arms. Let her lead him upstairs to his bed and make love to him with a tenderness that drained away every ounce of his tension and hurt.

Holly had no intention of falling asleep and spending the night in Benny's bed and arms. But she hadn't been able to stop from giving herself that small gift. His anguished tears had touched her deep down, until she hurt for him. Until she loved him.

He wasn't a man to love.

Not only was he her client by chance, but he sold his body for money on a regular basis. He didn't have room for a woman in his life. He might not even have room for a woman in his heart.

She'd done her best to heal his emotional scars and make him see there were so many better ways to rid his tension and pain than cutting himself. Last night, with the tender yet desperate way he allowed her to make love to him and that he made love to her in return, she believed she reached him.

Finally, she'd helped someone.

And now it was time to let that someone go. It was already nearing dawn, and so she'd gotten twice the time with Benny that she was supposed to have today.

Holly closed her eyes and savored the warmth of his big body against hers another minute and then she slipped from his bed. Grabbing her clothes, she went downstairs to the living room to dress. With her clothes on and her purse in hand, she planned to make her silent getaway, leaving no physical trace behind.

But she couldn't do it.

He'd implied he didn't have any friends, and she couldn't leave without knowing he had someone to turn to when he was ready to talk.

Pulling an old receipt and a pen from her purse, she scribbled her name and number on the back of the receipt, along with the words to call if he ever needed her . . . and then she walked out the door, hoping foolishly that he would.

5

Eight months ago, Saturday night at six o'clock would have found Nash and Thad at McCleary's Pub, indulging in their weekly routine of burgers and beer. Benny was counting on them standing by that routine and being here tonight.

Holly had been out of his life for almost three days, but her words lingered on, until he could no longer ignore them.

While she didn't love him, to end things so easily once her paid time was up, she also wasn't a mind fuck. Rather, she was right—his emotions didn't belong hidden away in the back of his head. He had to start confiding his feelings in others, the way he'd once done with his foster mother, if he was ever going to stop relying on sex as a way to circumvent his urges to lash out at people and hurt himself.

There were only two guys he wanted to confide in. The friends he'd used and abused, not so differently than the way his blood parents had mentally used and abused him. The difference was he was better than his parents, stronger. With Holly's influence guiding him, he could admit how much he missed his friends.

He just hoped to hell they missed him too.

Tension mounted as Benny cleared the front door of the pub and found their usual Saturday-night table empty.

"Hey, stranger." Brenna, the busty, redheaded nighttime bartender, flashed a crooked smile at him from behind the bar. "Haven't seen your face in here in months."

Returning her greeting, he moved up to the bar and dropped down on a backless stool. "The guys still come in on Saturdays?"

"Sometimes. Not as much the last while. Can I get you a beer?"

The tension intensified, licking along his spine. Shit, he was too late. They'd given up on the routine. Given up on him and moved on.

Smiling at Brenna in a way that felt brittle, he stood. "Nah. I'm good. If Nash or Thad stop by—"

"They're building a fast-track house over on Thompson, which is why they haven't been in much. I'd try tracking them down on the construction site."

Relief sighed through Benny. The tension eased off. They hadn't given up on him. Construction business was just finally keeping them busy—enough that they needed a third worker on board again?

Hopeful, he stood from the stool. "Thanks. I'll make it a point to drop by."

Just not tonight.

Temperatures had reached the mid-nineties today and he could guess the guys would be zapped of energy and irritable from the heat and humidity. He would approach them in the morning, when they were liable to be more forgiving of what an ass he'd been in the days before he quit speaking to them.

Exiting the bar, Benny went to his car parallel parked along the downtown street. His stomach growled as he started for home. This time last week, he'd just finished grilling cheeseburgers for Holly and himself. She'd downed hers in about a minute flat, she'd been so anxious to crawl under the picnic table and wrap her lips around his dick.

What was she doing tonight? Using the vocal skills they'd practiced to get some other guy off?

Since she didn't care about him, the answer shouldn't matter. But it did matter. Did turn his gut and weigh his shoulders with strain. She told him to confide in another when the emotional stress mounted. But the only two guys he wanted to confide in weren't available just yet. The only girl he wanted to confide in was her.

Before the fear of opening himself up could stop him, Benny grabbed his cell phone from the car's center console and punched in the number she'd left on the back of a receipt and he'd memorized without questioning the rationale.

Holly answered on the first ring. "Hello."

Her voice was soft, low, soothing. The strain melted from his shoulders. She might not care about him, but he cared about her despite his best intentions not to.

"Hey. This is Benny." He kept his voice casual, while inside his heart pounded. "I had some unexpected time come up and wondered if you wanted to get together tonight. Free of charge. We don't even have to have sex."

"Ummm. Just a second." In the background, he could hear her talking to someone.

Another man. The one he guessed would be benefiting from their time together by succumbing to Holly's newfound dirty-talking side.

Hell, he should never have called. Never allowed her to get to him on a level beyond the physical. What a fucking idiot.

He was ready to jab the power button and end his misery when she came back on the phone. "Mom and I are having dinner and then going to a movie. Why don't you join us?"

Benny's heart slowed. He sighed. Not with another man, but with her mother and inviting him to join them.

Holly might not love him, but at the very least she liked him. Unless it was an invitation based on sympathy. "I don't want to ruin your girls' night."

"You won't be ruining it. Mom likes to look at hot guys as much as any woman."

The words seared through him, leaving his fingers clenching around the steering wheel and the phone, and his body painfully tight. He shouldn't have expected her to think of him any differently, but hearing her say he was just another hot guy hurt like a bitch and had him gasping aloud.

"Hey, that was a joke." Holly's concern was as clear as if she sat beside him. "I'm still working on my verbal skills and obviously doing a bad job of it. Join us. Please."

Benny smiled for real for the first time in months. She did care. And he would confide in her, anything she wanted to know just as soon as they were alone together.

"Quit begging already," he teased—damn, he forgot he knew how to do that. "You're going to give me a big head. Just tell me where to meet you gals and I'm there."

Holly probably shouldn't have asked Benny to join her and her mother for their bimonthly dinner and movie outing. But she had, and he'd had a noticeably great time. More than once he'd told her mother how much she reminded him of his own. Holly could only assume he meant his foster mother, given the way he'd smiled when he spoke the words.

She'd always found him attractive, mouthwateringly sexy. But when he smiled for real like that, she found it next to impossible to keep her hands off him.

Even so, sex wasn't the reason she was going to his house after dropping her mother back at her parents' place.

Benny was fast on the way to being completely healed, but she still worried how he might respond to coming down from their night of fun. Depression was a nasty beast that could settle in without warning, and she wouldn't let him regress because of it.

Pulling into his subdivision driveway, she cut the engine on her car and stepped out. This time she didn't even make it to his front door before he had it opened. This time he didn't greet her mostly naked or scowling up a storm.

He smiled all the way to his eyes. "Weren't ready to go home?"

Holly sighed. She wanted to sink into his smile, wanted to lose herself in his strong arms. But she couldn't do that any more than come right out and tell him why she was here. "My mother's wonderful, but she can also be overbearing at times. I wanted to make sure you escaped her personality."

Humor flashed in his eyes and he laughed. "I was serious when I said how much I like her. But I am glad making sure of it brought you here." His amusement died away and he stepped back into the house. "Come inside."

Not so sure she would be happy with the results, she moved past him and into his house. Everywhere she looked she could see the two of them, naked, moving together, crying out with release.

"Have a seat," Benny said from behind her.

His deep voice had the same effect on her as it did that first day, making her wet as she crossed to the couch. She sat down and automatically tipped her head back to eye the spot where he'd first gone down on her.

She should have known from that first, dizzying orgasm he would prove to be more man than what she could keep her mind and body from wanting.

"I know why you're here," he said.

Holly brought her eyes down to Benny's. He'd slid onto the couch a couple feet away and eyed her so seriously it flushed every hot, sweaty, naked thought from her mind. "You do?"

"Yes, and I'm okay. It was lonely when I first got home. But it wasn't depressing lonely. It just made me look forward to seeing my old friends again."

"You have friends?"

"I hope so. I haven't talked to them in months. They would try to come over, call." He smirked self-deprecatingly. "I was an asshole and drove them away."

She reached out to take hold of his arm without thought. "You were in pain. How you acted was beyond your control at the time."

Benny looked down at her hand. She almost pulled it away, but then he lifted his gaze to hers and his smile returned, warm, friendly, so inviting she wanted to touch the rest of him too. "How is it you understand me so well?"

God, she wanted to tell him. But he wasn't likely to respond too well to hearing she was a therapist. If they remained friends and she opted to go back to work as she was almost convinced she was ready to do, he would find out in time.

But those were some pretty big ifs.

For one thing, with the way he was looking at her mouth, like he couldn't get his on it fast enough, and for another, with the way her sex was clenching with the want to feel him sliding into it, they wouldn't make very good friends. "Probably just because I've been around a lot of people who are going through tough times and need a little help to see them through."

"Thank you." The words fell softly from his mouth. His grip on her hand, as he lifted hers from his arm and joined their fingers, was anything but soft.

Benny jerked her onto his lap. The breath wheezed out of her as he slammed her breasts up against his hard chest. His mouth crashed down over hers. His tongue pushed between her lips, licking urgently, needfully at hers while his hands moved between their bodies and found her breasts through her tank top.

She had every plan to be good. To recognize sleeping with

him again would be a very bad idea. But he made her feel so very good. And it was more than she could do to turn him, or her own body's raging want, down.

It was all she could do to kiss him back and move her own hands between their bodies, tug up his T-shirt, and palm his rock-solid torso.

Growling into her mouth, he pushed her back on the couch. He had her naked in an instant. His own clothes were off just as quickly. He found a condom in seconds, and then he was over her, hard, huge, hot.

He grabbed her hands in his and dragged them over her head, pinning them against the arm of the couch. Her small breasts thrust into the air, inches from his mouth. And then inside his mouth, as he took a throbbing nipple between his teeth and twisted.

Holly arched up, crying out with the delicious sensations zinging through her. The head of his cock pushed against her swollen pussy lips with the move and she cried out again, wriggling her hips. "Fuck me, Benny. Now. Please!"

"Holly, honey, your dirty mouth is beautiful, just like your pussy." He guided his cock to her opening and surged inside as his own dirty mouth came back over hers, moist, warm, attacking her with kisses that left her breathless and still wanting more.

He gave her more, kissing her lips, her face, her neck, all the while pumping inside her, shoving his cock deep with each of her upward thrusts.

His mouth returned to her nipple. His gateau chafed across the puckered red skin. She was a goner. Lost in the throes of a soul-shaking, mind-numbing climax. He came seconds after her, gripping her fingers in his, biting down on her nipple and sending her straight into another rippling orgasm.

Limply, Holly lay beneath him, struggling to find the energy to breathe. She didn't come close to having the energy to talk, to tell him it was a bad idea to take her up to his bed and fall asleep with her in his arms.

So he did just that, and she gloried in being back there again. And when the light of dawn came, she slipped back downstairs, silently dressed, and left without any physical trace she'd been there.

Feeling like a ton of bricks rested on his shoulders, Benny climbed out of his car and stepped onto the freshly packed dirt of the construction site. Forty feet in front of him, Nash pounded together two-by-fours for one of the house's exterior walls.

His pulse thrumming, Benny started toward him.

"'Bout time you showed up," Thad said from behind Benny, seconds before he would have reached Nash. "The way this place is going up so far, we thought we were going to have to hire on part-time help to make the deadline."

Thad moved next to him and Benny looked over, expecting to see something on his face— What, he didn't know. Maybe loathing. At the very least, disappointment. But Thad just looked like his normal self, carefree despite his words.

Benny attempted to sound just as casual. "What's the deadline?"

"End of the month." Nash didn't look back. He also didn't act any more surprised than Thad that Benny was at the construction site.

Had Brenna tipped them off?

Thad gave the in-progress home a sweeping once-over. "It might look impossible. But if we meet it, there's a shiny bonus in the form of six grand. I don't think there's a one of us who can't use an extra two thousand." With that, he started around to the section of wall that was already up. He stopped just before he would have disappeared behind the sheetrock to frown at Benny. "You plan on standing around with your fingers up your ass all day or getting to work and earning your fair share?"

The words were so entirely the Thad he remembered, the weight lifted off Benny's shoulders and he found himself smiling. Then he realized how much hadn't been said. He couldn't pretend nothing had been wrong the last eight months. These guys were just too good to him for that. "I'm sorry."

"Apologies don't pay the bills," Nash tossed over his shoulder. "There's an extra tool belt in the back of my truck."

"I meant I'm sorry for being such an ass." Finally, Nash looked around. Benny looked over to make sure Thad was listening, and then drew in a breath and started confiding. "You guys were one of the few good things in my life for years and the second things got a little rough, I shit on you."

Amusement entered Nash's eyes. "You should consider a job with Hallmark."

Thad smirked, while Benny laughed out loud, because he'd made the same remark to Nash months ago, when he'd been drunk off his ass and pissed at the world over his foster mother's death. "I might just do that." He grinned at the guys who were like the brothers he'd never had and he'd missed too damned much. "After we get this bitch done on deadline."

Holly's cell phone rang as she was about to step out of her car and head into Tia's estate house. Her cousin had called her up shortly after four to tell her today was officially dubbed "tan your buns" day. The plan was to sunbathe buck naked on the front lawn and give all of Deevy Isle a heart attack.

Knowing the pretense Tia put up to keep her grandparents' name respected, they wouldn't actually end up sunbathing in the buff, but getting out in the sun at all while spending time with her cousin sounded like exactly what she needed to get her mind off thoughts of Benny.

Holly gave her phone a glance where it rested in the cup holder portion of the center console. She considered leaving voice mail to pick it up, then curiosity got the better of her and she grabbed it.

Caller ID displayed Benny's name, and her heart felt like it was lodged in her throat.

She shouldn't want to talk to him again so soon. But she wanted to talk to him again so soon that she punched the Send button and voiced a breathless "Hello."

"Hey." She could hear his smile through the phone line. "I just had one of the best days of my life and wondered if you would be interested in hearing about it."

"Of course."

"I'd prefer to tell you about it in person."

Holly sighed. She shouldn't want to see him again so soon, either, but she did. "I just got to my cousin's house, but you're more than welcome to come over. Let me give you directions."

On the other end of the phone line, Benny jotted the directions down on the pad of paper he kept in his car. Learning Tia lived on Deevy Isle made him think of Nash's girlfriend, Gen. Gen no longer called Deevy Isle home, instead living in Crichton with Nash, but the island was small and the odds were good the women had met at some point. Nash had invited him over for dinner tomorrow, so maybe he would ask Gen about it then.

For now, the only thing on his mind was getting to Holly. Sharing his day with her. Hell, just seeing her, pulling her into his arms, kissing her.

If she allowed it.

Nah, there wasn't going to be any ifs about it. She might have slipped off in the night again last night, but the way she held him before that, the passion in her kisses and lovemaking, told him she cared. Told him she might even love him the way he'd fallen for her.

Tension drifted through him with the idea. Good tension. The kind that had him grinning all the way to Tia's massive estate house and double front doors. He pushed the doorbell and an older, balding man in formal clothes and a name badge answered, letting him know Tia and her guests were out back sunning.

The man led him around to the rear of house and onto a huge wooden deck overlooking Lake Erie. Three women—one he quickly recognized as Holly by her tawny ponytail—sat in laying down lawn chairs facing the breeze-rippled water.

Benny thanked the man and was about to make his presence known to the women when Holly said, "How are things going with Nash?"

One of the women shifted her upper body toward Holly, revealing her profile to Benny in the process, revealing her as Gen. "Absolutely imperfect. I've never been happier."

That certainly answered his question if Tia and she knew each other. He started the fifteen feet toward the women's chairs when Gen asked, "How are things going with getting back to your mental health work?"

He thought the woman with the short, flame-orange hair, he assumed to be Tia, would respond. Instead, Holly said, "I think I'm ready."

Benny froze. What were they talking about?

"There's no thinking necessary," Tia said. "You are ready. Client number three was the lucky charm. No more dead bodies to feel guilty over."

Client number three? Were they talking about him? Was she a fucking shrink?

Anger tore through him, because he knew beyond a doubt she was. Knew exactly how it was she'd been able to get to him so effectively. Knew every moment they'd spent together was a lie.

It was just too big of a coincidence, her being a shrink and him being a mostly reformed mental case, for him to believe anything else.

Holly looked over at Tia and shook her head. "I swear sometimes I don't know if I love you or hate you more."

"I know exactly how you feel," Benny snapped.

Holly pushed up in her chair. She turned around in a skimpy red bikini and flashed a welcoming smile. "Hey. I was just thinking about you."

Tia came to her feet. Gen quickly followed, swiveling around to eye him in horror. "Benny! What are you doing here?"

He smirked. Gen had always seemed so nice, sweet, but obviously she was just as conniving as the company she kept. "As if you don't know."

Holly's smile vanished. Her eyes widened confusedly. "What are you talking about?"

Hell, he wanted to believe her innocent act, but he wouldn't play the fool twice. "Don't play stupid with me. I fell for it the first time, when you had your so-called cousin call up and beg me to help you learn to be more vocal with your lovers, but I'm not about to fall for it again. I was just a client to you. I get it."

She blinked, then shook her head. "No. You weren't—"

"I'm sorry, Benny." Guilt in her eyes, Gen cut off whatever additional lies Holly might have voiced. "Nash and Thad thought—"

"They were in on this?" Apparently, Brenna hadn't tipped the guys off to his coming to the construction site this morning. Apparently, they'd known all along his sorry ass would be there, just as soon as their ordered-up shrink worked her magic.

"They love you," Gen said.

"Most people express their feelings in words. I get a shrink sent to my door to fuck the pain out of me." He turned his glare back on Holly. "Congratulations. It's gone."

Only, it wasn't gone. The pain was alive and kicking through him, all but blinding in its intensity, just for an entirely different reason this time around.

6

Heart racing, Holly watched Benny storm from her cousin's house. She wanted to go after him, make him see she really had no idea what was going on. But he was so angry right now, and feeling betrayed by her and all those he held close, that he wasn't liable to listen to a word she, or anyone else, had to say.

Her own fury raged forth as she turned back to glare at Tia and Gen. "Is he right? Did you send me to him to make him better?"

Gen closed her eyes and nodded. "I'm so sorry, Holly. I thought it would be a win–win situation."

Tia shrugged but for once had the decency to look guilty. "Like I said before, the worst that could happen was you had multiple orgasms. The best was you forgot about your guilt over your past clients and got the orgasms too. It worked."

"Yeah, it worked. It made the guy I love think I'm an evil bitch who only slept with him for the sake of her job. God, he was doing so good. He was almost completely healed. But after this... After this, I wouldn't expect to hear from him anytime soon."

Holly hurried inside the house. She grabbed her purse and

clothes and, with the thought of admitting she loved Benny spinning in her head, rushed out to her car and far away from her manipulative cousin and the woman's conniving best friend.

No one worth speaking to would show up at his door before nine in the morning. Benny only answered the knocking because his body had been strung tight as hell for two days now and he wanted to bite some prick's head off for disturbing him.

Then he opened the door and saw he would actually get to bite two pricks' heads off.

He sneered at Nash and Thad. "What the fuck do you want?"

"You to get over yourself and accept we give a shit," Nash supplied, as he pushed his way into the house. "So Gen had her friend convince her cousin to come to you in an attempt to feel better about herself, so what?"

Benny backed up, planting himself on the couch in the living room. He wasn't afraid of either man, but the last time they'd ganged up on him like this, he'd ended up with them sitting on him for two hours and sore nuts for several days thereafter. "What do you mean, feel better about herself?"

Thad sat down on the other end of the couch. "Holly took on her first solo client last year and the woman ended up killing herself. Then she took on another guy and he killed himself, too, and blamed her therapy sessions for it. After that, she gave up on her psychiatric work. Gen knew how worried Tia was about her and she knew how worried we were about you, and it just came together that maybe if we could get the two of you together, you could help each other."

Tia really was Holly's cousin and Holly really didn't know she'd been a plant? She hadn't been lying to him that whole time? Holy shit. "I'm the first person she's ever helped who hasn't turned around and killed themselves?"

From where he stood, just past the end of the couch, Nash shrugged. "You know what they say, third time's a charm."

"Yeah, I guess," Benny mumbled, his thoughts spinning with the hurtful way he'd accused Holly of being involved in his friends' and her cousin's plotting.

"Holly makes you happy, yeah?" Thad asked.

He nodded, feeling numb. Feeling afraid he might have fucked up things with her beyond fixing. Feeling so damned alive with the prospect of spending the rest of his life making it up to her, if that was what it took to earn her love.

"Then we can expect to see your ass at work tomorrow?"

Benny smiled past the emotions shooting through him—incredible emotions he had no plan to cage. "I'll be there. I'd come over today, but it just occurred to me I have a hell of a lot of groveling to do thanks to you two idiots." He laughed. "Of course if it weren't for you two idiots, I never would have met Holly and I'd still be a miserable ass."

Nash grinned. "Working on another Hallmark card?"

"You know it. I love you guys." He stood and gestured toward the door. "Now, get your asses down to the construction site. Someone needs to put time in today if we're going to get that bonus."

Holly hit the Mute button on the television remote and grabbed her ringing cell phone from the coffee table in front of her couch. She considered chucking the phone across the room. It was probably Tia again, attempting to earn her forgiveness. How many times could she tell her cousin she wasn't going to be forgiven anytime soon, so she might as well call back after New Years?

Apparently, one more time. The phone no sooner stopped ringing than it started again.

She jabbed the Send button and growled over the line, "What do you want?"

"I'm not feeling so well, Holly."

Relief to hear Benny's voice, and then concern over the low, raspy quality of it spiked through her. Her heart constricted.

"What's the matter?" she asked gently, fearing she already knew. That by very little fault of her own, she'd managed to make his healing do a one-eighty.

"I just... I'm having bad thoughts. I—hell, I can't talk about it over the phone. Sorry I called."

"Wait!" she shouted into the cell. "Where are you?"

"Home."

"I'll be there as soon as I can. Don't do anything we'll regret."

His house was almost fifteen miles from hers. She managed it in just over ten minutes and, thank God, ticket free. She planned to go back to her therapy work in the next couple weeks, but in the meanwhile she didn't have any extra money to waste.

Holly hurried out of her car and up to his front door. He didn't open the door when she reached it, so she let herself inside and darted her gaze around, frantically searching him out.

He wasn't anywhere within sight, so she raced up the stairs, but he wasn't on the second floor. The basement and bathrooms were empty as well.

Jesus, if she was too late...

No, she wouldn't let her thoughts wander that route. He was here, alive, somewhere, waiting for her to save him from the painfully emotional trappings of his mind.

The kitchen was the only place she'd yet to check. She raced inside and shouted Benny's name... and smelled hamburgers.

What the hell?

"Out back," he called casually, like he didn't have a care in the world. Like he wasn't getting ready to do serious bodily injury to himself.

She stepped through the screen door and was hit with the

urge to cross over to where he stood happily grilling burgers and slap the shit out of him.

"What is this?" Holly's voice vibrated with fury as she indicated the patio, looking exactly the way it had two weeks ago, when he'd started on his quest to teach her to be more verbal with her lovers.

He looked up from flipping burgers with a spatula. His smile was wide, genuine, yet wobbly with nerves. "My attempt at making us feel better by remembering happier times."

The anger dissolved out of her. She wanted to tell him exactly how much she loved it when he smiled for real. But she couldn't forget the very real panic in his voice, when they spoke on the phone less than fifteen minutes before. "You said you were having bad thoughts that you couldn't talk about over the phone."

Benny's lips flattened. He nodded solemnly. "I was. They were of my life without you in it."

"Oh." Oh God. He was so sincere. So sweet. So healed.

He set the spatula on the wood shelf built into the side of the grill and came over to her. Close enough that she could see his affection for her in his eyes. Close enough that she could reach out and touch, pull him into her arms without any effort at all.

But Holly couldn't reach out. He was confiding in her, and she would never stop him from doing that.

"We both got duped by people we trust. But they did it for our own good, so I forgave them. I hope you can too. And forgive me for assuming you were in on things."

She couldn't touch, but she could smile, let her feelings for him come through in her voice. "It was a natural reaction."

"It was me letting out my emotions instead of bottling them up."

"That's right. A good thing."

Benny's smile returned, the ends of his lips curving up to his blond mustache, the warmth of it reaching well into his golden brown eyes. "Know what I think a good thing is?" She shook her head, and he reached out and tugged her up against his chest, into his arms. "How well you and I go together."

His body was warm, comforting. His mouth bare inches from hers. Her lips ached for his kiss. "But I don't date clients."

His smile never waned. "Then it's a good thing I'm not one."

"Or guys who get paid for sex."

"Then it's a good thing I'm not doing that anymore."

His hips moved against hers, a subtle nudge that was enough to heat her through, enough to have her nudging him back, harder, stirring his cock to life against her belly.

Holly rose up on her toes and slanted her mouth over his, brushed his lips softly, tenderly, in a way she could imagine very few women had ever done. "I think I love you."

"Then it's a good thing I know I love you." He kissed her back in the same slow, tender manner.

Then his hands moved to her ass and he lifted her up his body and kissed her for real, pushing his tongue between her lips, stroking hers with wild hunger, raw need.

Unconditional love.

She whimpered over the loss when he pulled back. But Benny didn't put her down, just held her legs around his waist and walked them both over to the grill and turned off the fire.

He took her into the kitchen and set her down on the counter, freeing the buttons of her shirt. She hadn't bothered with a bra, and his mouth closed over her breast the instant the sides of her shirt parted.

Sensation after glorious sensation jolted from her throbbing nipple to her core, filling her sex with cream, making it ache with the burning need to feel his cock inside her, claiming her.

Holly denied her fingers shaking with want to strip the clothes from his body. Tia had claimed he held the power to free a woman's mind of all thought, and she'd been accurate.

Once he was naked and she was naked and they were joined, her mind would be mush, her body a slave to ecstasy.

Before that happened, she took his head between her hands and broke his lips' contact with her breast.

He tipped his face back to look at her. She smiled, happily, sensually, tenderly. "I know I love you too."

He grinned. "And I know you're not leaving my bed again tomorrow morning before I wake up. Or at all the rest of this week, if I have my way."

Laughing, Holly urged his mouth back down to her breast and let him have his wicked way with her.

Turn the page for a peek at
THIGH HIGH!
On sale now!

1

DM's voice rolled over her, whiskey smooth, pebble rough. With the deft hand of a master, he took her into the realm of the sensual. Throaty and hot, the distinctive sound rolled like rumbling skies around the master cabin. The poetry he read of love, loss and betrayal followed paths he created along her searing need, until she found her most needful flesh and, with a lover's touch, tipped herself over the edge toward release.

Fingers slid through slick, tender flesh, moist and plump. Around. Around. Trickles of need whispered to her womb deep and empty.

Her whole life was empty these days. But she couldn't think of that, not when release beckoned. Her breath slowed, deepened as her lungs reached for air. Her heart thumped, pulse beats rose as sensation took over again, thought drowned.

His voice came back seductive and deep and pulled her again into the quiet of rising expectation. She closed her eyes as his voice entered her, hot against her heart. The remembered weight of a chest pressed to hers, of thighs pushing with power between her own, flesh sliding into flesh, pulling along nerve endings so taut they screamed. His voice in her ear, strong, sexy and low, carrying her along. Taking, stroking her neck, her chest, nipples and down with slow strokes of his tongue.

With two fingers inside, she rolled her precious pearl of nerves with her other hand until she crested, weak and small.

Music rose all around, sweeping through her as the last pulses ebbed. It was enough. It had to be.

She wasn't about bar prowls for sex, and she couldn't have a relationship. Not now, maybe not ever again.

Rolling to her side, she listened to the song he played for her, just for her, full of pain and loss. When it was over, she threw back the covers and went to wash her hands.

DM's voice came back on, quieter, more seductive than before. The man was good. The man was cool. The poetry was gone now, replaced by his rolling commentary on the blues songstress highlighted tonight.

Victoria's CHOK blues-in-the-night radio disk jockey was the hottest thing this place had going for it. Well, him and the guy over on the houseboat side of the marina who stared at her all the time.

Francesca Volpe couldn't remember squat about numbers. Never could. So she wrote important ones down until they stuck in her memory. Sooner or later, she'd remember the combination of this safe. But sooner wasn't now, so she yanked at the piece of paper in her shorts pocket and flattened it out on the wall in front of her while she dialed the combination.

Finally, the safe door clicked open.

Blown away by the fact that she even had to use a safe, she dug way into the back. Fiona's thong was in here somewhere.

Cold, hard diamonds against warm, soft velvet filled her hand, and she lifted the scrap of material gently. Fiona should have kept the thong in the designer's box, but no; her sister had decided the rich didn't give a rat's ass about their possessions so she didn't have to either.

The thong caught on a corner of a thick manila file. Anxious not to tear the velvet, she set it down, then pulled out of the safe everything that could possibly be in the way.

She took out a fireproof box that contained so many important papers her head swam. It held her sister's will, her sister's house deed, her sister's insurance policy. Next came file folders, then a copy of her parents' will. Everything came out, even the ownership papers for the yacht.

A yacht, for cripes sake.

Frankie Volpe was standing in the saloon of a yacht with four staterooms. Up to her armpit in a wall safe and she still couldn't believe it. Go figure!

And since when was a living room called a saloon? They belonged in old westerns, not on million dollar floating palaces.

She leaned in tight to the wall and winked at the scruffy brown dog that had all but adopted her. "Hey boy, how you doin'?"

He cocked his head and wagged his stubby tail. She'd decided he must've had it caught in a door when he was a puppy. It wasn't cropped exactly, more like he just lost the tip. He was her kind of dog, lost, lonely, a little rough around the edges, but lovable.

"Ah! Got it. Finally." She pulled out the thong and set it carefully on the coffee table in front of the leather settee. Looked more like a built-in sofa to her, but she still had a lot of boating terms to learn.

She considered the thong. Diamonds, glittering and cold, littered the front vee of black velvet. She shivered to think of all those sharp edges so close to the joy button. *Oh, ugh.*

The deep safe had been stuffed full. She took care to set all the papers and files back into the safe in reverse order, to be sure they fit.

When she turned back to talk to Scruffy, all she saw was his stubby tail and wet feet heading topside. He'd snatched the thong off the table and taken off with it!

"Hey! You little pervert! Give me back that thong!"

But he was gone when she got to the deck. His bouncing short tail was just visible as he raced along the floating dock toward the houseboats tied up a couple of docks over. A small community of houseboaters called the marina home.

Her former doggy pal must live over there in one of the houseboats.

She took off at a dead run after him, not caring that she was barefoot; night was falling and the floating dock was strewn with heavy gauge rope and chains. She picked her way as quickly as she could through the obstacles, keeping one eye on the scruffster as she went.

She wasn't quick enough. He disappeared for a full minute, but she'd bet anything he'd taken off for the waterfront park on Dallas Road. Oh shit, if he got to the off-leash part of the park, he'd drop the thong for sure.

She ran faster, no longer needing to watch him except in her mind's eye. He was a playful mutt, sure to have doggy pals. She imagined a tug of war, the velvet tearing into several pieces, the diamonds flying in every direction. "Shit! Shitshitshit!"

Her thighs burned with her run, her lungs strained, but her heart knew she'd lost him. She bit back a sob, gathered strength and picked up her pace again.

She reached the bottom of the ramp, steep now because it was low tide. Grabbing onto the rail for support, she dashed up the incline. She dragged in a heaving breath. Her chest blazed hot, and she could swear she felt the beginnings of a heart attack.

Oh man, how did she ever get this out of shape?

She wheezed once more and launched her aching self up the ramp, metal surface rough against her bare feet. The hard metal honeycomb was there to prevent slipping in heavy weather, but for bare feet, it was a killer.

She reached the halfway point when the dog reappeared at the top of the ramp and headed straight down toward her, tongue lolling out of his mouth.

Lolling out of his empty mouth.

She stopped, put her hands on her knees and dragged in a deep, burning breath. Her grateful lungs expanded.

"You . . . you . . . lost it . . . I'll . . . I'll . . . kill . . . kill . . ."

He licked her hand as he trotted past her down the ramp. At the bottom he turned right toward the houseboats.

Frankie dragged her body the remaining few feet to the top of the ramp, then searched the immediate area, but there was no thong in sight. He'd disappeared for long enough to bury it, or tear it up or, worse, hand it off to another dog whose owner would recognize the diamonds for what they were. A bonanza.

Lightheaded, she sank to her butt and laid her head to rest on the rail support. That thong was worth fifty thousand dollars!

She had to get it back.

If she was lucky, they'd find it when they did the dog's autopsy. She scanned the marina laid out below her.

The floating dock was cement and ran from right to left with several docks running perpendicular, like straight fingers out into the harbor. Each finger contained several slips. To the left was the marina side or the visitor's pier with visiting boats of varying sizes. Farther down were the fishing boats. To the right of the ramp were three fingers for houseboats. A subdivision of them, in fact.

She'd liked them, and the idea, at first sight.

But the sight she wanted now was of the dog, heading to the one he called home.

His bouncy rear end showed up as he reached the third finger.

A man, correction, *the* man who'd been watching her every time she was within view, whistled to Scruffy. The dog bounded faster.

She couldn't lose sight of the dog again, so she dashed down the ramp as fast as her bare feet on the rough steel would allow.

Whistling for the scruffy little dog might not mean a thing. Maybe the hunk was just another soft touch who fed the beast, the way she did. Either way, he hadn't seen her mad dash because he turned away and sat on one of the chairs on his deck. He faced away from her toward the inner harbor and put his feet up on the deck rail. Settling in for the night, she assumed. Great. He could help her search for the thong.

Daniel Martin cracked open a beer and settled in to watch the ferry to Seattle churn out of the harbor. One beer before work took the edge off, warmed his throat, soothed his nerves and put him into a blues frame of mind. He'd gone from domestic brands to beer from all over the globe to test the effects of each one. Tonight's was Dutch. He tilted the bottle away, glanced at the label out of habit, ran his tongue around his teeth to gather the flavor then took another sip. Not bad.

He put his feet up on the rail of his floating home and nearly dropped his brew when Barkley jumped into his lap. "Easy there, boy, you'd think you'd know better than to squish the package. Oof! Get off." He picked Barkley's back paw out of his crotch with a grunt. Instant relief.

The dog licked his chin.

"Is that... is that... your dog?" asked a husky, heavy-breathing female voice from behind him. He craned his neck around and dropped his feet to the deck at the same time.

It was the hottie he'd noticed from the yacht on the marina side. "You could say that. He's been mooching off me so long, I guess he does live here."

Good thing his paw hadn't damaged the goods. The goods in question sprang to life, as usual, at the sight of the compact, dark-haired dynamo.

The woman was built just for him, he was sure of it. And it was about time she showed up. They'd been glancing each other's way ever since she'd washed ashore.

He grinned, thinking the dog was good for at least three doggie snacks for delivering her. "Has Barkley caused trouble?"

Her chest heaved in and out a couple times, breasts rising and falling with each heave. He did his best not to look, but she was in a bikini top that left little to the imagination. And Daniel had a great imagination. "Down, boy," he said, not sure if he was talking to Barkley or his libido.

"He took a thong. And I didn't see where. It's not anywhere near the top of the ramp, because I followed him."

"I see. Was it leather? He's got a thing for leather." So did Daniel, but it wasn't the time to mention it. "Shoes, that is." Maybe after he got her shoe back for her, she'd be grateful.

"Not a shoe. A thong." She looked exasperated. "You know." Deep heave. "Underwear." Her breath was still labored, still entertaining him with soft jiggles of flesh and cleavage.

The image of her fine behind parted by a thin strip of leather made him sit up fast and straight. He put his hands up in surrender. "Oh, I see. As much as he loves leather, he loves women's underwear even more." The count was now officially up to four dog biscuits. "His favorite day of the week is when Bitsy Mayer, two slips over, does her laundry. He takes her panties all the time."

"I don't give a rat's ass about Bitsy somebody's underwear."

He played at being offended. "Bitsy does. She's on a fixed income and the underwear she favors is expensive," he quipped.

His reward? A reluctant lopsided grin that winded him with its hesitant charm. He went on, digging for more. "They come with that heavy-duty flat panel in the front to firm the belly and some kind of stitching up the back to make the most of her butt."

Damn things cost him a fortune every month. "I'm beginning to suspect Bitsy enjoys the idea of me shopping for her undies." He gave an exaggerated shiver. "Bitsy's sixty-eight."

Her raised eyebrows put an end to the fun. Her smile disappeared. So, okay, she wasn't impressed with his comedy. He'd always been better with the blues.

But still, a lady shouldn't have to fight with Barkley over her underwear.

"Are you sure you want your thong back after he's dragged it all over the pier? He chows down on them sometimes. Tears the crotches right out."

"Yes, I want it back! Regardless of the condition. He ran up the ramp with it, and I've got to get it back. Do you know if he has a hidey hole anywhere? Does he bury stuff?"

She looked about to cry.

"Hey, it's a thong. I'll buy you a new one." He liked that idea. Much more fun than buying for Bitsy.

"It's a special thong. My sister needs it. She's on her honeymoon and she called to have me send it to her." Her voice got higher and more agitated with every syllable. She sounded desperate now.

"It's not yours?" That was too bad; he liked the idea of fantasizing about her in a thong. He'd never seen the sister.

"You can buy your sister another. I'll take you to a nice lingerie store I know." That could be fun.

She looked about to spit nails. "I've got to find that one. It's special."

"How special?"

"Very. Look, it's got sentimental value. She bought it to celebrate her engagement and planned to take it on her honeymoon. Now she's *on* her honeymoon and she wants it."

"I see." He pretended to think hard when all he could really think about was the spectacular rise and fall of her breasts. He didn't want to be a pig, but he was a red-blooded male and there they were: round and pert with the nipples that pointed upward like two perfect pearls. "You could still buy her a replacement," he suggested.

She took another deep breath, but this time he figured it was one of those looking-for-patience deep breaths that women did so well, not an out-of-breath-from-running kind of heave.

And a woman looking for patience was not likely to agree to a date. "I'm sorry, but I don't have a clue where he'd bury it. But I can help you look for it first thing in the morning. I get home from the station around five A.M."

It wouldn't kill him to stay up a few extra hours after his shift to wait for her.

"You're leaving?" She looked at the beer bottle rising from his lap, condensation slipping and sliding down onto his hands. Kinda looked like his . . .

"Yep. I'm on the air at midnight. It takes fifteen minutes to get to the station." He stood. "I take an hour to prep, so I'd better get moving. I can wait for you to wake up before I hit the sack for the day. But if you wait until much after seven I'll be pretty useless. So, I'll see you bright and early?" The question was all about her name, not about when he'd see her.

"Frankie. I'm Frankie Volpe. And I hate early mornings. So, if I don't find it, I'll still be searching the park when you get home. Look for me there."

"You sure that's a good idea? That park's not the healthiest place to be after eleven or so. It's used by all the normals until then. A lot of people take their dogs for the last walk of the night along the path."

"I'll be fine. I've been in tougher neighborhoods and survived." Her eyes glittered and her chin came up, stubborn and cute as hell.

"What's this thing look like anyway?"

"It's sparkly. Very sparkly. Black velvet. With rhinestones all over it."

"Sounds like it would hurt."

She rolled her eyes. "Looks even worse," she said, and gave Barkley a scowl before she turned and headed back down the float.

"You must love this sister a lot if you're willing to search all night," he called after her.

She waved a hand without turning back.

"Barkley, man, I owe you big time. Frankie Volpe is definitely the catch of the day." Then he remembered she hadn't cared to ask his name.

"Hey!" he called again, aware that everyone on this side of the marina could hear him. "I'm Daniel and I'm on CHOK radio, the blues show from midnight to four. Give me a listen tonight. Maybe I can figure out where Barkley hid it."

She gave him a salute and took her fine ass up the ramp.